Alira's Deadly Sins

Volume 1

Sean Taylor

ALIRA'S DEADLY SINS

A Four-Book Thriller Series

Copyright © 2025 by Sean Taylor

All rights reserved.

This is a work of fiction. Names, characters, businesses, places, events, locales, and incidents are either the products of the author's imagination or used in a fictitious manner. Any resemblance to actual persons, living or dead, or actual events is purely coincidental.

Content Warning: This book contains mature themes including violence, sexual assault (discussed but not graphically depicted), and vigilante justice. Reader discretion is advised.

Published by Sean Taylor

ISBN: 979-8-9930145-2-4 (Paperback)

First Edition: December 2025

Printed in the United States of America

10 9 8 7 6 5 4 3 2 1

CONTENTS

Book One – The First Sin

CONTENTS

Book Two – The Second Fall

Book One

The First Sin

LUXURIA *Lust*

———

"The predator does not see a person. He sees only prey."

Prologue

The Breaking Point

The fluorescent lights of Riverside Care Facility cast harsh shadows across the common room where Sierra Sinclair sat surrounded by coloring books and puzzles designed for children half her age. At thirty-six, she should have been teaching developmental psychology at a prestigious university, publishing groundbreaking research on childhood trauma recovery, and mentoring the next generation of therapists who would help damaged children heal.

Instead, she colored within the lines of cartoon animals with the careful concentration of a seven-year-old, occasionally looking up to smile at her younger sister with the innocent joy of someone who no longer understood why Alira visited so often or why her eyes were always red from crying.

"Look, Alira!" Sierra said, holding up a picture of a purple elephant she'd been working on for twenty minutes. "I stayed inside all the lines this time!"

"It's beautiful, Sierra," Alira replied, her voice carefully controlled to hide the rage and grief that threatened to overwhelm her every time she visited her damaged sister. "You're getting so good at coloring."

Sierra beamed with pride, her brain-damaged mind unable to comprehend the devastating irony of a brilliant academic reduced to celebrating achievements that actual children would find mundane. The traumatic injury she'd suffered ten years ago had stolen everything that made her exceptional, leaving behind only fragments of the person she'd been before Dr. Marcus Webb had drugged, raped, and beaten her until her skull fractured and her brilliant mind shattered.

Alira watched her sister return to her coloring book, and felt something fundamental shift inside her. She'd spent the past decade trying to work within legal systems, believing that justice would eventually be served through official channels if she just remained patient and persistent. She'd filed complaints with the university, contacted police investigators, hired attorneys, and exhausted every legitimate avenue for holding Webb accountable for what he'd done to Sierra.

But Webb had died peacefully in his sleep three months ago, his reputation intact, his career celebrated, his crimes unpunished and largely unknown beyond the small circle of victims he'd systematically abused and discredited. The university had issued a glowing obituary praising his contributions to psychological research and his dedication to mentoring graduate students, with no mention of the women whose lives he'd destroyed through that supposed mentorship.

Sierra would never recover, would never reclaim the life and career that had been stolen from her, would never receive justice through the legal systems that had protected her attacker while abandoning her to institutional care facilities and permanent disability.

But Alira could ensure that other predators wouldn't be allowed to escape consequences the way Webb had. She could become the justice that institutional systems refused to provide, the consequence that powerful men believed their privilege would allow them to avoid forever.

The decision crystallized in that moment, watching Sierra color her purple elephant with childlike concentration. Alira would stop trying to work within systems that were designed to protect predators, and she would start eliminating them using methods that those systems couldn't prevent or deflect.

Her first target was already identified: Richard Blackwood, a wealthy real estate developer with a documented history of sexual assault spanning three decades. Blackwood had used his wealth and legal connections to silence dozens of victims, paying settlements that required non-disclosure agreements while continuing to prey on vulnerable women who needed jobs or housing or any of the other resources that his money could provide.

The planning had already begun, the research was nearly complete, and Alira had acquired the skills and resources necessary to ensure that Richard Blackwood would become the first predator to face consequences that no amount of wealth or institutional protection could prevent.

As she left Riverside Care Facility that evening, Alira made a silent promise to her damaged sister: Sierra's suffering would not be meaningless. Every predator that Alira eliminated would be one less threat to vulnerable women, one less monster using power and privilege to escape accountability for destroying innocent lives.

The first sin was about to be committed, but it would be in service of a justice that legal systems had proven themselves incapable of delivering.

Chapter 1

The Perfect Disguise

The photography studio occupied a converted warehouse space in the arts district, its exposed brick walls and industrial lighting creating the kind of authentic urban aesthetic that appeared effortlessly spontaneous in photographs while actually requiring meticulous planning and professional expertise to achieve. Alira had selected the location carefully after reviewing portfolios from dozens of photographers, looking for someone whose work could create the specific impression she needed for Sophia Gardner's dating profile.

"So you're looking for lifestyle shots that feel natural and unposed?" asked Marcus Rivera, the photographer she'd hired for the session. He was reviewing the shot list Alira had provided, his expression showing professional interest in the technical challenge she was presenting. "You want to look approachable and cultured, but not like you're trying too hard or presenting an artificially perfect version of yourself."

"Exactly," Alira replied, speaking in the slightly uncertain tone she'd been developing for Sophia Gardner's persona. "I want to seem like someone who has interesting hobbies and cultural interests, but who's also dealing with real financial constraints that make me relatable rather than intimidating."

The psychology behind Sophia's visual presentation had been carefully calculated based on months of research into Blackwood's preferences and selection criteria. Men like Blackwood were attracted to a specific combination of qualities that created the vulnerability they sought to exploit—intelligence and cultural sophistication suggested someone worth spending time with beyond purely sexual purposes, while visible economic struggle indicated someone who could be controlled through promises of financial support.

Marcus nodded thoughtfully. "I think we can definitely achieve that. I'm thinking we do some shots at the contemporary art museum—that's got great natural light and suggests cultural engagement without being pretentious. Then maybe some casual street photography in the historic district, showing you exploring the city in a way that feels authentic rather than staged."

"That sounds perfect," Alira said. "I also thought maybe some shots in coffee shops or bookstores? Places that suggest I'm intellectually engaged but in accessible, everyday ways rather than in ways that might seem elitist or unapproachable."

The shot list they'd developed together included specific locations and poses designed to create a comprehensive visual narrative about who Sophia Gardner appeared to be. Each photograph would tell part of the story about a cultured, educated young woman struggling financially but maintaining her intellectual interests and cultural engagement despite economic constraints.

Over the next six hours, Marcus photographed Alira in a dozen different locations throughout the city. At the contemporary art museum, she posed studying abstract paintings with expressions that suggested genuine intellectual engagement rather than mere aesthetic appreciation. In the historic district, she appeared wandering through cobblestone streets with the curiosity of someone who found pleasure in exploring her environment rather than consuming it as mere backdrop for social media presentation.

The coffee shop shots were particularly important for establishing Sophia's economic vulnerability in ways that wouldn't be immediately obvious but would register subconsciously with someone like Blackwood who'd spent decades identifying and exploiting financial desperation. Alira made sure to be photographed with a basic laptop computer that was several years old rather than the latest model, suggesting someone who couldn't afford regular technology upgrades. Her coffee was from the budget menu rather than expensive specialty drinks. Her clothing was tasteful and appropriate but showing signs of wear that indicated limited resources for wardrobe replacement.

Every detail had been calibrated to create the impression of someone maintaining dignity and cultural sophistication despite financial constraints—exactly the combination that would appeal to Blackwood's particular psychology.

"These are coming out great," Marcus said as he reviewed images on his camera between locations. "You've got a really natural quality in front of the camera. Most people look stiff when they're being photographed, but you seem completely comfortable."

The observation was ironic given how carefully Alira was controlling every aspect of her presentation, but the effectiveness of her performance validated months of preparation. She'd practiced Sophia's expressions and body language until they appeared completely spontaneous, studying photographs of genuinely candid moments to understand how authentic emotional states translated into visual presentation.

By the end of the session, Marcus had captured over three hundred images that would provide Alira with extensive material for creating Sophia Gardner's dating profile and social media presence. The photographs presented a comprehensive portrait of a young woman who was intelligent, cultured, financially struggling, and subtly vulnerable in ways that would register as attractive to predators seeking victims they could control through economic leverage.

Back in her apartment that evening, Alira began the meticulous process of selecting and editing photographs that would bring Sophia Gardner to life as a fully realized identity. The dating profile would feature six images carefully chosen to present different aspects of Sophia's personality and circumstances while maintaining consistent visual narrative.

The primary photograph showed Alira at the art museum, studying a contemporary painting with an expression that combined intellectual engagement with a hint of wistfulness that suggested someone who appreciated beauty but couldn't afford to own it herself. The image communicated cultural sophistication while subtly reinforcing economic vulnerability.

Additional photographs showed Sophia in the coffee shop working on her laptop, wandering through the historic district with a vintage camera, browsing in an independent bookstore, attending an outdoor concert in a public park, and sitting on the steps of a university building. Each image reinforced specific aspects of the identity she was creating—intellectual ambition, cultural engagement, creative interests, and the ability to find pleasure in experiences that didn't require significant financial resources.

But the photographs were only one component of the comprehensive false identity Alira had been constructing for the past two months. Sophia Gardner needed to exist as a verifiable person with documented history and authentic presence across multiple platforms that background investigators might examine if Blackwood's legal team decided to research her before or after their encounter.

The social media accounts Alira had created for Sophia were masterpieces of detailed fabrication designed to withstand casual investigation while requiring minimal ongoing maintenance. Sophia's Instagram account featured photographs dating back three years, showing a consistent visual narrative of someone pursuing graduate education while dealing with financial constraints and maintaining active cultural interests.

Early posts from three years ago showed Sophia celebrating acceptance to a master's program in art history at the state university, expressing excitement about educational opportunities mixed with anxiety about financing her studies. Subsequent posts documented her graduate school experience through carefully curated images—library study sessions, museum visits, coffee shop work sessions, apartment life with visible budget furnishings.

The account's follower count was modest but authentic—approximately three hundred followers consisting of real accounts belonging to actual people rather than fake profiles or purchased followers. Alira had built the follower base gradually by engaging with content from art history communities, museum education programs, and graduate student support networks, creating genuine social connections that would make Sophia appear to be a real person with legitimate educational interests and authentic social relationships.

Sophia's Facebook account presented a more comprehensive biographical narrative, with a timeline extending back to her supposed undergraduate years at a public university in another state. The account included photographs from college experiences, tagged connections with people who appeared to be classmates and friends, and posts documenting the transition from undergraduate to graduate studies.

Alira had created this historical content using a combination of stock photographs carefully selected to maintain visual consistency with her own appearance, images from actual university events that could plausibly have included Sophia as an attendee, and creative editing that inserted Sophia into group photographs in ways that appeared authentic rather than artificially composed.

The LinkedIn profile completed Sophia's professional presence with a detailed work history that explained her financial situation while establishing intellectual credentials that would appeal to someone like Blackwood. The profile showed a progression from undergraduate research assistant positions through graduate teaching assistantships and part-time work in museum education programs—exactly the kind of resume that demonstrated intellectual capability while explaining why someone with Sophia's credentials might be struggling financially.

Each element of these online presences had been designed to tell consistent stories that would reinforce each other if examined by investigators or background researchers. The Instagram posts about museum visits corresponded to events documented on Facebook. The LinkedIn work history aligned with educational timeline shown across social platforms. Even small details like Sophia's listed interests and hobbies remained consistent across all platforms, creating the impression of a coherent identity rather than artificially constructed persona.

Beyond social media, Alira had created additional documentation that would support Sophia's existence if deeper investigation occurred. A university email account was established using the state university's public system, with correspondence in the account dating back three years showing interactions with professors, classmates, and administrative offices. A Google Voice phone number provided Sophia with a functioning telephone contact that would appear in online directories and could receive verification calls from dating services or other platforms requiring phone authentication.

Financial records were more challenging to fabricate but equally important for creating a fully realized identity. Alira had established a bank account in Sophia's name using falsified identification documents, maintaining small balances and transaction histories that reflected graduate student financial circumstances—modest deposits from teaching assistantships and part-time work, regular withdrawals for rent and living expenses, occasional overdrafts that suggested someone living on the edge of financial stability.

The identification documents themselves had been obtained through connections Alira had developed during her research into how legal systems could be manipulated and circumvented. The driver's license, student ID, and other credentials were genuine documents issued by legitimate authorities, but based on falsified applications that had exploited vulnerabilities in verification systems designed to prevent exactly this kind of identity fabrication.

Creating Sophia Gardner had required expertise in multiple domains—graphic design for social media content, photography for visual consistency, writing for biographical narratives and online interactions, technical knowledge for establishing digital footprints across multiple platforms, and understanding of bureaucratic systems for obtaining genuine documentation based on false information.

But the most challenging aspect of creating Sophia had been psychological rather than technical. Alira needed to inhabit this identity completely when interacting with Blackwood, maintaining perfect consistency in speech patterns, emotional responses, body language, and behavioral patterns that would make Sophia appear authentic rather than performed.

She'd spent weeks developing Sophia's voice through practice conversations recorded and analyzed for consistency. Sophia spoke with slight regional accent from the Midwest, reflecting her supposed undergraduate education in that region. Her vocabulary was sophisticated but not pretentious, demonstrating intellectual capability while remaining accessible and non-threatening. Her emotional expressions were slightly more open and vulnerable than Alira's natural presentation, suggesting someone who hadn't yet developed the protective guardedness that came from repeated negative experiences with powerful men.

With all the groundwork in place—photographs, social media presence, documentation, voice and mannerisms perfected—Alira was ready to create Sophia's profile on Elite Companions, the exclusive dating service where Blackwood regularly sought vulnerable women to exploit.

The profile she crafted was a masterpiece of psychological manipulation disguised as earnest self-presentation:

"Graduate student in art history seeking mentorship and support from successful professional. I'm passionate about art, culture, and intellectual conversation, but I'm struggling to finance my graduate education. I'm looking for a generous arrangement with someone who appreciates sophisticated companionship and understands that I need to focus on my studies rather than constantly worrying about rent and expenses. I have to admit I'm somewhat new to these kinds of arrangements, but I'm open to exploring mutually beneficial relationships with the right person. Discretion and respect are very important to me."

Every word had been chosen to appeal to Blackwood's specific psychology while maintaining plausible deniability about the transactional nature of what was being offered. The emphasis on being "new to these arrangements" suggested naivety that would appeal to his predatory instincts. The mention of financial struggles and needing to "focus on studies" established economic vulnerability that made her controllable. The reference to "discretion" signaled willingness to keep their relationship private, exactly what someone like Blackwood needed to continue his pattern of assault without legal consequences.

The profile went live on Elite Companions at 8:47 PM on a Tuesday evening. Alira knew from her research that Blackwood checked the service regularly, usually in the evenings after returning from work. She expected to hear from him within twenty-four to forty-eight hours if her profile successfully matched his preferences.

The response came even faster than anticipated. At 11:23 PM that same evening—less than three hours after the profile went live—Alira received a message notification from Elite Companions. The sender was Richard Blackwood.

"Sophia," the message read, "I was struck by your profile and the thoughtful way you describe your interests in art and culture. I'm a successful real estate developer who appreciates intelligent conversation and sophisticated companionship. I've been involved in several arrangements similar to what you're describing, and I think I understand exactly what you're looking for. I'd enjoy the opportunity to discuss a mutually beneficial relationship over dinner at my penthouse. I think you'll find that I can be quite generous with someone who understands what I'm looking for and who values discretion as much as I do. Would you be interested in meeting to explore whether we're compatible?"

The language was carefully calibrated to communicate sexual expectations without stating them explicitly, maintaining the plausible deniability that had protected Blackwood throughout his predatory career. "Mutually beneficial relationship" meant sex in exchange for money. "Generous with someone who understands what I'm looking for" meant he expected sexual compliance without complaints or resistance. "Values discretion" meant she would never discuss what happened between them, accepting that any attempt to report assault would be met with legal and financial retaliation.

Alira crafted Sophia's response with equal care, portraying enthusiasm mixed with carefully calculated naivety:

"Mr. Blackwood, thank you so much for your message! I'm really flattered by your interest in my profile. I have to admit I'm somewhat nervous about all of this since I've never done anything like this before, but I'm very interested in finding someone who can help me focus on my graduate work without constantly worrying about finances. Your message suggests you're someone who appreciates intellectual companionship and cultural sophistication, which is exactly what I was hoping to find. I would definitely be interested in meeting you to discuss what kind of arrangement might work for both of us. When would be convenient for you?"

The response hit all the right notes—enthusiastic enough to maintain his interest, inexperienced enough to appeal to his predatory instincts, and financially desperate enough to suggest that Sophia would be willing to accept his terms in exchange for economic support.

His reply came the following morning: "Sophia, I'm delighted by your enthusiasm and your obvious intelligence. I'm traveling for business over the next few weeks, but I'd very much like to meet you when I return. Why don't we plan for three weeks from this Thursday—that will give us both time to get to know each other better through phone and email, and it will give you time to feel comfortable with the arrangement before we meet in person. When we do meet, I'll arrange for dinner to be delivered to my penthouse, and we can spend the evening getting to know each other and discussing how I might be able to help with your financial situation. Does that timeline work for you?"

The three-week delay was actually perfect for Alira's purposes. It would give her time to conduct comprehensive surveillance on Blackwood's movements and security arrangements while building the relationship through increasingly personal email and phone conversations. By the time they met in person, Blackwood would feel confident that he understood Sophia well enough to control her, while Alira would have all the intelligence she needed to ensure his death appeared natural and undetectable.

"That sounds perfect, Mr. Blackwood," Alira replied as Sophia. "Three weeks will give me time to finish my current semester coursework and feel more comfortable about meeting you. I'm looking forward to getting to know you better over email and phone in the meantime. Thank you so much for being patient with me—I really appreciate how understanding you're being about my nervousness."

"Of course, Sophia," his response came quickly. "I understand completely. Take your time getting comfortable with this. I'll call you this weekend and we can start getting to know each other better. I think you'll find that I'm very easy to talk to, and that this arrangement will be exactly what you're looking for."

The trap was set, with a three-week timeline that would allow Alira to prepare comprehensively for the most important night of her life. She had three weeks to conduct surveillance, finalize her acquisition of the potassium chloride that would stop Blackwood's heart, build a relationship that would make him comfortable and confident, and rehearse the victim persona that would ensure her survival when police investigated his death.

As she closed her laptop that evening, Alira felt the weight of what she was planning settle over her like a physical presence. In three weeks, she would commit her first murder. She would cross a line that separated victims' family members seeking justice from something else entirely—a hunter of predators who'd decided that some consequences couldn't be delivered through legal systems that were designed to protect powerful men.

Sierra's coloring books flashed through her mind— the purple elephant, the childlike pride in staying within the lines, the brilliant mind reduced to celebrating achievements that actual children would find mundane. Webb had destroyed Sierra and faced no consequences. But Blackwood would be different.

The first sin was three weeks away, and Alira Sinclair would use every day of that time to ensure that when it came, it would be executed with perfect precision.

The perfect disguise was complete. Now came the surveillance, the preparation, and finally, the kill.

SUPERBIA *Pride*

———

"The only thing necessary for the triumph of evil is for good men to do nothing." — Edmund Burke

Chapter 2

The Predator's Pattern

The law offices of Kellerman, Price & Associates occupied the entire forty-second floor of the Tower Financial Building, a gleaming monument to corporate power in the heart of the city's legal district. For the past three decades, the firm had specialized in a particular type of legal work that existed in the shadows between legitimate defense and systematic obstruction of justice—protecting wealthy clients from the consequences of sexual misconduct through aggressive legal tactics that destroyed accusers while preserving their clients' reputations and freedom.

Richard Blackwood had been their most lucrative client for twenty-eight years.

Alira sat in the reading room of the city's central law library, surrounded by boxes of court documents that told the story of Blackwood's predatory career through the clinical language of legal filings and settlement agreements. She'd spent the past six months obtaining these records through a combination of legitimate research requests, strategic relationships with court clerks who could be convinced to overlook certain access restrictions, and careful exploitation of public records laws that required disclosure of information that parties involved would have preferred to keep confidential.

The earliest case in her files dated back to 1995, when Blackwood had been thirty years old and just beginning to build his real estate empire. The plaintiff was Michelle Torres, a twenty-three-year-old administrative assistant who'd been hired to work in Blackwood's development office. According to her complaint, Blackwood had subjected her to months of increasingly aggressive sexual harassment before assaulting her in his office after a company party where he'd encouraged her to drink heavily.

Torres had reported the assault to police and filed both criminal charges and a civil lawsuit seeking damages for sexual assault and workplace harassment. The criminal case had been dropped after six months of investigation, with prosecutors citing "insufficient evidence" and "credibility concerns" that Alira now understood were the result of Kellerman, Price & Associates' behind-the-scenes work to undermine Torres's testimony and character.

The civil case had proceeded further, but ultimately had been settled for $75,000 in exchange for Torres's agreement to sign a comprehensive non-disclosure agreement that prohibited her from ever discussing Blackwood, the assault, or the settlement terms with anyone. The settlement agreement Alira had obtained included language that went far beyond standard confidentiality provisions—Torres had been required to affirm that the settlement did not constitute any admission of wrongdoing by Blackwood, that she would never make any public statements that could damage his reputation, and that violation of these terms would result in immediate legal action seeking return of the settlement payment plus substantial additional damages.

The legal strategy had been devastatingly effective. Torres had taken the money and disappeared from public view, her allegations permanently buried under the weight of the non-disclosure agreement. Blackwood had continued building his business empire, apparently learning from the experience that wealthy men could purchase silence from their victims through strategic application of legal and financial pressure.

What followed over the next twenty-eight years was a systematic pattern of assault, legal intimidation, and strategic settlement that had allowed Blackwood to victimize at least forty-three women that Alira had been able to document, with likely many more whose cases had never resulted in formal complaints or legal action.

The files spread across Alira's library table painted a comprehensive portrait of institutional failure on a massive scale. Each case followed a similar trajectory: a woman would report being assaulted or harassed by Blackwood, either to police or through civil legal action. Kellerman, Price & Associates would immediately launch a coordinated response designed to destroy the accuser's credibility while protecting Blackwood from any meaningful accountability.

The firm's tactics had evolved and improved over the years as they refined their approach through repeated practice. Early cases had relied primarily on attacking accusers' credibility through conventional means—questioning their sobriety during alleged assaults, suggesting financial motivations for their accusations, highlighting inconsistencies in their accounts that were actually the predictable result of trauma rather than fabrication.

But by the mid-2000s, Kellerman, Price & Associates had developed a far more sophisticated and comprehensive strategy that Alira recognized as a template for how powerful men could systematically evade accountability for sexual violence.

The strategy had several interconnected components, each designed to achieve specific objectives in isolating and silencing Blackwood's victims:

Immediate Investigation and Evidence Gathering: Within hours of learning about accusations against Blackwood, the firm would deploy private investigators to conduct comprehensive background research on accusers. These investigators had access to databases and information sources that allowed them to compile detailed profiles including financial records, employment history, medical records, social media activity, and personal relationships.

The goal wasn't to find evidence of Blackwood's innocence, but rather to identify any information that could be weaponized to undermine accusers' credibility or create alternative narratives that would cast doubt on their allegations. Past mental health treatment became evidence of instability and unreliability. Previous financial difficulties became proof of mercenary motivations. Social media posts showing the accuser drinking or partying became evidence of irresponsible behavior that supposedly made their testimony suspect.

Strategic Media Management: For cases that threatened to become public, Kellerman, Price & Associates worked with crisis management firms and friendly journalists to shape media coverage in ways that favored Blackwood. Stories would appear questioning accusers' motivations, highlighting supposed inconsistencies in their accounts, or suggesting that Blackwood was the victim of false accusations by women seeking financial settlements.

The firm had cultivated relationships with reporters at major publications who could be relied upon to give favorable coverage to Blackwood's side of disputes. These journalists would be provided with selective information from Blackwood's legal team, often including details from accusers' backgrounds that had been obtained through the investigation process. The resulting stories would create public narratives that made accusers appear unreliable or dishonest, poisoning potential jury pools and creating social pressure on accusers to abandon their claims.

Economic Warfare: Accusers who persisted despite media attacks and legal intimidation would find themselves facing coordinated economic pressure designed to make continued legal action financially impossible. The firm would file aggressive motions that forced accusers to spend money on legal fees and court costs. They would drag out discovery processes to maximize expenses. They would file counter-suits alleging defamation or other torts that required accusers to defend themselves at additional cost.

Simultaneously, private investigators would contact accusers' employers with questions designed to create concerns about the accusers' judgment or reliability, often resulting in termination or forced resignation. Landlords would receive similar contacts, sometimes resulting in lease terminations or eviction proceedings. Even family members might be contacted with information designed to create conflict or withdrawal of financial and emotional support.

The economic pressure was designed to force accusers into settlement negotiations from positions of complete desperation, where they would accept minimal payments in exchange for comprehensive non-disclosure agreements rather than continuing to fight cases that were destroying them financially and professionally.

Aggressive Legal Tactics: In cases that actually reached trial, Kellerman, Price & Associates employed legal tactics that pushed the boundaries of professional ethics while staying just barely within the rules governing attorney conduct. Defense attorneys would subject accusers to brutal cross-examinations designed not to elicit truth but to humiliate and intimidate them. Questions about sexual history, personal relationships, and intimate details of accusers' lives would be framed in ways designed to suggest that accusers were promiscuous, unstable, or motivated by financial gain rather than genuine trauma.

Expert witnesses would be called to testify about the unreliability of trauma memories, the prevalence of false accusations in sexual assault cases, and psychological theories that could be twisted to suggest that accusers were motivated by unconscious desires for attention or financial compensation rather than by actual experiences of assault.

The trials themselves became additional trauma for accusers, with the legal process functioning as punishment for daring to challenge powerful men rather than as mechanisms for achieving justice or accountability.

Alira had documented case after case where these tactics had been deployed with devastating effectiveness. She'd read transcripts of cross-examinations that had reduced accusers to tears on the witness stand as defense attorneys questioned their morality, sanity, and motivations in language that was technically permissible but clearly designed to humiliate and intimidate. She'd reviewed expert testimony that distorted legitimate psychological research to suggest that accusers were delusional, mercenary, or motivated by unconscious psychological needs rather than by actual experiences of assault.

The cumulative effect of these tactics had been to create a system where reporting assault by Richard Blackwood virtually guaranteed that accusers would experience additional trauma, professional destruction, and economic ruin, while Blackwood himself faced no meaningful consequences and continued preying on vulnerable women with complete impunity.

Of the forty-three cases Alira had documented, only seven had actually reached trial. Of those seven, five had resulted in verdicts favoring Blackwood, one had resulted in a hung jury that was followed by a settlement, and one had resulted in a verdict in favor of the accuser that was subsequently overturned on appeal. Not a single case had resulted in a final judgment requiring Blackwood to pay damages or acknowledge wrongdoing.

The other thirty-six cases had been settled through the strategic application of legal, economic, and media pressure that forced accusers to accept payments and sign non-disclosure agreements as the only way to end the destruction that opposing Blackwood had brought into their lives.

But the settlements themselves told only part of the story. Alira had tracked down many of Blackwood's victims despite their non-disclosure agreements, promising them anonymity in exchange for their willingness to describe what had happened to them and how the legal process had failed them. What she'd learned had convinced her that legal accountability for men like Blackwood was essentially impossible within existing institutional frameworks.

Jennifer Morrison had been a twenty-five-year-old marketing coordinator when Blackwood assaulted her in 2008. She'd reported the attack to police and filed a civil lawsuit seeking damages, believing that the justice system would protect her and hold Blackwood accountable. Instead, she'd endured eighteen months of legal warfare that destroyed her career, depleted her savings, and left her psychologically shattered.

"They investigated every aspect of my life," Jennifer had told Alira during their interview six months before her suicide. "My medical records, my sexual history, my finances, my relationships. They contacted my employer and made me sound like I was unstable and seeking money. They contacted my family and suggested I was making false accusations for attention. By the time we settled, I had nothing left— no job, no savings, no reputation, no belief that the legal system would ever protect women like me from men like him."

Jennifer had taken the settlement of $125,000 primarily to make the destruction of her life stop rather than because she believed it represented fair compensation for what Blackwood had done to her. Six months later, unable to find employment in her field and suffering from severe depression and PTSD related to both the assault and the legal process, she'd taken her own life.

Her suicide note, which Alira had obtained from Jennifer's sister, included a detailed description of both Blackwood's assault and the systematic destruction she'd experienced through the legal process. "I thought reporting what he did to me would lead to justice," Jennifer had written. "Instead, it led to a second violation that was worse than the first. He raped my body, but the legal system raped my entire life. I can't live with what they've done to me."

Katherine Ford had been a successful marketing executive before she'd made the mistake of challenging Blackwood legally. Her assault had occurred in 2012, when Blackwood had used his authority as a potential client to engineer a situation where he could attack her during what was supposed to be a business dinner. Katherine had been confident that her professional reputation and clear evidence of Blackwood's predatory behavior would ensure justice through legal channels.

Instead, she'd endured two years of coordinated attacks that destroyed her career and left her homeless and addicted to drugs. Kellerman, Price & Associates had used their investigation to uncover a brief period of marijuana use during her college years, which they'd weaponized to suggest that she was a drug user whose testimony couldn't be trusted. They'd contacted her employer with questions that led to her termination. They'd used media contacts to plant stories suggesting she was making false accusations for financial gain.

By the time Katherine accepted a settlement of $200,000, she'd lost her career, her apartment, and her psychological stability. The money had gone primarily to paying legal fees and debts accumulated during the two years of fighting Blackwood. Within a year of settling, she was living on the streets, using drugs to cope with the trauma of both the assault and its aftermath.

Alira had found Katherine living in a homeless encampment three months ago, barely recognizable from the professional photograph that appeared in court documents. "I tried to do the right thing," Katherine had told her, her words slurred from whatever substances she'd used to get through another day. "I thought the truth mattered. I thought evidence mattered. I thought justice was possible. I was wrong about everything."

Maria Rodriguez's story had been perhaps the most heartbreaking of all. She'd been a law student when Blackwood assaulted her in 2015, attacked when she'd gone to his office to discuss a potential internship with his real estate development company. As someone studying law, Maria had believed she understood how to navigate the legal system and hold Blackwood accountable.

Instead, her legal training had simply allowed her to understand in precise detail exactly how thoroughly the system was rigged against victims like her. She'd watched defense attorneys use procedural tactics she'd learned about in her classes, but deployed in ways designed to obstruct justice rather than serve it. She'd seen expert witnesses distort research she'd studied, twisting legitimate psychological findings to suggest that she was delusional or dishonest.

The psychological impact of understanding exactly how she was being destroyed, of seeing legal principles she'd believed in weaponized against her, had been too much for Maria to handle. She'd suffered a complete psychological breakdown during her trial, requiring hospitalization in a psychiatric facility where she'd remained for eight months.

"I went to law school because I believed in justice," Maria had told Alira during a visit to the care facility where she now lived. "Watching what they did to me destroyed that belief. The legal system isn't designed to protect people like me from people like him. It's designed to protect people like him from accountability. Understanding that cost me my career, my sanity, and my future."

These stories, multiplied across forty-three documented victims and likely many more who'd never filed formal complaints, painted a comprehensive picture of systematic failure that had convinced Alira that legal accountability for predators like Blackwood was essentially impossible. The institutions that were supposed to protect victims instead protected their attackers, using the machinery of justice to punish anyone who dared to challenge powerful men.

But institutional power, while extensive, wasn't absolute. Blackwood's wealth couldn't protect him from physical harm if that harm was delivered with sufficient planning and sophistication. His legal team couldn't defend him if he was dead before they could be mobilized. His media connections couldn't manage crisis coverage of a death that appeared natural and unremarkable.

The pattern of predation that Alira had documented so carefully would soon be ended, not through legal proceedings or institutional accountability, but through the simple application of lethal force by someone who'd learned exactly how and why the justice system failed victims of powerful predators.

Alira had spent days in this law library, reading case after case, settlement after settlement, watching the same tactics deployed again and again with devastating effectiveness. Each document reinforced her conviction that what she was planning wasn't murder in the conventional sense—it was the execution of justice through the only means available when institutional systems had been corrupted beyond redemption.

As she packed up her research materials and prepared to leave the law library that afternoon, Alira felt the moral certainty that came from understanding that Thursday evening's encounter with Blackwood wasn't just about eliminating one predator. It was about demonstrating that power and money couldn't ultimately protect men who used those resources to destroy vulnerable women.

Blackwood had spent twenty-eight years perfecting the art of evading accountability through legal and financial means. But on Thursday evening, he would discover that some consequences couldn't be purchased, litigated, or intimidated away.

The predator's pattern was about to end, permanently and irrevocably. And when it did, at least forty-three women whose lives Blackwood had destroyed would know that he'd ultimately paid a price for what he'd done to them—not through legal channels that had consistently failed them, but through the kind of direct action that institutional systems were designed to prevent but couldn't ultimately stop.

Two more days until Thursday evening. Two more days until Richard Blackwood's reign of terror finally ended.

AVARITIA *Greed*

———

"Power without accountability is not power—it is tyranny wearing a suit."

Chapter 3

The Surveillance

Three weeks before she would kill Richard Blackwood, Alira Sinclair sat in a rented sedan parked across the street from the Meridian Tower, a luxury high-rise in the city's financial district where Blackwood maintained a penthouse apartment worth seven million dollars. The vehicle was registered to a nonexistent business address, rented using one of the carefully constructed false identities she'd been developing over the past year in preparation for this moment.

It was 11:47 PM on a Wednesday night, and this was the sixteenth consecutive evening that Alira had been conducting surveillance on Blackwood's movements. She'd documented his routines, catalogued his habits, and identified patterns that would allow her to approach him without triggering the security measures that protected wealthy predators from the consequences of their actions.

Through her telephoto lens, she watched Blackwood exit his private car service and enter the building's marble lobby, moving with the confident stride of someone who'd never faced real accountability for anything he'd done. At fifty-eight, Blackwood was still physically imposing—over six feet tall, athletic despite his age, carrying himself with the arrogance that came from decades of using power and money to get whatever he wanted.

The surveillance operation had begun the same day that Sophia Gardner's dating profile went live on Elite Companions, three weeks ago. Alira had known that Blackwood would respond quickly to a profile that matched his preferences so perfectly, and she'd wanted to have comprehensive intelligence about his movements and security arrangements before their first in-person meeting.

The Meridian Tower itself was a fortress of wealth and privilege, its lobby staffed twenty-four hours by uniformed security personnel who screened visitors and monitored an extensive network of surveillance cameras. But Alira had learned through her observation that the building's security was focused primarily on preventing unauthorized entry rather than monitoring the activities of residents once they were inside their units.

Blackwood's penthouse occupied the entire top floor of the tower, accessible only through a private elevator that required a keycard for activation. The elevator opened directly into his residence, meaning that anyone who gained access to the elevator would enter his home without passing through additional security checkpoints or encountering building staff.

This arrangement provided Blackwood with the privacy he needed for his predatory activities—women could be brought to his penthouse without creating documented records of their visits, and what happened inside his residence occurred beyond the view of building security cameras or staff. The isolation that protected his criminal behavior also created the perfect environment for what Alira was planning.

Over the past sixteen days, Alira had documented Blackwood's daily routine with meticulous precision. He left for his office between 8:15 and 8:45 each morning, driven by his car service to a high-rise building in the business district where his real estate development company occupied three floors. He typically returned to the Meridian Tower between 7:30 and 9:00 PM, depending on whether he had business dinners or social engagements.

Twice during her surveillance period, Alira had observed Blackwood bring women to his penthouse in the evening—young women who matched the profile of the vulnerable targets he sought through dating services and business contacts. Both women had arrived separately from Blackwood, entering through the lobby with the confidence of people who'd been given instructions about bypassing standard visitor protocols.

The first woman had arrived at 8:45 PM on a Friday evening, spending approximately three hours in Blackwood's penthouse before departing at 11:52 PM. Even from her surveillance position across the street, Alira could see that the woman's demeanor had changed dramatically between arrival and departure—she'd entered appearing confident and well-put-together, but she'd left with the slightly disoriented expression and unsteady gait that suggested either heavy drinking or psychological trauma.

The second woman had arrived at 7:30 PM on a Tuesday, staying until nearly midnight. Her departure had been even more troubling—she'd practically run from the building's entrance, her distress visible even from a distance. Alira had watched her collapse on a bench two blocks from the Meridian Tower, sitting with her head in her hands for nearly twenty minutes before finally calling a car service to take her home.

These observations had reinforced Alira's conviction that what she was planning was necessary and just. Blackwood was continuing to victimize vulnerable women even after twenty-eight years of documented predatory behavior and legal battles that should have taught him that his conduct carried consequences. The legal system had failed utterly to stop him, leaving vigilante justice as the only remaining option for protecting future victims.

Beyond documenting Blackwood's routine and security arrangements, the surveillance had allowed Alira to observe his psychological state and behaviors in ways that would inform her approach during their Thursday evening encounter. Through high-powered binoculars and telephoto photography, she'd watched him in his penthouse during the evenings when he was alone.

Blackwood displayed the casual confidence of someone who'd never experienced real consequences for his actions. He moved through his luxury apartment with proprietary satisfaction, often standing at the floor-to-ceiling windows that overlooked the city with a glass of expensive wine, surveying his domain like a feudal lord assured of his power and position.

The apartment itself was decorated with the kind of sophisticated minimalism that suggested professional interior design rather than personal taste—modern furniture, contemporary art, carefully curated collections of books and sculptures that created an impression of cultural sophistication whether or not Blackwood actually possessed such qualities. It was exactly the kind of environment designed to impress and intimidate young women who'd never experienced such wealth, making them feel simultaneously privileged to be included in this world and acutely aware of the power differential between themselves and their host.

Alira had also used the surveillance period to verify that Blackwood maintained the security arrangements she'd identified during her earlier research. His home security system was professionally installed but relatively standard for luxury residences—door and window sensors, motion detectors in unoccupied areas, and camera coverage of entrance points. The system could be armed and disarmed through a keypad near the elevator entrance, but Blackwood appeared to leave it disarmed when he was home and expecting visitors.

More importantly, the penthouse's interior wasn't monitored by cameras—a deliberate choice that allowed Blackwood to assault women without creating video evidence that might later be used against him. This absence of internal surveillance meant that whatever happened inside the penthouse during Alira's visit would be known only to the participants, exactly the situation she needed for her plan to succeed.

The surveillance period had also allowed Alira to maintain and deepen the relationship she was building with Blackwood through Sophia Gardner's persona. Over the past three weeks, their email and phone conversations had gradually escalated from polite discussion of potential arrangements to increasingly explicit expectations about what their Thursday evening meeting would entail.

"I've been thinking about Thursday," Blackwood had said during their most recent phone conversation, two days ago. "I want to make sure you understand what kind of arrangement I'm proposing. I can be very generous—I could easily cover your rent and living expenses, maybe even help with tuition costs. But I need someone who's flexible and understanding about what I'm looking for in return."

The euphemism had been transparent—"flexible" meant being willing to do whatever he wanted sexually, "understanding" meant accepting that resistance or complaints would result in withdrawal of financial support and potential legal retaliation.

"I understand," Alira had replied in Sophia's voice, maintaining the persona of someone eager for financial support but naive about the dangers of entering into arrangements with predatory men. "I really appreciate your generosity, Mr. Blackwood. I'm willing to be very flexible if it means I can focus on my studies without constantly worrying about money. I just want to make sure we're compatible and that this arrangement will work for both of us."

The response had been perfect for Blackwood's purposes—it confirmed Sophia's financial desperation while suggesting just enough inexperience to make her seem like an ideal victim for someone who enjoyed the psychological dimension of corrupting and controlling vulnerable women.

"I think we'll be very compatible," Blackwood had replied, his voice taking on a proprietary tone that suggested he'd already mentally claimed ownership of Sophia. "I'm looking forward to Thursday evening. Come dressed nicely but not too formally—think sophisticated but approachable. And Sophia? Don't be nervous. I promise I'll take very good care of you if you take good care of me."

The implied threat beneath the reassurance had been unmistakable—comply with his expectations and be rewarded financially, resist or complain and face consequences he had extensive experience deploying against women who challenged his authority.

Now, on this Wednesday evening exactly one day before their scheduled meeting, Alira sat in her surveillance vehicle watching Blackwood's penthouse lights go out one by one as he prepared for bed. Tomorrow evening, he would be expecting Sophia Gardner to arrive at 8:00 PM for dinner and the beginning of what he believed would be a profitable arrangement that would give him sexual access to another vulnerable young woman.

Instead, tomorrow evening would be the last night of Richard Blackwood's life.

Alira started her vehicle and pulled away from her surveillance position, driving through the empty streets toward her own modest apartment across the city. The surveillance phase of her operation was complete—she had comprehensive intelligence about Blackwood's routines, security arrangements, and psychological state. She knew the layout of his penthouse, the capabilities of his security systems, and the patterns of building staff who might potentially witness her arrival or departure.

More importantly, the three weeks of surveillance had reinforced her moral conviction that what she was planning was necessary and just. She'd watched Blackwood victimize at least two additional women during her observation period, continuing his pattern of predatory behavior despite decades of accusations and legal battles that should have resulted in accountability.

The legal system had demonstrated its complete failure to protect vulnerable women from powerful predators like Blackwood. Forty-three documented victims over twenty-eight years, millions of dollars in settlements, countless lives destroyed—and Blackwood continued operating with complete impunity, confident that his wealth and legal protections made him untouchable.

Tomorrow evening, Alira would prove that some consequences couldn't be avoided through legal maneuvering or financial pressure. Tomorrow evening, the predator would finally become prey.

Back in her apartment, Alira reviewed her final preparations one last time. The potassium chloride solution was prepared and loaded into a medical syringe concealed in a specially modified section of her purse. The injection technique had been practiced dozens of times on simulation equipment until she could deliver the dose smoothly and accurately even under stress conditions.

The victim persona had been rehearsed until it was flawless—the traumatized shock, the defensive wounds that would appear authentic, the 911 call that would convey appropriate emotional distress while providing the narrative that would shape police understanding of events. She'd studied audio recordings of genuine assault survivors calling for help, analyzing the vocal patterns and emotional expressions that distinguished authentic trauma from performed distress.

Her clothing for tomorrow evening had been carefully selected—a dress that was sophisticated but not overly sexual, professional but approachable, exactly what Blackwood had requested when he'd told Sophia to dress "nicely but not too formally." The dress also provided easy access to the concealed syringe while appearing completely innocent to casual observation.

Most importantly, Alira had mentally prepared herself for the psychological reality of what she was about to do. Tomorrow evening, she would commit premeditated murder, crossing a line that separated victims' family members seeking justice from something else entirely—a killer who'd decided that some people deserved death regardless of what legal systems might say about vigilante violence.

The moral justification was clear in Alira's mind. Blackwood had destroyed at least forty-three women's lives over twenty-eight years, and he showed no signs of stopping. The legal system had proven itself completely incapable of holding him accountable or protecting future victims. Eliminating him through extralegal means wasn't murder in the conventional sense—it was execution of a predator who'd evaded legitimate justice through corruption and manipulation of institutional systems.

Sierra's face flashed through Alira's mind—not the damaged sister coloring pictures in the care facility, but the brilliant graduate student she'd been before Webb had destroyed her. Sierra had believed in justice through official channels, had trusted that reporting her assault would lead to accountability for her attacker. That belief had been betrayed by every institution that should have protected her.

Alira wouldn't make the same mistake. She'd learned that justice sometimes required working outside systems that were designed to protect predators rather than victims. Tomorrow evening, she would deliver the consequences that Richard Blackwood had evaded for twenty-eight years.

As she prepared for bed, Alira felt remarkably calm considering what she was planning. There was no doubt, no hesitation, no moral ambiguity about whether what she was doing was right. Blackwood deserved death for what he'd done to dozens of women, and the legal system's failure to deliver that consequence didn't make it less deserved.

Tomorrow evening at 8:00 PM, Sophia Gardner would walk into Richard Blackwood's penthouse for what he believed would be the beginning of another successful exploitation of a financially desperate young woman. Instead, he would encounter someone who'd spent months learning exactly how to kill him in ways that would appear natural and undetectable.

The hunter's preparation was complete. The surveillance was finished. The moral justification was absolute.

Tomorrow came the kill.

Chapter 4

Final Preparations

Alira woke at 6:47 AM on Thursday morning, three minutes before her alarm was scheduled to sound. She'd slept surprisingly well considering what the day would bring—six hours of dreamless sleep that had left her feeling alert and focused rather than anxious or uncertain. The clarity was remarkable, almost unsettling in its completeness. There was no doubt, no hesitation, no last-minute moral crisis about what she was planning to do in thirteen hours.

She lay in bed for several minutes, watching early morning light filter through her apartment windows and mentally rehearsing the sequence of events that would unfold beginning at 8:00 PM. The rehearsal had become a ritual over the past three weeks, a form of meditation that reinforced each element of her plan until the entire operation felt as natural and inevitable as any routine daily activity.

Sophia Gardner would arrive at the Meridian Tower at precisely 8:00 PM, telling the doorman she was expected by Mr. Blackwood in the penthouse. She would be escorted to the private elevator, riding it alone to the top floor where it would open directly into Blackwood's residence. He would greet her with the superficial charm he employed with all his victims, offering wine and making small talk designed to help her "relax" before he began the assault he'd been planning since their first communication three weeks ago.

But Blackwood's assault would never reach completion. At some point during his attack—the exact timing would depend on circumstances Alira couldn't fully predict—she would retrieve the concealed syringe from her purse and inject the potassium chloride solution directly into his carotid artery or another major blood vessel. The injection would cause immediate cardiac arrest that would be indistinguishable from natural heart attack in any autopsy that didn't specifically test for potassium levels in the injection site.

Blackwood would collapse, and Sophia would transform into a traumatized assault survivor who'd just watched her attacker die during his attempt to rape her. She would call 911 in appropriate distress, providing a narrative that would shape police understanding of events. By the time investigators arrived, the scene would tell a clear story—wealthy predator attempts to assault young woman, suffers fatal heart attack from stress and exertion, woman survives traumatic experience but is too shaken to provide detailed testimony.

The plan was elegant in its simplicity and devastating in its effectiveness. Alira had spent three weeks identifying every potential vulnerability and developing contingencies for complications that might arise. But she'd also recognized that no plan survived contact with reality unchanged, and that her ultimate success would depend on her ability to adapt to circumstances while maintaining the core narrative that would protect her from investigation.

She rose from bed and began her morning routine with the same methodical precision she brought to all aspects of the operation. Shower, breakfast, coffee—each activity performed with careful attention to maintaining normal patterns that would later be documented if police became suspicious and investigated her movements on the day of Blackwood's death.

At 8:30 AM, Alira drove to Riverside Care Facility for what she'd decided would be her final visit with Sierra before committing her first murder. The visit served multiple purposes—it would reinforce her moral justification for what she was planning, it would establish her normal routine for the day, and it would allow her to see her sister one last time before crossing the line that would transform her from victim's family member into something else entirely.

Sierra was in the common room when Alira arrived, working on a jigsaw puzzle designed for children ages five to seven. The puzzle featured cartoon animals in a farm setting—cows, chickens, pigs, horses—each piece large and brightly colored to make assembly easy for small hands and developing minds.

"Alira!" Sierra exclaimed with the unfiltered joy of someone whose damaged brain could no longer moderate emotional expression. "Look, I'm almost done with the puzzle! Just need to find the last three pieces!"

"That's wonderful, Sierra," Alira said, sitting beside her sister and studying the nearly completed puzzle. "You're getting so good at these."

Sierra beamed with pride, then returned her attention to the scattered pieces still waiting to be placed. Her fingers moved with careful deliberation, testing each piece against the remaining gaps until she found the correct fit. The concentration on her face was absolute—this puzzle represented the full extent of her current intellectual capacity, a task that the brilliant graduate student she'd been before Webb's assault would have completed in seconds without conscious thought.

Watching Sierra work on the puzzle, Alira felt the familiar mixture of grief and rage that had become the emotional foundation of her existence. This was what powerful predators did to vulnerable women—they destroyed not just bodies but minds, futures, the entire trajectory of lives that would have contributed beauty and knowledge and healing to a world that desperately needed those things.

Webb had stolen Sierra's brilliant mind and replaced it with childlike simplicity that found satisfaction in completing puzzles designed for kindergarteners. Blackwood had destroyed at least forty-three women's lives through assault, legal intimidation, and systematic character assassination. And the legal systems that were supposed to protect victims had instead protected their attackers, using institutional machinery to punish anyone who dared challenge powerful men.

Tonight, that would change. Tonight, at least one predator would face consequences that no amount of wealth or legal sophistication could prevent.

"Alira?" Sierra said, looking up from her puzzle with the innocent curiosity of a child. "Why do you look sad? Did something bad happen?"

The question struck Alira with unexpected force. Sierra's damaged mind could no longer understand complex causation or remember events beyond immediate experience, but she could still read emotional states with the intuitive accuracy that had made her such an effective therapist before Webb had destroyed her.

"I'm not sad, Sierra," Alira replied, forcing a smile that felt brittle and artificial. "I'm just thinking about some things I need to do today. Important things that might help other people who've been hurt the way you were hurt."

Sierra's expression showed confused concern, her limited cognitive capacity struggling to process the abstract concept of helping people through actions not yet taken. But after a moment, her face brightened with understanding that was heartbreakingly simplified.

"That's good," Sierra said with absolute conviction. "Helping people is good. That's what I was going to do before... before I got hurt. I was going to help children who were sad and scared. I don't remember very well, but I know that's what I wanted to do."

The fragment of memory, emerging unexpectedly from Sierra's damaged consciousness, nearly broke Alira's carefully maintained composure. Sierra rarely remembered anything about her life before the assault, her brilliant academic career and therapeutic aspirations lost along with the cognitive capacity that would have allowed her to achieve them. But occasionally, brief moments of lucidity would surface like debris from a shipwreck, reminding Alira of everything that had been stolen from her sister.

"Yes," Alira said, her voice thick with suppressed emotion. "That's exactly what you wanted to do. You were going to help damaged children heal from trauma and abuse. You would have been extraordinary at it, Sierra. You would have saved so many lives."

"I wish I could remember better," Sierra said wistfully. "But it's okay. You remember for me, right? You remember what I wanted to do?"

"I remember everything," Alira promised. "And I'm going to make sure that what happened to you means something. I'm going to make sure that bad men who hurt people face consequences, even when the police and lawyers can't stop them."

Sierra nodded with the solemn understanding of a child receiving an important truth from a trusted adult. She couldn't comprehend the full implications of what Alira was saying, but she understood that her sister was trying to do something good, something that would help people who'd been hurt the way she'd been hurt.

"That's good," Sierra repeated. "Helping people is good."

Alira stayed with Sierra for another hour, helping her complete the puzzle and then starting a new one—this time featuring Disney princesses that Sierra approached with the same careful concentration she'd brought to the farm animals. The visit reinforced everything Alira needed to feel certain about what she was planning. Sierra's destroyed brilliance, her childlike simplicity, her complete dependence on institutional care—all of it was the direct result of a predatory man's violence and the legal system's failure to deliver accountability.

Tonight, Alira would ensure that at least one predator faced the consequences he'd evaded for twenty-eight years.

She left Riverside Care Facility at 11:30 AM, driving directly to a medical supply warehouse on the industrial side of the city. Over the past two weeks, she'd been assembling the equipment she needed for Blackwood's murder, purchasing items from different suppliers using different false identities to avoid creating patterns that might later be traced back to her.

The warehouse specialized in supplying small medical practices, research laboratories, and institutional healthcare facilities with equipment and chemicals that didn't require the same level of scrutiny as controlled pharmaceutical substances. Alira had established a relationship with the warehouse manager three weeks ago, presenting herself as a research assistant for a university biochemistry laboratory that needed supplies for ongoing studies.

"Morning, Dr. Gardner," the warehouse manager greeted her as she entered. He'd never questioned Sophia Gardner's academic credentials or her authority to purchase medical supplies on behalf of a university laboratory that didn't actually exist. "What can I help you with today?"

"I need to pick up an order of potassium chloride solution," Alira replied, presenting a purchase order she'd created using falsified university letterhead. "We're running low on stock and have some time-sensitive experiments scheduled for the next few weeks."

The manager checked his computer system, verifying that the order had been prepared and was ready for pickup. "Looks like we have everything ready for you. That'll be four 500-milliliter bottles of potassium chloride solution at medical grade concentration. Sign here and I'll have someone bring it out from the stockroom."

Alira signed the release form using Sophia Gardner's practiced signature, knowing that even if police eventually traced the purchase, it would lead to a false identity rather than her real name. The potassium chloride itself was a common laboratory chemical with legitimate medical and research applications, making its purchase unremarkable and unsuspicious.

Five minutes later, she was driving away from the warehouse with four bottles of the solution that would stop Richard Blackwood's heart. The amount she'd purchased was far more than needed for a single injection—the excess would be disposed of in ways that would prevent any later discovery that might connect her to Blackwood's death.

Back at her apartment, Alira spent the early afternoon conducting final preparations with the meticulous attention to detail that had characterized her entire three-week planning process. She assembled the equipment she would carry to Blackwood's penthouse: a modified cosmetics bag that concealed a medical syringe pre-loaded with 10 milliliters of potassium chloride solution, a small bottle of hand sanitizer that would serve as cover for the chemical smell if anyone noticed it, and the usual items women carried in their purses—wallet, phone, lipstick, compact mirror.

The syringe itself was a marvel of concealment engineering. Alira had purchased a standard medical syringe and modified it to fit inside a hollowed-out tube of lipstick, creating a device that would pass casual inspection while remaining accessible for rapid deployment when needed. The needle was covered by a protective cap that would prevent accidental injection while allowing quick removal when the moment came.

She practiced the retrieval and deployment sequence twenty times, timing herself to ensure she could access the syringe, remove the protective cap, and position it for injection in under three seconds. The speed was crucial—Blackwood would be physically stronger than her, and she would have only a brief window of opportunity when his guard was down or his position was vulnerable.

The injection itself would need to be delivered with precision into a major blood vessel—ideally the carotid artery in his neck, but potentially the femoral artery in his thigh or another accessible vessel that would allow rapid distribution of the potassium chloride throughout his cardiovascular system. She'd studied vascular anatomy until she could identify injection sites by touch, and she'd practiced the injection motion until it felt as natural as any habitual physical movement.

At 3:00 PM, Alira began preparing herself psychologically for the evening's performance. She'd spent weeks developing Sophia Gardner's persona, but the character who would meet Blackwood tonight needed to be perfect in every detail—voice, mannerisms, emotional responses, the subtle behaviors that distinguished genuine naivety from conscious performance.

She stood before her bathroom mirror, practicing Sophia's facial expressions and vocal patterns. Sophia was nervous but excited about meeting Blackwood, grateful for his willingness to help with her financial situation, naive about the dangers of entering into arrangements with predatory men. Her smile was slightly uncertain, her laugh a bit too eager, her body language open and unguarded in ways that suggested someone who hadn't yet learned to protect herself from men who viewed vulnerability as invitation.

"Thank you so much for inviting me, Mr. Blackwood," Alira said to her reflection in Sophia's voice, slightly higher and more tentative than her natural tone. "Your penthouse is absolutely beautiful. I've never been anywhere this nice before."

The performance was flawless—enthusiastic enough to flatter Blackwood's ego, inexperienced enough to appeal to his predatory instincts, financially desperate enough to suggest complete compliance with whatever he might demand.

But Sophia would need to transform the moment Blackwood's assault began. The naive graduate student would become a traumatized victim fighting for her life, someone whose defensive response would seem completely justified and whose ultimate survival would be attributed to luck rather than planning. Alira practiced that transformation as well, watching her expression shift from nervous anticipation to genuine fear, hearing her voice change from tentative enthusiasm to panicked desperation.

"No, please stop! I don't want this! Stop!" The words came out with authentic terror, the vocal patterns matching recordings she'd studied of assault survivors calling for help. "Someone help me! Please, I don't want this!"

The performance would need to be perfect because police would later ask Sophia to describe what had happened, and her account would need to match physical evidence while establishing the narrative that would protect her from suspicion. Wealthy predator invites young woman to his penthouse. Assault begins. Woman fights back. Predator suffers fatal heart attack during struggle. Woman survives but is traumatized by experience.

At 5:00 PM, Alira prepared her final insurance policy—the defensive wounds that would corroborate her story of fighting back against Blackwood's assault. She used a specialized abrasive pad to create shallow scratches on her arms and shoulders, injuries that would be consistent with struggling against someone trying to restrain her. She applied controlled pressure to create bruising on her wrists that would suggest someone had grabbed her forcibly.

The injuries were painful but superficial, exactly what would be expected from a woman defending herself against assault. They would be photographed by police forensic technicians, documented in medical examinations, and ultimately serve as physical evidence supporting Sophia's account of events.

At 6:00 PM, Alira began the process of becoming Sophia Gardner for what would be the final and most important performance of the character she'd created. She showered carefully, washing away any trace evidence that might later connect her apartment to the crime scene. She styled her hair in the slightly uncertain way that Sophia favored—not quite professional enough to suggest confidence, but put together enough to show she'd made effort for the evening.

The dress she'd selected was perfect for Blackwood's instructions to dress "nicely but not too formally"—a navy blue cocktail dress that was sophisticated but not overtly sexual, professional but approachable. The neckline was modest, the hem fell just above her knees, and the overall impression was of someone trying to look mature and put-together despite limited resources for expensive clothing.

She applied makeup with careful attention to creating Sophia's aesthetic—minimal foundation that suggested someone who couldn't afford expensive cosmetics, neutral eye shadow that looked professional without being dramatic, lipstick in a shade that was appropriate but not memorable. The overall effect was pleasant but unremarkable, exactly what someone like Blackwood would expect from a financially struggling graduate student trying to look nice for an important meeting.

Jewelry was minimal—small earrings, a simple necklace that had supposedly belonged to Sophia's grandmother. The watch was inexpensive but functional, several years old and showing slight wear consistent with someone who couldn't afford to replace accessories regularly.

At 7:15 PM, Alira conducted a final equipment check. The modified lipstick containing the syringe was secured in her purse, easily accessible but invisible to casual inspection. Her phone was fully charged and set to record audio automatically when activated—the recording would capture Blackwood's assault and her resistance, providing additional evidence that would support her narrative if needed.

She'd programmed three emergency contacts into the phone under fake names—if something went catastrophically wrong and she needed immediate help, she could trigger calls to burner phones she controlled that would create the appearance of having friends or family she could reach out to for support.

At 7:30 PM, Alira left her apartment and walked to the parking garage where she'd stored the rental car she would use to drive to the Meridian Tower. The vehicle was registered under Sophia Gardner's false identity, providing another layer of protection if police later investigated her movements on the evening of Blackwood's death.

During the twenty-minute drive to the Meridian Tower, Alira maintained Sophia's persona completely, speaking her nervous thoughts aloud in the car to reinforce the character she would need to sustain for the next several hours.

"It's going to be fine," she said in Sophia's voice, practicing the slightly uncertain tone of someone trying to convince herself of something she didn't quite believe. "Mr. Blackwood seems really nice, and he's going to help me with my financial problems so I can focus on school. I just need to be flexible and understanding like he said. Everything is going to work out."

The self-reassurance was exactly what someone like Sophia would engage in before walking into a situation she knew might be dangerous but felt compelled to accept because of financial desperation. If police later questioned neighbors about whether they'd heard anything unusual from her car in the parking garage, the nervous self-talk would reinforce the narrative of someone who'd been genuinely uncertain about meeting Blackwood rather than someone who'd been planning his murder for three weeks.

At 7:52 PM, Alira pulled into a parking space two blocks from the Meridian Tower. She sat in the car for three minutes, taking slow breaths and centering herself for the performance that was about to begin. The nervousness she felt was authentic—not fear of what she was planning to do, but the natural anxiety that came from knowing the next few hours would determine whether she successfully eliminated a predator or ended up arrested for murder.

At 7:58 PM, she locked the car and began walking toward the Meridian Tower, her pace deliberately measured to arrive at exactly 8:00 PM. Punctuality would reinforce Sophia's eagerness to please and her naive belief that following Blackwood's instructions would result in the generous arrangement he'd promised.

The Meridian Tower's lobby was as opulent as Alira remembered from her surveillance—marble floors, contemporary art installations, uniformed doormen who existed primarily to reinforce the building's atmosphere of wealth and exclusivity. She approached the desk with Sophia's characteristic mixture of nervousness and excitement.

"Good evening," she said to the doorman, her voice slightly breathless from the walk and from practiced performance. "I'm Sophia Gardner. I'm expected by Mr. Blackwood in the penthouse?"

The doorman checked his tablet, verifying that Sophia Gardner was indeed on the approved visitor list for the evening. "Yes, Miss Gardner. Mr. Blackwood is expecting you. I'll escort you to his private elevator."

As they walked across the lobby toward the elevator bank, Alira maintained perfect composure despite knowing that in approximately thirty minutes, she would commit her first murder. The doorman made polite small talk about the weather and the building's amenities, completely unaware that he was escorting a killer to her victim.

The private elevator required the doorman's keycard for activation. He swiped the card, the elevator doors opened, and Alira stepped inside the confined space that would carry her directly into Richard Blackwood's penthouse.

"Have a pleasant evening, Miss Gardner," the doorman said as the doors began to close.

"Thank you," Alira replied in Sophia's voice. "I'm sure I will."

The elevator began its ascent to the penthouse, and Alira felt her consciousness shift into the heightened state of awareness that would sustain her through everything that was about to happen. Sophia Gardner was about to meet Richard Blackwood for dinner and discussion of their potential arrangement.

But Richard Blackwood would never see another morning.

The hunt was about to begin, and the hunter was ready.

Chapter 5

The Penthouse

The elevator rose smoothly toward the top floor of the Meridian Tower, its motion so fluid that Alira could barely detect the sensation of upward movement. The interior was paneled in dark wood with brass fixtures that gleamed under recessed lighting, creating an atmosphere of understated luxury that was designed to impress without overwhelming. A small security camera was positioned in the upper corner, its red recording light blinking steadily as it documented her ascent.

Alira kept her expression neutral with just a hint of nervous anticipation, exactly what would be expected from someone like Sophia Gardner arriving for her first meeting with a wealthy man who'd promised financial support in exchange for "flexible companionship." The camera footage would later be reviewed by police investigators looking for any evidence of premeditation or suspicious behavior, and they would see only an anxious young woman arriving for what she believed would be a dinner meeting to discuss a mutually beneficial arrangement.

The elevator slowed as it approached the penthouse level, and Alira felt her heart rate increase slightly—not from fear, but from the physiological response to knowing that the next thirty to sixty minutes would determine whether she successfully committed her first murder or ended up arrested for attempted homicide. She took a slow breath, centering herself in the persona she'd spent three weeks perfecting.

The elevator chimed softly and the doors slid open, revealing not a hallway but the interior of Richard Blackwood's penthouse itself. The private elevator opened directly into his residence, exactly as Alira's surveillance had confirmed—a security arrangement that provided privacy while also creating the isolation that would make what she was planning possible.

Richard Blackwood stood approximately fifteen feet from the elevator, positioned in the center of his spacious living room with a glass of wine in his hand and an expression of proprietary satisfaction on his face. He was dressed casually but expensively—dark slacks, a white dress shirt with the sleeves rolled up to his elbows, no tie. The outfit projected relaxed confidence while subtly emphasizing his physical presence and the muscular forearms that suggested he maintained his athletic build despite his age.

"Sophia," he said warmly, his voice carrying the smooth charm he'd deployed in their phone conversations. "Welcome. Please, come in. Don't be shy."

Alira stepped out of the elevator into the penthouse, allowing Sophia's nervous energy to show in her body language while her eyes quickly catalogued details of her surroundings that would be crucial for what was coming. The living room was exactly as she'd observed through her telephoto surveillance—floor-to-ceiling windows offering panoramic views of the city, modern furniture arranged in conversation areas, contemporary art on the walls, a kitchen visible through an open doorway to her left.

More importantly, she noted the locations of potential weapons or obstacles—a heavy glass sculpture on a side table, the distance to the kitchen where knives would be accessible, the arrangement of furniture that could either provide cover or create impediments to movement. The layout of the space would determine how the confrontation unfolded once Blackwood's assault began and Alira needed to create the opportunity for injection.

"Mr. Blackwood," she said in Sophia's slightly breathless voice, "thank you so much for inviting me. Your home is absolutely beautiful. I've never been anywhere this nice before."

The compliment was calculated to flatter his ego while reinforcing her supposed economic vulnerability—she was someone who could be impressed and controlled through exposure to wealth she'd never personally experienced. Blackwood's expression showed satisfaction at her reaction, confirming that she was responding exactly as he'd expected.

"Please, call me Richard," he said, moving toward her with the confident stride of someone completely comfortable in his environment and certain of his control over the situation. "Sophia is such a lovely name. Chinese heritage?"

"Yes, on my father's side," Alira replied, maintaining Sophia's background story. "Though I was born here and I'm afraid my Mandarin is pretty terrible. My parents always wanted me to be more connected to that part of my heritage, but I was more interested in Western art history."

The biographical detail was irrelevant to what was about to happen, but it reinforced Sophia as a real person with authentic background rather than a constructed persona. Blackwood wouldn't care about her family heritage—he was making small talk designed to help her "relax" before he began the assault he'd been planning since their first communication.

"Well, you've certainly chosen an interesting field of study," Blackwood said, gesturing toward his living room. "Though I have to admit, art history isn't known for being particularly lucrative. That's why you're looking for arrangements like this, I assume?"

The directness was clearly intentional—Blackwood was establishing immediately that their relationship was transactional, that her financial desperation was the leverage that would ensure her compliance with whatever he demanded.

"Yes," Alira said, allowing embarrassment to color Sophia's voice. "I love what I'm studying, but the financial reality is pretty challenging. Graduate stipends barely cover rent, and I've been working multiple part-time jobs just to stay afloat. When I saw your profile on Elite Companions, it seemed like exactly what I needed—someone who could help me focus on my studies rather than constantly worrying about money."

"Well, I think we can definitely help each other," Blackwood replied, his tone becoming slightly more intimate as he moved closer to her. "Why don't you come sit down? I had dinner delivered—nothing too heavy, just some appetizers and wine. We can eat and talk about what kind of arrangement might work for both of us."

He gestured toward a seating area near the windows, where a coffee table had been arranged with several plates of expensive-looking appetizers—cheese, crackers, olives, cured meats, fruit. Two wine glasses sat beside an opened bottle of red wine that Alira recognized from her research as costing several hundred dollars per bottle.

The setup was classic Blackwood—create an atmosphere of sophistication and generosity, offer alcohol to lower inhibitions and create legal complications if the victim later claimed assault, establish the transactional nature of the relationship while maintaining plausible deniability about the sexual expectations underlying the arrangement.

Alira allowed Sophia to be impressed by the display, moving toward the seating area with the slightly uncertain gait of someone who wasn't quite comfortable in such an expensive environment. She sat on the edge of the sofa, positioning herself so that her purse remained easily accessible while her posture conveyed nervous anticipation rather than threat.

Blackwood poured wine into both glasses, filling them nearly to the rim—far more than would be appropriate for casual dinner conversation, clearly intending to encourage rapid consumption that would impair Sophia's judgment and physical capabilities.

"This is a 2015 Bordeaux from a small vineyard I visited a few years ago," he said, handing her one of the overfilled glasses. "I think you'll find it's excellent. Not too dry, very smooth finish."

Alira accepted the glass with Sophia's grateful smile, bringing it to her lips and taking a small sip while ensuring that very little of the wine actually entered her mouth. The taste was indeed excellent—rich and complex in ways that justified its expensive price—but she had no intention of consuming enough alcohol to impair her cognitive function or physical coordination.

Over the next twenty minutes, as Blackwood made small talk about art, culture, and his real estate development business, Alira engaged in a carefully choreographed performance of pretending to drink while actually consuming minimal alcohol. She would bring the glass to her lips frequently, appearing to take substantial sips while barely wetting her mouth with wine. When Blackwood wasn't looking directly at her, she would discreetly pour small amounts of wine into the potted plant positioned conveniently near her seat.

The deception was crucial—Blackwood expected his victims to become intoxicated and therefore more vulnerable to assault while also creating legal complications about consent that would protect him if they later tried to report his crimes. But Alira needed to maintain complete control of her faculties for what was coming.

"You know, Sophia," Blackwood said after his third glass of wine—he was drinking genuinely while she was performing consumption—"I have to say I'm impressed by how sophisticated you are for someone your age. Most of the women I meet through these services are... well, let's just say they don't have your level of intellectual engagement with culture and ideas."

The compliment was backhanded and revealing—he was comparing her favorably to other women he'd exploited through dating services, suggesting an extensive history of exactly the kind of predatory behavior that Alira had documented through her research.

"Thank you," she said in Sophia's voice, allowing herself to appear flattered by the attention. "I've always believed that financial struggles shouldn't prevent someone from pursuing intellectual interests. Art and culture belong to everyone, not just people who can afford expensive educations and luxury lifestyles."

"A noble sentiment," Blackwood replied, moving closer to her on the sofa. "Though I have to admit, I appreciate when intelligence comes in such an attractive package. You're really quite beautiful, Sophia. The photographs in your profile didn't do you justice."

The transition was beginning—Blackwood was shifting from superficial conversation to more personal and physical attention, testing her boundaries and assessing how she would respond to increasingly intimate remarks. This was the pattern Alira had identified through her research into his previous victims: establish superficial rapport, offer alcohol to lower inhibitions, make increasingly forward comments and physical advances, then escalate to assault when the victim was too impaired or intimidated to effectively resist.

"That's very kind of you to say," Alira replied, maintaining Sophia's slightly uncertain demeanor. "I have to admit I'm not always very confident about my appearance.

Grad school doesn't leave much time or money for keeping up with fashion or beauty routines."

"Well, I think you look perfect exactly as you are," Blackwood said, reaching out to touch her arm in a gesture that appeared casual but was clearly testing her response to physical contact. "Natural beauty is much more appealing than artificial enhancement."

His hand remained on her arm, fingers applying slight pressure that suggested ownership rather than friendly contact. Alira allowed the touch to continue for several seconds before shifting her position slightly—not pulling away completely, which might suggest suspicion or resistance, but creating subtle distance that appeared unconscious rather than deliberate.

"Would you like to see the rest of the penthouse?" Blackwood asked, his tone making clear that this was less an invitation than an expectation. "I have a beautiful view from the bedroom, and I think you'd appreciate the art collection I have displayed there."

The bedroom. Of course. The assault would happen there, in the location where Blackwood had attacked dozens of women over his twenty-eight-year predatory career. The bedroom would provide the privacy he needed while also creating the psychological dynamic he sought—bringing victims into his most intimate space established dominance and control while making them feel complicit in what was about to happen to them.

"I'd love to see more of your home," Alira said, maintaining Sophia's eager-to-please tone despite knowing exactly what Blackwood intended. "The art you have displayed out here is already so impressive. I'd be fascinated to see what else you've collected."

Blackwood stood and offered his hand to help her up from the sofa—a gentlemanly gesture that concealed the proprietary nature of his intentions. Alira accepted the assistance, rising with the slightly unsteady movement of someone who appeared to have consumed more wine than she actually had.

They moved through the penthouse toward the bedroom, passing through a hallway lined with contemporary art that Blackwood described with the superficial knowledge of someone who'd purchased pieces for status rather than genuine appreciation. Alira responded with Sophia's enthusiastic interest, asking questions that made her appear intellectually engaged while her tactical awareness catalogued the layout and identifying potential escape routes if something went wrong.

The bedroom was exactly as she'd observed through her surveillance—king-sized bed with luxury linens, more floor-to-ceiling windows offering city views, additional art on the walls, and most importantly, relative isolation from the living areas where sound might carry to neighboring units or building security.

"This is the piece I wanted you to see," Blackwood said, gesturing toward a large abstract painting that dominated one wall. "It's from a Japanese artist whose work is just starting to gain international recognition. I acquired it at auction last year for significantly less than I expect it will be worth in five years."

The art discussion was transparent pretense—Blackwood had brought Sophia to the bedroom not to appreciate his collection but to create the setting for assault. But protocol required that they maintain the fiction of cultural conversation while he positioned her where he wanted her and prepared to make his move.

Alira moved toward the painting with Sophia's apparent fascination, studying the abstract forms and colors while maintaining awareness of Blackwood's position behind her. This was the moment when his assault would likely begin—he would move close, perhaps place his hands on her shoulders or waist, make increasingly intimate physical contact while gauging her response and preparing to escalate to force if she showed resistance.

"The color composition is really striking," she said, maintaining focus on the painting while her peripheral vision tracked Blackwood's approach. "The way the artist uses negative space to create tension and movement is—"

Blackwood's hands settled on her shoulders, gripping with pressure that was too firm to be merely friendly. "You really are quite beautiful, Sophia," he said, his voice taking on a different quality—no longer charming and sophisticated, but something darker and more predatory. "I think we're going to have a very satisfying arrangement."

His hands moved from her shoulders down her arms, the touch no longer even pretending to be appropriate or consensual. This was the transition Alira had been waiting for—the moment when Blackwood revealed his true intentions and began the assault that would end with his death rather than another successful exploitation.

"Mr. Blackwood—Richard—I'm not sure I'm ready for—" Alira began in Sophia's voice, allowing nervousness to become more pronounced as she started to turn away from him.

But Blackwood's grip tightened, preventing her movement. "Shh, it's okay," he said in a tone that was meant to be reassuring but carried an unmistakable threat. "Just relax. I told you I'd take care of you, and I will. You just need to trust me and be flexible like we discussed. This is part of the arrangement, Sophia. This is what you agreed to when you came here tonight."

The words were calculated to create doubt and compliance—suggesting that she'd somehow consented to what he was about to do, that resistance would be inappropriate and might result in withdrawal of the financial support he'd promised. It was the same psychological manipulation he'd deployed against dozens of women, using their economic desperation and social conditioning to secure compliance with assault.

But Alira wasn't actually Sophia Gardner, and she'd come prepared for exactly this moment.

"No, I didn't agree to this," she said, her voice shifting from Sophia's uncertainty to something clearer and more forceful. "I thought we were going to talk about arrangements, not—please let go of me. You're hurting me."

Blackwood's expression hardened at the resistance, his charming façade dissolving to reveal the predatory nature that had always existed beneath it. His grip on her arms tightened to the point of pain, and he pulled her back against his body with force that eliminated any pretense of consensual contact.

"Listen to me carefully, Sophia," he said, his voice now carrying open threat. "You came to my home voluntarily. You drank my wine, you allowed me to touch you, you came into my bedroom. If you try to claim this wasn't consensual, no one will believe you. I have lawyers who've handled situations like this dozens of times, and they know exactly how to make women like you look like liars and opportunists. So I suggest you relax and let this happen, because fighting me will only make things worse for you."

The threat was explicit and comprehensive—Blackwood was telling her that resistance was futile, that the legal and financial resources he commanded would destroy her if she tried to report what he was about to do. It was the same threat he'd delivered to forty-three women over twenty-eight years, the same institutional power he'd weaponized to escape accountability for a career of sexual violence.

But tonight, that institutional power would fail him.

Alira allowed genuine fear to show in her expression—not performance, but authentic response to being physically restrained by someone significantly stronger than herself. The fear was necessary for what came next, for the narrative she would provide to police about fighting back against assault in genuine terror for her safety.

"Please don't do this," she said, her voice carrying the panic of someone realizing they'd made a terrible mistake coming to this penthouse. "I'll leave right now, I won't tell anyone about this, just please let me go."

"Too late for that," Blackwood replied, beginning to force her toward the bed. "You're going to give me what I want, and then we'll discuss how much financial support you'll receive to keep quiet about our arrangement. This is how these relationships work, Sophia. The sooner you understand that, the easier this will be for you."

His hands moved to the zipper of her dress, beginning to pull it down while maintaining his grip on her arm with his other hand. The assault was escalating exactly as Alira had anticipated, following the pattern she'd identified through research into his previous victims' accounts.

This was the moment. Blackwood was focused on restraining her and removing her clothing, his attention divided and his defensive awareness minimal. His neck was exposed as he bent toward her, the carotid artery clearly visible beneath his skin.

Alira's right hand moved to her purse, which she'd deliberately positioned so it remained accessible during their movement toward the bed. Her fingers found the modified lipstick tube, extracting it with practiced efficiency while her left hand pushed against Blackwood's chest in apparent resistance.

"No! Stop! I don't want this!" she shouted, her voice carrying the genuine panic that would be necessary for the 911 call she would make in approximately ninety seconds.

Blackwood's response was to increase the force of his restraint, pulling her more tightly against him while his hand continued working at her dress zipper. His face was inches from hers, his breathing heavy with exertion and arousal, his complete focus on overpowering her resistance.

He never saw the syringe.

Alira's right hand came up in a smooth arc that she'd practiced hundreds of times, the protective cap already removed from the needle, the injection positioned for optimal penetration of the carotid artery. The motion took less than one second from the moment her hand left her purse to the moment the needle entered Blackwood's neck.

His eyes widened in shock and confusion as he felt the sharp pain of penetration, his grip loosening slightly as his brain processed the unexpected sensation. But recognition came too late—Alira had already depressed the plunger, delivering 10 milliliters of concentrated potassium chloride solution directly into his carotid artery where it would reach his heart within seconds.

"What—what did you—" Blackwood stammered, his hand moving toward his neck where the needle still protruded from his flesh.

Alira pulled the syringe free and stepped back, watching with clinical detachment as the potassium chloride began its lethal work. Blackwood staggered, his hand pressed against the injection site, his expression shifting from anger to confusion to the first stirrings of genuine fear as his cardiovascular system began to fail.

"What did you do to me?" he demanded, his voice already showing signs of distress as his heart rhythm became erratic. "What did you give me?"

"Justice," Alira replied, her voice no longer carrying any trace of Sophia Gardner's uncertainty. "Something you've managed to avoid for twenty-eight years. Something the legal system was too corrupted to deliver to the forty-three women whose lives you destroyed."

Blackwood lurched toward her, whether to attack or to seek help she couldn't determine, but his movements were already becoming uncoordinated as the potassium chloride disrupted his cardiac function. He took two steps before his legs buckled, sending him crashing to his knees with an impact that would have been painful if his nervous system hadn't been failing too rapidly to properly process sensation.

"You... you can't..." he gasped, his hands clutching at his chest as his heart began to fibrillate. "Lawyers... police... they'll..."

"They'll find a wealthy predator who died of a heart attack while attempting to assault a young woman," Alira said calmly, watching as Blackwood's face began to turn grayish-blue from oxygen deprivation. "They'll find defensive wounds on my arms where you grabbed me. They'll find evidence of struggle. They'll find your history of settlement payments and accusations. And they'll close the case as a tragic but unremarkable death—a man whose lifestyle and stress levels caught up with him at an inopportune moment."

Blackwood tried to respond, but his respiratory system was shutting down along with his cardiovascular function. He collapsed fully onto the bedroom floor, his body convulsing as his heart's electrical system failed completely. His eyes remained open, staring at Alira with an expression that combined disbelief, rage, and the dawning understanding that he was dying and there was nothing his wealth or lawyers could do to prevent it.

Alira stood watching until the convulsions stopped and Blackwood's chest ceased its labored attempts at breathing. The entire process from injection to death had taken approximately ninety seconds—faster than she'd anticipated, suggesting that her dosage calculations had been accurate and that the direct carotid injection had achieved optimal distribution of the potassium chloride throughout his cardiovascular system.

Richard Blackwood was dead. The predator who'd destroyed at least forty-three women's lives over twenty-eight years had finally faced consequences that no amount of institutional protection could prevent.

Now came the performance that would ensure Alira's survival and freedom.

She dropped the empty syringe into her purse—it would be disposed of later in ways that would prevent discovery—and retrieved her phone. Her hands were steady despite what she'd just done, her breathing controlled, her mind clear about the sequence of actions that would transform her from killer to survivor in the police narrative that would soon be constructed.

She used her phone to take several photographs of Blackwood's body, documenting his position and the scene from multiple angles. The photographs would never be seen by police—they were for her own records, proof of what she'd accomplished and insurance against any future doubts about whether Blackwood had truly deserved death.

Then she opened the camera app and switched it to video mode, positioning the phone to record herself as she delivered the performance that would shape official understanding of events.

Alira took several deep breaths, allowing tears to form in her eyes—not from grief or guilt, but from the deliberate triggering of stress responses that would create authentic physiological markers of trauma. When she spoke, her voice carried the shaking quality of genuine panic rather than performed distress.

"Oh my god. Oh my god, he's not breathing. I think he's dead. He tried to—he was trying to—oh god, what do I do?"

She allowed herself to collapse to the floor several feet from Blackwood's body, her breathing becoming rapid and shallow in a textbook presentation of panic attack. The performance needed to be perfect because police would later review this video if they had any suspicions about her account of events.

After thirty seconds of recorded panic, Alira ended the video and opened her phone's dial pad. Her finger hovered over the emergency call button for a moment as she centered herself for the most important performance of the evening—the 911 call that would establish the official narrative of Richard Blackwood's death.

She pressed the button and brought the phone to her ear, listening to it ring twice before an operator answered.

"911, what's your emergency?"

"Please help me," Alira said, her voice breaking with authentic terror. "I'm at the Meridian Tower penthouse and there's a man—he tried to assault me and I fought back and now he's not breathing and I think he might be dead and I don't know what to do—"

"Ma'am, I need you to slow down and tell me exactly what happened. Are you injured? Are you in immediate danger?"

"No, I don't think so. He's on the floor and he's not moving. I think he had a heart attack or something. We were struggling and he just—he just collapsed and now he won't wake up."

"Okay, ma'am, I'm dispatching emergency services to your location right now. Can you tell me if the man is breathing?"

Alira moved closer to Blackwood's body, maintaining her panicked breathing while she performed the check that 911 operators always requested. "No, I don't think so. His chest isn't moving and his eyes are open but he's not responding."

"Do you know how to perform CPR?"

The question was expected, and Alira had her response prepared. "I—I don't think I can. I'm too scared. What if he wakes up and tries to hurt me again? Please just send someone. Please."

"Emergency services are on their way, ma'am. They should arrive in approximately five minutes. I need you to stay on the line with me. Can you tell me your name?"

This was the crucial moment—the point where Alira would abandon the Sophia Gardner persona and provide her real identity to authorities. Maintaining the false identity beyond this point would create legal problems and raise suspicions that would undermine her entire defense.

"My name is Alira Sinclair," she said, speaking clearly despite the panic in her voice. "I used a different name—Sophia Gardner—on the dating profile where I met him. I thought it would be safer to use a fake name online. A lot of women do that. But my real name is Alira Sinclair."

"Okay, Alira, can you tell me what happened? How did you come to be in this penthouse?"

This was the narrative that would guide police understanding of events. Alira delivered it with perfect combination of panic and coherence, someone traumatized but still capable of providing essential information.

"I met him through a dating service called Elite Companions. I used the name Sophia Gardner on my profile because I didn't want to use my real identity online—it's safer that way. He contacted me and we talked for about three weeks through email and phone. He seemed nice, and he said he could help me with my finances while I'm in graduate school. Tonight was supposed to be our first meeting to talk about what kind of arrangement we could work out. But when I got here he started drinking heavily and then he tried to—he tried to force himself on me. I told him to stop but he wouldn't listen. We were struggling and then he just collapsed. I think his heart gave out or something. Oh god, is he really dead?"

"Stay calm, Alira. Help is almost there. Did he injure you during the struggle?"

"He grabbed my arms really hard. It hurts. I have scratches from trying to push him away."

"Okay, when the police and paramedics arrive, they'll make sure you receive medical attention for your injuries. You're doing great, Alira. Just keep breathing and stay with me."

Through the penthouse windows, Alira could see the flashing lights of emergency vehicles arriving at the Meridian Tower. The first responders would be entering the building within seconds, ascending in the elevator that would carry them to the scene of what they would believe was a tragic but unremarkable death—a wealthy man whose attempted assault had ended with fatal heart attack rather than another successful exploitation.

Richard Blackwood's pattern of predation had finally ended.

And Alira Sinclair's transformation from victim's family member into hunter of predators was complete.

IRA *Wrath*

"Justice delayed is justice denied." — William Gladstone

Chapter 6

The Investigation

The first responders arrived at the penthouse at 8:47 PM—exactly fourteen minutes after Alira had injected the potassium chloride into Richard Blackwood's carotid artery. The elevator doors opened to reveal two paramedics in their late twenties, both carrying emergency medical equipment and moving with the practiced efficiency of professionals who'd responded to countless crisis situations.

"FDNY Paramedics," the lead medic announced as they stepped into the penthouse. "We received a call about an unresponsive male?"

Alira was sitting on the floor approximately ten feet from Blackwood's body, her knees drawn up to her chest and her arms wrapped around herself in the classic posture of traumatized withdrawal. She'd positioned herself so that she appeared too frightened to approach the body but close enough to have theoretically attempted to help if she hadn't been paralyzed by fear and shock.

"He's in the bedroom," she said, her voice carrying the trembling quality of someone barely maintaining coherent speech. "I think he's dead. I couldn't—I was too scared to check properly. He tried to attack me and then he just collapsed."

The paramedics moved quickly toward the bedroom, their focus immediately shifting to the potential patient rather than the traumatized woman who'd called for help. Alira remained in her position on the living room floor, watching through the bedroom doorway as they began their assessment of Blackwood's condition.

The lead paramedic knelt beside Blackwood's body, immediately checking for pulse and respiration while his partner prepared emergency equipment. After approximately fifteen seconds of examination, the lead medic looked up at his partner with an expression that confirmed what they both already suspected.

"No pulse, no respiration, fixed and dilated pupils," he reported in the clinical tone that medical professionals used to maintain emotional distance from death. "Appears to have been down for at least ten to fifteen minutes based on presentation. Beginning assessment for resuscitation viability."

The paramedics worked quickly, checking Blackwood's body temperature, examining his skin color and rigor mortis development, assessing whether there was any realistic possibility of successful resuscitation. Their training required them to attempt revival in most circumstances, but they also understood that some deaths were too far advanced to be reversed through medical intervention.

"Body temp suggests he's been deceased for at least ten minutes, possibly longer," the partner reported. "Significant cyanosis and early rigor in the extremities. I'd estimate time of death at approximately 8:30 to 8:35 PM."

The timing was perfect—it placed Blackwood's death at exactly when Alira's 911 call had reported the emergency, supporting her narrative that he'd collapsed during their struggle and that she'd called for help immediately rather than allowing time to pass while she staged the scene.

"What's your recommendation?" the lead paramedic asked his partner.

"Deceased beyond viable resuscitation. We should call it and wait for police to arrive before disturbing the scene further."

The lead paramedic nodded, then stood and walked back toward the living room where Alira remained in her traumatized position on the floor. His expression had softened from professional assessment to something approaching compassion—he'd apparently been briefed by the 911 dispatcher about the circumstances leading to Blackwood's collapse.

"Ma'am—Alira?—I need to ask you some questions about what happened here tonight. Are you able to talk with me?"

Alira looked up at him with an expression that combined fear, confusion, and the desperate need for reassurance that what had happened wasn't somehow her fault. "Is he dead? I couldn't tell if he was breathing. I tried to check but I was too scared to get close to him after he collapsed."

"Yes ma'am, I'm afraid he is deceased. It appears he suffered some kind of cardiac event. But I need you to tell me exactly what happened. Can you do that?"

This was the first of many times Alira would need to recount her narrative about the evening's events, and the consistency of her story across multiple retellings would be crucial for maintaining the fiction that Blackwood's death had been a tragic accident rather than premeditated murder. She took a shaking breath and began the performance she'd rehearsed for three weeks.

"I met Richard—Mr. Blackwood—through a dating service called Elite Companions. I used a fake name on my profile—Sophia Gardner—because I thought it would be safer not to use my real identity online. A lot of women do that on dating sites. He contacted me about three weeks ago and said he was interested in someone who appreciated culture and intelligent conversation, and that he could help me with my financial situation while I'm in graduate school. We talked through email and phone calls using my fake identity, and tonight was supposed to be our first in-person meeting to discuss what kind of arrangement we might be able to work out."

The paramedic listened attentively, his expression neutral and professional. "Okay. What happened when you arrived?"

"He was very nice at first. We had wine and appetizers in the living room, and he talked about his art collection and his real estate business. Everything seemed fine. But then he wanted to show me a painting in his bedroom, and when we got there he started... he started touching me in ways that weren't appropriate. I told him I wasn't comfortable, that I thought we were just going to talk about arrangements, but he said I'd agreed to this by coming here and that I needed to be 'flexible' like we'd discussed."

Alira allowed her voice to break slightly, conveying the emotional impact of recounting traumatic events. The paramedic's expression showed sympathy, and he made notes on a tablet while maintaining appropriate professional distance.

"What happened next?"

"He grabbed my arms—hard—and he started trying to take my dress off. I told him to stop, that I wanted to leave, but he said his lawyers would destroy me if I tried to report that anything non-consensual had happened. He said he'd done this dozens of times before and he knew exactly how to make women like me look like liars."

The detail about Blackwood's threat was crucial—it established his pattern of predatory behavior while explaining why Alira might have been too frightened to fight back effectively. The paramedic's expression darkened slightly at the description, suggesting he'd understood the implication that Blackwood had been a serial predator.

"So there was a physical struggle?" the paramedic prompted.

"Yes. I was trying to push him away and he was trying to restrain me and get my dress off. We were struggling for maybe thirty seconds, maybe a minute—I don't really remember exactly how long. And then he just—his eyes got really wide and he made this gasping sound and he collapsed. Just dropped to the floor like someone had cut his strings. I thought maybe I'd hit him or something, but I don't remember striking him. He just fell."

"Did he say anything when he collapsed? Indicate what he was feeling?"

"He said 'what' or maybe 'wait'—something like that. And he grabbed at his chest like it hurt. Then he was on the floor and he was convulsing or shaking, and then he just stopped moving. I didn't know what to do. I was scared he might wake up and attack me again, but I also thought he might be dying and I should try to help. So I called 911."

The narrative was perfect—detailed enough to seem authentic, consistent with the physical evidence, and psychologically plausible for someone experiencing genuine trauma. The paramedic made additional notes, then asked the follow-up question that Alira had been anticipating.

"You mentioned he grabbed your arms. Are you injured? Do you need medical attention?"

"I don't know. My arms hurt where he grabbed me. And I have some scratches from when I was trying to push him away. But I don't think I need to go to the hospital or anything."

"I'd like to examine your injuries if you're comfortable with that. And when the police arrive, they'll probably want to photograph them as evidence. Is that okay?"

"Yes, that's fine. Whatever you need to do."

The paramedic conducted a brief examination of Alira's arms, documenting the bruises and scratches she'd carefully created hours earlier during her final preparations. The injuries were exactly what would be expected from someone defending herself against forcible restraint—linear abrasions from fingernails, contusions in hand-shaped patterns on her biceps and forearms, minor swelling around her wrists.

"These are consistent with defensive injuries from physical struggle," the paramedic noted, taking photographs with his tablet. "You'll probably have significant bruising over the next few days. I'd recommend ice and over-the-counter pain medication, and you should follow up with your regular doctor to document these injuries for any potential legal proceedings."

"Legal proceedings?" Alira asked, allowing confusion to show in her expression. "What do you mean?"

"Well, based on what you've described, there may be questions about whether Mr. Blackwood's death occurred during the commission of a sexual assault. The police will want to investigate thoroughly, which means they'll need to document everything that happened here tonight."

As if summoned by the mention of police investigation, the elevator chimed and two NYPD officers stepped into the penthouse. They were both in their forties, one male and one female, both carrying themselves with the alert professionalism of experienced patrol officers responding to a potential crime scene.

"NYPD," the male officer announced. "We received a report of an unresponsive male at this location. What's the situation?"

The lead paramedic approached the officers, speaking in the low tone that medical and law enforcement professionals used when discussing sensitive information within earshot of traumatized witnesses. Alira couldn't hear the specific words, but she could see the paramedic gesturing toward Blackwood's body in the bedroom and then toward her position on the living room floor.

After approximately two minutes of consultation, the female officer approached Alira while her partner moved toward the bedroom to assess the scene. The officer's expression was carefully neutral, maintaining professional detachment while also projecting the kind of reassurance that was supposed to make traumatized witnesses feel comfortable providing information.

"Miss Sinclair? I'm Officer Rodriguez. I understand you've had a very difficult evening. I need to ask you some questions about what happened here. Are you able to talk with me right now?"

"Yes," Alira replied, maintaining her traumatized demeanor. "I already told the paramedic what happened. Do I need to go through it again?"

"I'm afraid so. I know it's difficult, but I need to hear the account directly from you so I can document it properly in my report. Can you tell me why you came to this penthouse tonight?"

Alira repeated the narrative she'd provided to the paramedic, maintaining perfect consistency in details while allowing appropriate emotional variation in her delivery—someone recounting genuine trauma would show slight differences in emphasis and phrasing across multiple tellings, while someone reciting a rehearsed script would maintain unnatural consistency.

"I met Mr. Blackwood through a dating service called Elite Companions about three weeks ago. I used a fake name—Sophia Gardner—on my profile because I didn't want to use my real identity online. It's pretty common for women to do that for safety reasons. We communicated using that fake name through emails and phone calls, but my real name is Alira Sinclair. Tonight was our first in-person meeting, and it was supposed to be just dinner to discuss a potential arrangement where he would help me financially while I'm in graduate school."

Officer Rodriguez took detailed notes, occasionally asking clarifying questions about timing, physical positions, and specific statements Blackwood had made during the assault. The questions were professional and appropriate, showing no indication that the officer suspected anything other than what Alira's account claimed—an attempted sexual assault that had ended with the assailant's death from apparent cardiac event.

"Can you describe the moment when Mr. Blackwood collapsed? What exactly did you observe?"

"We were struggling and he was trying to pull my dress down. I was pushing against his chest trying to get him away from me. And then he just—his whole body kind of jerked, and his eyes got really wide, and he made this gasping sound like he couldn't breathe. He let go of me and grabbed at his chest, and then he fell. First to his knees, then onto his side. He was shaking or convulsing for a few seconds, and then he stopped moving."

"Did you see him take any medication before he collapsed? Or did he mention having any medical conditions?"

"No, nothing like that. He seemed perfectly healthy. We'd been drinking wine, but he didn't seem drunk or impaired. He was strong and in control right up until the moment he collapsed."

The detail about Blackwood's apparent health was important—it would support the medical examiner's eventual conclusion that his death resulted from an undiagnosed cardiac condition rather than any external cause that might trigger suspicion of foul play.

Officer Rodriguez's partner returned from the bedroom, speaking quietly with the female officer before they both approached Alira with expressions that suggested they'd reached a preliminary assessment of the situation.

"Miss Sinclair," Officer Rodriguez said, "based on what we've observed and what you've told us, it appears that

Mr. Blackwood suffered a fatal cardiac event during an attempted sexual assault. We're going to need you to come to the precinct to provide a formal statement, and we'll need to have forensic technicians photograph and document your injuries. Are you willing to cooperate with that process?"

"Of course. Whatever you need. I just want to understand what happened. One minute he was attacking me, and the next he was dead on the floor. I don't—I can't—" Alira allowed her voice to break convincingly, conveying the overwhelmed confusion of someone trying to process traumatic events.

"I understand this is very difficult," Officer Rodriguez said with practiced sympathy. "But you did the right thing by defending yourself and calling 911. We're going to make sure you receive appropriate support and that this incident is properly investigated."

Over the next thirty minutes, the penthouse filled with additional personnel—crime scene technicians, a medical examiner's investigator, a supervisor from the detective division who would oversee the investigation into Blackwood's death. Alira remained in her position on the living room floor, answering questions when asked but primarily maintaining the posture of traumatized withdrawal that was expected from assault survivors.

The crime scene technicians photographed everything—Blackwood's body from multiple angles, the bedroom where the struggle had occurred, the living room where Alira claimed they'd initially met, the wine glasses and appetizers that supported her account of having dinner before the assault began. They also photographed Alira's injuries extensively, documenting the defensive wounds that would corroborate her story of physical struggle.

At 10:15 PM—approximately ninety minutes after she'd killed Richard Blackwood—Alira was escorted from the penthouse by Officer Rodriguez and transported to the local precinct for formal statement and additional documentation. The officer maintained appropriate professional distance during the transport, making small talk designed to keep Alira calm while avoiding questions about the incident that might later be challenged as obtained outside proper interview protocols.

The precinct was busy with the typical Thursday night activity—arrests from bar fights, domestic disturbances, drug offenses, and various other infractions that kept patrol officers occupied in a major metropolitan area. Alira was taken to a private interview room and offered water, coffee, and access to a bathroom before the formal statement process began.

At 10:47 PM, Detective Marcus Hale entered the interview room carrying a folder of preliminary documentation about the incident. He was in his early forties, with the weathered appearance of someone who'd spent fifteen years working homicide and sex crimes investigations. His expression was carefully neutral, showing neither suspicion nor sympathy as he introduced himself and explained the interview process.

"Miss Sinclair, I'm Detective Hale. I'm going to be overseeing the investigation into Mr. Blackwood's death. I know you've already provided an account of what happened to the responding officers, but I need to hear it directly from you and ask some additional questions that will help me understand the full context of this incident. Everything we discuss is being recorded, and you have the right to have an attorney present if you choose. Do you understand?"

"Yes," Alira replied. "Do I need an attorney? Am I in trouble?"

"You're not in trouble," Detective Hale said, his tone remaining neutral and professional. "At this point, you're a victim and witness rather than a suspect. But you have the right to legal representation if you want it, and I need to make sure you understand that right before we proceed."

"I don't think I need an attorney. I just want to tell you what happened and go home. I'm exhausted and I just want this to be over."

Detective Hale nodded, activating the recording equipment and beginning the formal documentation process. "For the record, please state your full name and date of birth."

"Alira Marie Sinclair. Date of birth is March 15, 1991."

"And can you explain why you were using a different name—Sophia Gardner—when communicating with Mr. Blackwood?"

This was the crucial explanation that would justify her use of a false identity without raising suspicion about premeditation or criminal intent. Alira delivered it with the right mixture of embarrassment and pragmatism.

"I used a fake name on my dating profile because I didn't want to connect my real identity to that kind of service. Elite Companions is for people seeking financial arrangements, and I was worried about privacy—I didn't want anyone from my graduate program or my academic life to find out I was looking for that kind of relationship. A lot of women use fake names on dating sites for safety and privacy reasons. I was planning to tell him my real name eventually if we ended up having an ongoing arrangement, but for the initial contact I thought it was safer to use a fake identity."

The explanation was entirely plausible—women frequently used false names and limited personal information on dating platforms to protect their privacy and safety. Detective Hale nodded, making notes but showing no indication that the use of a false identity raised any red flags about her credibility or intentions.

"And how did you come to meet Richard Blackwood?"

Alira repeated her narrative again, maintaining consistency with previous tellings while allowing natural variation in phrasing and emphasis. She described creating her profile on Elite Companions using the name Sophia Gardner, receiving Blackwood's initial message, three weeks of email and phone conversations, and tonight's dinner meeting that was supposed to discuss potential arrangements.

Detective Hale listened attentively, occasionally making notes but primarily focusing on her delivery and demeanor. His questions were probing but not hostile, designed to elicit detail rather than challenge credibility.

"When Mr. Blackwood brought you to the bedroom, what was your understanding of his intentions?"

"I thought he genuinely wanted to show me his art collection. He'd been talking about art all evening, and he knew I was studying art history, so it seemed natural that he'd want to share pieces he was proud of. But when we got there, his whole demeanor changed. He stopped being charming and conversational and became... predatory. Aggressive."

"Can you describe specifically what he did or said that made you feel threatened?"

"He put his hands on my shoulders from behind while I was looking at the painting. At first it seemed like it might just be friendly or casual, but then his grip got harder and his hands started moving down my arms in a way that felt sexual rather than appropriate. I tried to turn away from him but he held me in place. That's when he said I was beautiful and that we were going to have a 'very satisfying arrangement.' The way he said it made it clear he was talking about sex rather than the kind of financial mentorship arrangement we'd discussed."

"What happened next?"

"I told him I wasn't ready for that kind of physical contact, that I thought we were going to talk about arrangements first. But he said this was part of the arrangement, that I'd agreed to be 'flexible' when I came to his penthouse. He said if I tried to claim things weren't consensual, his lawyers would make me look like a liar who was just seeking money. He said he'd dealt with situations like this dozens of times before and he knew exactly how to handle them."

Detective Hale's expression remained neutral, but Alira could see his attention sharpen at the mention of Blackwood's threat. The detective would certainly run Blackwood's background and discover his history of settlement payments and accusations—information that would support Alira's account while providing context for why she might have feared that resistance would be futile.

"So you believed he was going to assault you regardless of your consent?"

"Yes. He made it very clear that he expected me to comply with whatever he wanted, and that fighting back or trying to report him would only result in my own destruction. He said women like me—meaning women who were financially desperate—had no power against men like him. That the system was designed to protect people with money and connections, not people like me who needed help."

The narrative was devastating in its accuracy—Alira was describing not just Blackwood's individual psychology but the entire institutional framework that had enabled his predatory behavior for twenty-eight years. Detective Hale would investigate these claims and find extensive documentation supporting everything she was saying.

"What did you do when you realized he intended to assault you?"

"I tried to get away from him. I pushed against his chest and tried to move toward the bedroom door. But he was much stronger than me, and he grabbed my arms hard enough to leave bruises. We struggled for what felt like a long time but was probably only thirty or forty seconds. I was trying to push him away and he was trying to hold me still and take my dress off."

"At any point during this struggle, did you strike Mr. Blackwood or use any kind of weapon against him?"

The question was the one Alira had been anticipating—Detective Hale was asking whether she'd done anything that might have contributed to Blackwood's death beyond simple defensive resistance. Her answer needed to be truthful enough to match the physical evidence while maintaining the narrative that his death was caused by cardiac event rather than external trauma.

"I don't think so. I was pushing against his chest with both hands, trying to create distance. I might have slapped at his arms or shoulders, but I didn't hit him with my fists or use any objects as weapons. I was just trying to get away from him, not hurt him."

"And then what happened?"

"He just—collapsed. One second he was holding me and trying to undress me, and the next second his whole body jerked and his eyes went wide and he made this awful gasping sound. He let go of me and grabbed at his chest like something hurt, and then he fell to his knees and then onto his side. His body was shaking or convulsing for a few seconds, and then he stopped moving and his eyes went blank."

"What did you do after he collapsed?"

"I backed away from him. I was terrified he might get up and attack me again. I waited maybe ten or fifteen seconds to see if he was going to move, and when he didn't I got closer to check if he was breathing. But I couldn't tell, and I was too scared to get close enough to check properly. So I called 911 and tried to explain what had happened."

Detective Hale made additional notes, then asked several follow-up questions about specific timing, physical positions during the struggle, and Alira's emotional state throughout the incident. All of her answers remained consistent with her initial narrative, maintaining the coherence that would be expected from someone recounting genuine experience rather than fabricated story.

Finally, after nearly forty-five minutes of questioning, Detective Hale sat back in his chair and studied Alira with an expression that suggested he was trying to assess her credibility and determine whether additional investigation was warranted.

"Miss Sinclair, I want you to understand that Mr. Blackwood's death will be investigated thoroughly. The medical examiner will conduct an autopsy to determine the exact cause of death, and we'll be reviewing all available evidence including security camera footage from the building, Mr. Blackwood's communication records, and any other information that might be relevant to understanding what happened in that penthouse tonight."

"I understand," Alira replied. "I want you to investigate thoroughly. I want to know why he died. One minute he was attacking me, and the next he was dead. I don't understand what happened to him."

"Based on preliminary assessment, it appears Mr. Blackwood suffered some kind of cardiac event— possibly a heart attack or arrhythmia brought on by physical exertion and stress. The medical examiner will be able to provide more specific information once the autopsy is complete. But I want to make sure you understand that if any evidence emerges suggesting that his death was caused by anything other than natural medical event, we'll need to revisit this investigation."

"Of course. I'll cooperate with whatever you need. I just defended myself against someone who was trying to rape me. I didn't want him to die. I just wanted him to stop attacking me."

Detective Hale nodded, apparently satisfied with her response. "Okay. We're going to need you to provide DNA samples and fingerprints for elimination purposes—we'll need to distinguish your biological evidence from anything else we might find at the scene. We'll also need you to surrender the clothing you were wearing tonight for forensic examination. Are you comfortable with that?"

"Yes, whatever you need."

Over the next hour, Alira provided the biological samples that would be used to exclude her DNA and fingerprints from the forensic analysis of Blackwood's penthouse. She surrendered her dress, shoes, and undergarments, changing into clothing provided by the precinct's victim services coordinator. The items would be examined for trace evidence, but they would reveal nothing except what her account claimed—evidence of physical struggle during attempted sexual assault.

At 12:23 AM—four hours after she'd killed Richard Blackwood—Alira was released from police custody and provided with transportation back to the parking garage where she'd left her rental car. Detective Hale had given her his business card with instructions to contact him if she remembered any additional details about the incident or if she needed any assistance with victim services resources.

"Get some rest, Miss Sinclair," he'd said as she prepared to leave the precinct. "I know this has been an incredibly traumatic experience. We'll be in touch once the medical examiner completes the autopsy and we have more information about what caused Mr. Blackwood's death."

"Thank you, Detective. I appreciate your kindness."

Alira drove back to her apartment in a state of heightened awareness, replaying every moment of the evening and analyzing whether she'd made any mistakes that might later be discovered during the investigation. The performance had been flawless— she'd maintained consistency across multiple retellings, provided a plausible explanation for using a false identity online, and delivered the narrative with appropriate emotional authenticity.

Most importantly, there was no evidence that would contradict her account of events. The potassium chloride injection would be undetectable unless the medical examiner specifically tested for elevated potassium levels in the carotid artery tissue— something that would only occur if there was reason to suspect poisoning rather than natural cardiac death. The syringe had been disposed of in a public trash bin miles from both her apartment and the Meridian Tower, the empty vial of solution had been crushed and scattered across multiple dumpsters throughout the city.

Richard Blackwood was dead, and Alira Sinclair had successfully committed her first murder.

As she entered her apartment at 1:47 AM, Alira felt the adrenaline that had sustained her through the evening finally beginning to fade, replaced by a profound exhaustion that went beyond mere physical fatigue. She'd spent three weeks preparing for tonight, and the psychological weight of finally executing her plan was only now becoming apparent.

She showered for thirty minutes, washing away any remaining traces of the evening while allowing herself to process what she'd done. A man was dead by her hand—not in abstract planning or hypothetical scenario, but in concrete reality. She'd watched the life drain from Richard Blackwood's eyes, had observed his final moments of consciousness as he realized that his wealth and power couldn't save him from the consequences of his crimes.

The moral weight of what she'd done was substantial, but not in the way that conventional ethics might suggest. Alira felt no guilt about Blackwood's death— he'd destroyed at least forty-three women's lives over twenty-eight years, and his elimination had prevented countless future victims from experiencing similar trauma. The world was objectively safer with Richard Blackwood dead, and the legal system's failure to achieve that outcome through legitimate means had made extrajudicial action necessary.

What troubled Alira was not the fact of killing, but the realization of how easy it had been. The planning, the execution, the performance of traumatized innocence— all of it had proceeded so smoothly that she couldn't help wondering if this was how serial killers felt after their first successful murder. The line between justice and murder was clearer in theory than in practice, and Alira understood that she would need to remain vigilant about her own motivations and methods if she wanted to avoid becoming the kind of predator she'd set out to eliminate.

At 2:30 AM, exhausted beyond the capacity for further introspection, Alira finally collapsed into bed. Tomorrow would bring news coverage of Blackwood's death, possibly follow-up questions from Detective Hale, and the beginning of whatever investigation the police deemed necessary.

But tonight, for the first time in ten years, Alira Sinclair slept with the knowledge that at least one of the predators who destroyed vulnerable women had finally faced consequences that no amount of wealth or institutional protection could prevent.

The first sin was complete.

And Richard Blackwood would never hurt anyone again.

INVIDIA *Envy*

"They wanted her silence. She gave them consequences."

Chapter 7

The Aftermath

Alira woke at 9:23 AM on Friday morning to sunlight streaming through her bedroom windows and the disorienting sensation of having slept far later than her usual routine. For a moment, she lay still in bed, her mind struggling to process why she felt so profoundly exhausted despite having slept for nearly seven hours. Then the memories of the previous evening returned in vivid detail—the penthouse, the assault, the injection, Blackwood's death, the police investigation that had lasted until after midnight.

She'd killed someone. The abstract planning and hypothetical scenarios that had occupied her thoughts for three weeks had been transformed into concrete reality. Richard Blackwood was dead by her hand, and the world had continued turning as if nothing particularly significant had occurred.

Alira reached for her phone on the nightstand, checking for any messages or calls that might indicate complications with the police investigation. There were three missed calls from an unknown number and a text message from Detective Hale sent at 8:47 AM: "Miss Sinclair, please call me when you're available. I have some preliminary information about last night's incident that I'd like to discuss with you."

The message was professional and neutral, giving no indication whether the "preliminary information" represented good news or emerging suspicions about her account of events. Alira sat up in bed, taking several slow breaths to center herself before returning the detective's call. The conversation would be important—Detective Hale's tone and the information he chose to share would reveal how the investigation was proceeding and whether she needed to prepare for additional scrutiny.

She pressed the callback button and waited through three rings before Detective Hale answered.

"Miss Sinclair, thank you for returning my call. I hope you were able to get some rest after the difficult evening you experienced."

"I slept, but I can't say it was particularly restful," Alira replied, maintaining the tone of someone still processing traumatic events. "I keep replaying what happened, trying to understand why he just collapsed like that. Have you learned anything about what caused his death?"

"That's actually why I'm calling. The medical examiner conducted a preliminary examination of Mr. Blackwood's body early this morning, and I wanted to share the initial findings with you. The autopsy revealed that Mr. Blackwood suffered a massive myocardial infarction—a heart attack—that appears to have been caused by a previously undiagnosed cardiac condition combined with the physical stress of the altercation you described."

Alira felt relief flood through her body, though she was careful to keep her voice appropriately confused and uncertain. "A heart attack? But he seemed so healthy. He was strong, he'd been drinking wine and talking normally all evening. There was no sign that anything was wrong with him until he suddenly collapsed."

"That's not uncommon with certain cardiac conditions," Detective Hale explained. "Some people have underlying heart problems that don't present any obvious symptoms until a stressful event triggers a catastrophic failure. The medical examiner found evidence of significant arterial blockage that had apparently been developing for years. Combined with the elevated stress hormones from physical exertion and the attempted assault, his cardiovascular system simply couldn't handle the strain."

The explanation was perfect—it attributed Blackwood's death entirely to natural medical causes while acknowledging the assault as a contributing stressor rather than the primary cause of death. The medical examiner had apparently conducted exactly the kind of routine autopsy that Alira had anticipated, looking for obvious signs of heart attack or stroke without any reason to suspect poisoning that would require specialized testing for substances like potassium chloride.

"So his death wasn't caused by anything I did?" Alira asked, allowing genuine uncertainty to show in her voice. "I've been worried that maybe I hit him harder than I realized, or that pushing against his chest somehow triggered the heart attack. I keep thinking that if I hadn't fought back, he might still be alive."

"Miss Sinclair, I want to be very clear about this: Mr. Blackwood's death was caused by his pre-existing cardiac condition, not by your defensive actions. The medical examiner found no evidence of traumatic injury that contributed to his death. You have absolutely no legal or moral responsibility for what happened. You were defending yourself against sexual assault, and Mr. Blackwood's underlying health problems caused his death during that assault. If anything, his decision to attack you is what triggered the cardiac event that killed him."

The detective's reassurance was exactly what Alira needed to hear—not because she felt guilty about Blackwood's death, but because it confirmed that the official narrative was proceeding exactly as she'd planned. Detective Hale had no suspicions about foul play, the medical examiner had attributed death to natural causes, and Alira was being treated as a victim rather than a suspect.

"What happens now?" she asked. "Do you need me to come back to the precinct for additional questioning? Will there be any kind of trial or legal proceedings?"

"No, nothing like that. Based on the medical examiner's findings and the evidence we collected at the scene, this case is being closed as a death by natural causes that occurred during the commission of an attempted sexual assault. You won't face any criminal charges—you were clearly the victim in this situation, and your actions were entirely justified as self-defense. We will need you to be available if Mr. Blackwood's family or estate decides to pursue any kind of civil action, but given his history of similar accusations, I doubt that will happen."

"His history?" Alira prompted, feigning surprise at the revelation.

"Yes. As part of our investigation, we ran a background check on Mr. Blackwood and discovered that he'd been accused of sexual assault or harassment by multiple women over the past three decades. Most of those cases were settled out of court with non-disclosure agreements, but the pattern is clear and well-documented. What happened to you last night wasn't an isolated incident—Richard Blackwood was a serial predator who used his wealth to silence his victims and avoid accountability."

Detective Hale's tone carried a mixture of disgust and professional detachment, suggesting that he'd seen enough similar cases to recognize institutional failures when they presented themselves. His willingness to share this information with Alira indicated that he viewed her as a victim who deserved to understand the full context of what she'd experienced.

"I had no idea," Alira said, maintaining her persona of naive graduate student who'd stumbled into a dangerous situation without understanding the risks. "When he told me last night that he'd dealt with 'situations like this' before, I thought he was just trying to scare me. I didn't realize he actually had a history of attacking women."

"Unfortunately, men like Blackwood often operate with impunity for years because the legal system makes it very difficult for victims to achieve accountability through official channels. The fact that his predatory behavior was finally ended—even if it was through his own medical condition rather than legal consequences—means that he won't be able to hurt anyone else."

The detective's words carried an undertone that Alira found interesting—there was almost a note of satisfaction in his voice, as if he viewed Blackwood's death during an attempted assault as a form of poetic justice. Detective Hale might not know the full truth of what had happened in that penthouse, but he apparently believed that the world was better off without Richard Blackwood in it.

"Thank you for letting me know," Alira said. "I appreciate you taking the time to explain everything. I was so worried that I'd be blamed for his death somehow, or that people would think I'd led him on and then panicked when things got physical."

"That's exactly the kind of victim-blaming that prevents women from reporting sexual assault," Detective Hale replied firmly. "You have nothing to be ashamed of, Miss Sinclair. You were invited to discuss a potential arrangement, you clearly communicated your boundaries when his behavior became inappropriate, and you defended yourself when he refused to respect those boundaries. Everything that happened last night was Richard Blackwood's fault, not yours."

They spoke for a few more minutes about practical matters—Alira could retrieve her clothing from evidence once the forensic examination was complete, she should contact victim services if she needed counseling or support resources, and Detective Hale would send her a copy of the final incident report once it was completed. The conversation ended with the detective's reassurance that she should reach out if she had any questions or concerns as she processed the traumatic experience.

After hanging up, Alira remained sitting on her bed for several minutes, processing the significance of what Detective Hale had told her. The investigation was closed. The medical examiner had attributed Blackwood's death to natural causes. She was officially classified as a victim rather than a suspect. The first kill had been executed perfectly, with no evidence linking her to murder and no reason for authorities to suspect that Blackwood's death had been anything other than a tragic medical event.

She'd gotten away with it.

The realization brought a complex mixture of emotions—satisfaction at having successfully eliminated a predator, relief that the legal system wouldn't punish her for delivering consequences that institutional channels had failed to provide, and a subtle unease about how easily she'd committed murder and convinced everyone that she was innocent.

At 10:15 AM, Alira made coffee and settled at her kitchen table with her laptop, pulling up news coverage of Blackwood's death to see how media outlets were framing the incident. She found several articles that had been published in the early morning hours, each telling slightly different versions of the story based on whatever information journalists had been able to gather from police sources and public records.

The New York Times article was the most comprehensive, published at 6:47 AM under the headline: "Real Estate Developer Richard Blackwood Dies During Alleged Sexual Assault"

Richard Blackwood, 58, a prominent real estate developer whose career was marked by both professional success and numerous allegations of sexual misconduct, died Thursday evening in his Meridian Tower penthouse during what police are describing as an attempted sexual assault.

According to police sources, Blackwood invited a 32-year-old woman to his residence Thursday evening to discuss a financial arrangement. During the encounter, Blackwood allegedly attempted to sexually assault the woman, who fought back in self-defense. During the physical struggle, Blackwood collapsed and died from what the medical examiner's preliminary findings indicate was a massive heart attack caused by pre-existing cardiac conditions.

The woman, whose identity is being withheld, called 911 immediately after Blackwood's collapse. She was treated for minor injuries consistent with defensive wounds and released from police custody after providing a statement. Police have indicated that she will not face any criminal charges, and the case is being closed as a death by natural causes.

Blackwood's death comes amid revelations about his extensive history of sexual misconduct allegations. Court records reviewed by the Times show that at least 17 women have accused Blackwood of sexual assault or harassment over the past three decades, with most cases settled out of court through confidential agreements. Legal experts suggest the actual number of victims may be substantially higher, as many women who experience assault by wealthy individuals with access to aggressive legal representation never file formal complaints.

The article continued with additional background about Blackwood's real estate career, his settlement history, and quotes from victim advocates about how the legal system frequently fails survivors of sexual assault by powerful men. The overall tone was sympathetic toward the unnamed woman who'd been attacked, while treating Blackwood's death as an almost inevitable consequence of decades of predatory behavior that had finally caught up with him.

Other media outlets had published similar articles, each emphasizing different aspects of the story but all arriving at the same basic conclusion: Richard Blackwood had died while attempting to assault a woman, and his death represented a form of karmic justice for decades of similar assaults that had gone unpunished through legal channels.

The New York Post had gone with a more sensational headline: "Karma Kills: Serial Predator Dies During Assault Attempt" while the Wall Street Journal had opted for restrained reporting: "Developer Richard Blackwood, 58, Dies of Heart Attack." But regardless of how outlets chose to frame the story, the fundamental narrative remained consistent—Blackwood's death was attributed to natural medical causes triggered by the stress of assaulting someone who'd fought back.

Alira closed her laptop, satisfied that the media coverage was reinforcing exactly the narrative she'd intended. Public perception of Blackwood's death would shape how people remembered him, and the consistent emphasis on his history of sexual misconduct meant that his legacy would be defined by his crimes rather than his professional achievements.

At 11:30 AM, Alira drove to Riverside Care Facility to visit Sierra. The visit felt necessary—not for establishing an alibi, since the police investigation was already closed, but for processing what she'd done and reconnecting with the moral foundation that had motivated her to kill Blackwood in the first place.

Sierra was in the common room when Alira arrived, working on a paint-by-numbers picture of a sunset over an ocean. The paint was mostly staying within the designated areas, though Sierra's coordination challenges occasionally resulted in colors bleeding across boundary lines in ways that created unintentional abstract effects.

"Alira!" Sierra exclaimed with her characteristic unfiltered joy. "Look what I'm painting! It's going to be a sunset when I'm finished!"

"It's beautiful, Sierra," Alira said, sitting beside her sister and studying the partially completed picture. "You're doing such a good job with the colors. The orange and pink blend together really nicely."

Sierra beamed with pride, returning her attention to carefully applying blue paint to a section designated as ocean. Her tongue stuck out slightly in concentration, her damaged brain requiring intense focus for tasks that her brilliant former self would have completed without conscious thought.

Watching Sierra paint, Alira felt the weight of what she'd done settle over her with renewed clarity. This—Sierra's destroyed brilliance, her childlike simplicity, her permanent dependence on institutional care—was what predatory men like Webb and Blackwood did to vulnerable women. They didn't just assault bodies; they destroyed entire lives, stealing futures and potential that could have contributed immeasurable beauty and knowledge and healing to the world.

Webb had stolen Sierra's brilliant mind and promising career. Blackwood had destroyed at least forty-three women's lives through assault, legal intimidation, and systematic character assassination. And the legal systems that were supposed to protect victims had instead protected their attackers, using institutional machinery to punish anyone who dared challenge powerful men.

Last night, Alira had ensured that at least one predator faced consequences that no amount of wealth or legal sophistication could prevent. Blackwood would never assault anyone again, would never deploy lawyers to destroy another victim's credibility, would never use his money to purchase silence from women whose lives he'd devastated.

"Alira?" Sierra said, looking up from her painting with curious concern. "Why do you look sad? Did something bad happen?"

The question—so similar to what Sierra had asked during Alira's previous visit—struck her with unexpected force. Sierra's damaged mind couldn't retain memories for more than brief periods, couldn't understand complex causation, couldn't comprehend the sophisticated planning and execution that had resulted in Blackwood's death. But she could still read emotional states with intuitive accuracy.

"Something bad happened to someone who hurt a lot of people," Alira replied carefully, speaking in language that Sierra's limited cognitive capacity might be able to process. "But he won't be able to hurt anyone anymore.

So even though it's sad that someone died, the world is safer now because he's gone."

Sierra's expression showed the confused understanding of someone processing concepts at the edge of their intellectual capacity. "Like... like when bad people go away and can't hurt children anymore? That kind of thing?"

"Yes, exactly like that," Alira confirmed. "Someone who hurt vulnerable women isn't able to hurt them anymore. It's sad that he died, but it's also good that he can't hurt anyone else."

Sierra nodded solemnly, accepting this explanation with the simple moral clarity that her brain damage had left intact even as it destroyed her capacity for complex reasoning. Good people helped others, bad people hurt others, and the world was better when bad people couldn't hurt anyone anymore. The philosophy was simplistic but fundamentally sound.

"I'm glad," Sierra said with conviction. "Bad people shouldn't hurt vulnerable women. They should face consequences."

The words—so close to Alira's own justification for what she'd done—nearly broke her composure. Sierra couldn't remember what had happened to her, couldn't understand the institutional failures that had allowed Webb to destroy her life with impunity. But somewhere in her damaged consciousness, there remained a fragment of moral conviction that perpetrators should face accountability for their crimes.

They spent another hour together, with Alira helping Sierra complete her paint-by-numbers sunset and then starting a new puzzle featuring farm animals. The simple activities were meditative, allowing Alira to process the previous evening's events while maintaining connection with the sister whose suffering had motivated her transformation from victim's family member into hunter of predators.

As Alira prepared to leave, Sierra looked up from her puzzle with an expression of unusual clarity. "You're doing important work, aren't you? Helping people who've been hurt?"

"Yes," Alira replied honestly. "I'm trying to make sure that people who hurt vulnerable women face consequences, even when the legal system fails to provide them."

"That's good," Sierra said, her face showing the simple satisfaction of someone who understood they'd grasped something meaningful despite their cognitive limitations. "You remember what I wanted to do, and you're doing it in a different way. That's really good, Alira."

The insight—that Alira was continuing Sierra's therapeutic mission through different means—was more profound than Sierra's damaged mind could fully comprehend. But she'd understood the essential truth: Alira was trying to protect vulnerable people from predators, just as Sierra had once planned to help traumatized children heal from abuse.

Alira left Riverside Care Facility at 1:15 PM feeling the moral certainty that had motivated her to kill Blackwood reinforced and validated. Sierra's destroyed life remained a constant reminder of why extrajudicial action was necessary when legal systems consistently failed to protect victims from powerful predators.

The rest of Friday passed in a strange blur of normalcy punctuated by moments of intense awareness about what she'd done. Alira went to the grocery store, cleaned her apartment, responded to emails from professors about graduate program requirements—all the mundane activities that comprised normal life for someone who hadn't committed murder less than twenty-four hours earlier.

But beneath the surface normalcy, Alira's mind was already beginning to contemplate next steps. Blackwood was dead, but he'd been just one predator among thousands operating with similar impunity throughout the country. The legal system that had protected him remained fundamentally unchanged, and the institutional failures that had enabled his twenty-eight-year career of assault would continue protecting other wealthy men who used power and privilege to escape accountability.

If Alira wanted to make a real difference—if she wanted Sierra's suffering to have meaning beyond just one eliminated predator—she would need to continue her work. Blackwood couldn't be her only kill; he needed to be the first of many.

That evening, sitting at her kitchen table with her laptop, Alira began researching her next potential target. She'd spent months identifying predatory men whose crimes were well-documented but who'd escaped legal accountability through wealth and institutional protection. Richard Blackwood had been the most accessible, but he hadn't been the only monster on her list.

The next target would need to be chosen carefully. Alira couldn't simply kill wealthy men accused of sexual assault in rapid succession—that would create patterns that might alert investigators to the possibility of a serial killer targeting predators. She would need to vary her methods, create different circumstances for each death, and allow sufficient time between kills to avoid raising suspicions about connections between seemingly unrelated deaths.

But she also couldn't wait too long. Every day that predatory men continued operating with impunity meant more victims, more destroyed lives, more women experiencing the kind of trauma that had devastated Sierra and the forty-three women Blackwood had assaulted.

As Alira reviewed her research files, one name kept drawing her attention: Senator William Hayes, a powerful politician with a well-documented history of sexually harassing and assaulting female staff members and interns. Hayes had used his political influence to silence victims and intimidate potential witnesses, creating a culture of fear that prevented anyone from challenging his behavior despite decades of credible accusations.

Hayes would be more challenging than Blackwood—he had government security, more sophisticated protective measures, and higher public profile that would attract more media attention to any suspicious death. But he was also responsible for destroying dozens of women's careers and lives, and his position of political power made him even more dangerous than a wealthy real estate developer.

Alira created a new research folder on her encrypted hard drive, beginning the meticulous documentation process that would eventually lead to Senator Hayes's death. The planning would take months—she would need to identify vulnerabilities in his security, develop access strategies, acquire appropriate materials, and create circumstances that would make his death appear natural and unremarkable despite his public profile.

But she had time. Blackwood's death had taught her that careful planning and patient execution could overcome even sophisticated protective measures. If she maintained the same meticulous approach with Hayes, she could eliminate another predator while continuing to evade detection by authorities who had no reason to suspect that an unassuming graduate student was systematically executing powerful men who'd escaped accountability through institutional failures.

At 11:47 PM on Friday evening—exactly twenty-seven hours after she'd killed Richard Blackwood—Alira finally went to bed. The exhaustion she felt was profound but different from normal fatigue. She'd crossed a line that separated her permanently from law-abiding citizens who trusted institutional systems to deliver justice, and there would be no going back to the person she'd been before Thursday evening.

But as she drifted toward sleep, Alira felt no regret about the transformation. Richard Blackwood had destroyed at least forty-three women's lives and would have continued his predatory behavior indefinitely if his own cardiac condition hadn't killed him during an assault attempt. Except it hadn't been his cardiac condition—it had been Alira's carefully planned injection of potassium chloride that stopped his heart.

The world was objectively safer without Richard Blackwood in it. And soon, it would be safer still without Senator William Hayes preying on vulnerable women who worked for him or sought his political support.

Alira's mission had begun with a single kill, but it wouldn't end there. She'd become something unprecedented—a systematic hunter of predators who'd learned that justice sometimes required working outside legal systems that were designed to protect powerful men rather than hold them accountable.

The first sin was complete, and Alira Sinclair was ready to commit the second.

Sierra's suffering would not be meaningless. Every predator that Alira eliminated would be one less threat to vulnerable women, one less monster using power and privilege to escape the consequences that institutional systems refused to deliver.

The hunt would continue, and the hunters would finally become the hunted.

The Hunter's Path

Six weeks after Richard Blackwood's death, Alira sat in the reading room of the city's central law library, surrounded by files that documented the political career and predatory behavior of Senator William Hayes. The research process had become familiar— court records, settlement agreements, victim statements obtained through promises of anonymity, patterns of institutional protection that had allowed a powerful man to operate with impunity for decades.

Senator Hayes's file was even more extensive than Blackwood's had been. Where Blackwood had destroyed forty-three documented victims over twenty-eight years, Hayes had leveraged his political authority to assault or harass at least sixty-two women over a thirty-three-year career in public service. The victims included congressional staffers, interns, campaign volunteers, lobbyists, journalists, and constituents who'd sought his assistance with federal matters.

The pattern was sickeningly familiar: Hayes would identify vulnerable women whose careers or objectives required his political support, create situations where they were isolated and dependent on his goodwill, then deploy a combination of charm and coercion to secure sexual compliance. Women who resisted faced professional destruction orchestrated through Hayes's extensive political network. Women who reported his behavior encountered legal and media strategies designed to discredit their accusations while protecting Hayes's reputation and political viability.

The institutional protections surrounding Hayes were even more sophisticated than what Blackwood had enjoyed. Where Blackwood had relied primarily on private attorneys and settlement agreements, Hayes had the full machinery of political power at his disposal—party leadership that valued his legislative effectiveness more than his victims' wellbeing, media contacts who could shape coverage in his favor, and government resources that could be weaponized against anyone who threatened his career.

But institutional power, while extensive, wasn't absolute. Hayes's security measures were designed to protect against conventional threats—political opponents, angry constituents, foreign intelligence services. They weren't designed to protect against someone like Alira, who'd learned exactly how to kill powerful men in ways that appeared natural and undetectable.

Alira closed the file she'd been reviewing—a deposition from a former staffer named Sarah Chen who'd been assaulted by Hayes in 2019 and subsequently driven out of politics through a coordinated campaign of professional sabotage—and allowed herself a moment of satisfaction about what she'd accomplished with Blackwood.

The police investigation into his death had been officially closed three weeks ago with a final report that attributed his death to cardiac arrest caused by pre-existing medical conditions. The medical examiner's autopsy had found no evidence of foul play, no indication that Blackwood's death had been anything other than a tragic medical event that occurred during an attempted sexual assault.

Detective Hale had called Alira personally to inform her of the case closure, his tone carrying the same mixture of professional detachment and subtle satisfaction that had characterized their previous conversations. "I wanted you to know that the investigation into Mr. Blackwood's death has been completed and the case is officially closed," he'd said. "The medical examiner's final report confirms that he died of natural causes—a massive heart attack triggered by stress and pre-existing cardiac disease. You bear no legal responsibility for his death, Miss Sinclair. You were defending yourself against sexual assault, and what happened to him was a consequence of his own medical condition and his decision to attack you."

Alira had thanked the detective for keeping her informed, maintaining the persona of a traumatized graduate student grateful for official validation that she wasn't responsible for Blackwood's death. In reality, she'd felt profound satisfaction that her planning and execution had been so successful that experienced investigators had found no reason to suspect murder.

The media coverage of Blackwood's death had followed the trajectory that Alira had anticipated. Initial stories had focused on the dramatic circumstances—wealthy developer dies during assault attempt, reveals decades of similar accusations. Subsequent reporting had explored his history of settlement payments and legal intimidation, with victim advocates using his death as an opportunity to discuss institutional failures that protected wealthy predators.

Within two weeks, the story had largely faded from public attention, replaced by newer scandals and tragedies that captured media interest. Richard Blackwood was dead, his legacy permanently defined by his crimes, and the world had moved on as if his existence had been of no particular consequence.

Which was exactly as it should be, Alira reflected. Predatory men like Blackwood didn't deserve elaborate eulogies or sympathetic remembrance. They deserved to be eliminated and forgotten, their deaths notable primarily for ending patterns of violence that legal systems had proven incapable of stopping through legitimate means.

But Blackwood's death, while personally satisfying, represented only the beginning of what Alira was planning. One eliminated predator was meaningful for his specific victims, but it did nothing to address the systemic failures that had enabled his career of assault and would continue enabling countless other powerful men who used wealth and privilege to escape accountability.

If Alira wanted to make a real difference—if she wanted Sierra's suffering to have meaning beyond personal revenge—she needed to establish herself as something unprecedented: a systematic hunter of predators who would continue eliminating powerful men until institutions either reformed themselves or ran out of monsters to protect.

Senator Hayes would be the second kill, and his death would need to be even more carefully planned than Blackwood's. Hayes had government security, sophisticated protective measures, and a public profile that would attract significant media attention to any suspicious death. The methods that had worked for Blackwood—fake identity, dating service approach, isolated assault scenario—wouldn't be appropriate for a prominent politician whose movements were documented and whose associates would notice any deviation from established patterns.

Alira had been developing a different approach for Hayes, one that would exploit the same political authority that made him such a dangerous predator. The plan was still taking shape, but the basic strategy was clear: she would need to get closer to Hayes's inner circle, establish herself as someone with legitimate political connections, and create circumstances that would allow her to eliminate him in ways that appeared to be natural death or unfortunate accident rather than murder.

Sarah Chen's deposition had given Alira an idea about how to accomplish this. Chen had been driven out of politics after reporting Hayes's assault, but her contacts and knowledge of his operation remained extensive. If Alira could recruit Chen—not as an accomplice to murder, but as an unwitting source of information about Hayes's vulnerabilities and patterns—she might be able to identify opportunities for elimination that would be impossible to discover through external surveillance alone.

The recruitment would need to be subtle and carefully managed. Chen had been devastated by what Hayes had done to her and by the institutional failures that had protected him while destroying her career. She was angry, disillusioned with the political system, and probably receptive to the idea that Hayes deserved consequences that legal channels would never deliver.

But Chen was also fundamentally law-abiding, someone who believed in reform rather than revolution. She would need to be manipulated carefully—given information that would help Alira without understanding how that information would be used, positioned as an advocate for victims rather than an accomplice to murder.

Alira made notes in her encrypted research file, documenting potential approaches for contacting Chen and establishing a relationship that could be exploited for intelligence gathering. The planning would take months, possibly longer than the three weeks she'd spent preparing for Blackwood's death. But Hayes represented a more challenging target, and his elimination would require correspondingly more sophisticated methods.

As Alira packed up her research materials and prepared to leave the law library, she felt the weight of what she'd become settling over her with renewed clarity. She was no longer Alira Sinclair, graduate student and victim's family member seeking justice through legitimate channels. She was something else entirely—a systematic killer who'd learned that some forms of justice required working outside institutional frameworks that were designed to protect powerful predators rather than hold them accountable.

The transformation was permanent and irreversible. There would be no returning to the person she'd been before Blackwood's death, no going back to trusting that legal systems would eventually provide accountability if she just remained patient and worked through official channels.

But Alira felt no regret about the transformation. Richard Blackwood had destroyed at least forty-three women's lives and would have continued his predatory behavior indefinitely if she hadn't stopped him. Senator Hayes had destroyed sixty-two documented victims and was currently leveraging his political authority to assault and harass vulnerable women who depended on him for professional advancement or political support.

The world was objectively better with Blackwood dead, and it would be better still once Hayes met a similar fate.

As Alira walked out of the law library into the afternoon sunlight, she thought about Sierra working on her paint-by-numbers pictures at Riverside Care Facility, her brilliant mind reduced to childlike simplicity by a predator who'd faced no consequences during his lifetime. Webb's peaceful death in his sleep had been a travesty of justice, an institutional failure that had motivated Alira to ensure that other predators wouldn't escape so easily.

Blackwood hadn't escaped. Hayes wouldn't escape. And after Hayes, there would be others—an ever-growing list of powerful men who used wealth, authority, and institutional protection to prey on vulnerable women while evading the accountability that legal systems consistently failed to deliver.

Alira had become something that didn't exist in conventional criminal taxonomies—not a serial killer driven by psychological compulsion, not a vigilante seeking personal revenge, but a systematic reformer who'd chosen murder as the most effective tool for achieving social change that couldn't be accomplished through legitimate channels.

The mission would continue until either she was caught or institutions reformed themselves sufficiently that extrajudicial action was no longer necessary. Given the depth of corruption and the comprehensiveness of protections surrounding powerful predators, Alira suspected she would be killing for a very long time before legal systems evolved to the point where women like her weren't required to deliver consequences that courts refused to impose.

But that was acceptable. Every predator eliminated was one less threat to vulnerable women. Every powerful man who died knowing that his wealth and privilege couldn't ultimately protect him sent a message to others who believed institutional protections made them invincible.

The hunt had begun with Richard Blackwood, but it wouldn't end with Senator William Hayes. There were too many predators, too many victims, too many institutional failures that enabled violence while punishing those who dared to challenge powerful men.

Alira Sinclair had transformed from victim's family member into hunter of predators, and she would continue her work until either justice was reformed or she was stopped.

Sierra's suffering would not be meaningless.

The first sin was complete.

The second was about to begin.

Book Two

The Second Fall

ACEDIA *Sloth*

———————

"The system did not fail. It worked exactly as designed—to protect the powerful."

Pattern Recognition

Detective Marcus Hale sat at his desk on a rainy Monday morning in early May, three months after Richard Blackwood's death, reviewing the closed case file one more time before consigning it permanently to archives. The investigation had been straightforward—wealthy businessman attempts sexual assault, victim defends herself, Blackwood suffers fatal cardiac arrest during the confrontation. Justified self-defense, no criminal charges filed, case closed.

But something about the encounter continued nagging at Hale's detective instincts, creating cognitive dissonance he couldn't quite articulate or resolve.

Alira Sinclair had presented as exactly what she claimed to be during their multiple interviews: a trauma survivor who'd defended herself against a predator using basic self-defense techniques that had fortunately proven effective despite Blackwood's significant size and strength advantages. Her account had been consistent across all interviews, her emotional responses appropriate for someone processing traumatic violence, and the forensic evidence had supported her narrative completely.

Case closed. Justice served. A sexual predator dead and his intended victim alive.

So why did Hale keep returning to the file, reviewing details that should have been unremarkable?

Part of his unease stemmed from Sinclair's fighting efficiency. The positioning of Blackwood's body, the minimal defensive injuries on Sinclair despite the violence of the encounter, the precision with which she'd apparently neutralized a much larger and stronger opponent—all of this suggested more sophisticated combat training than would be expected from someone with no documented martial arts background.

But self-defense classes were common among women concerned about sexual assault, and Sinclair might have simply been fortunate that her limited training had proven effective during a crisis situation. Hale couldn't justify continued suspicion based solely on the fact that a woman had successfully defended herself against an attacker.

More troubling was something Hale had discovered during routine background research on Sinclair. She had two sisters—Sierra, who lived in a specialized care facility after suffering traumatic brain injury during a sexual assault ten years ago, and Cassandra, who'd died seven years ago in New York under circumstances officially ruled suicide.

Sierra's assault had never been solved, the case remaining officially open but practically abandoned due to the victim's memory loss and lack of physical evidence. But Hale's research had revealed that Sierra had been a doctoral student working with Dr. Marcus Webb, a psychology professor who'd died of apparent heart failure shortly after accusations against him had been quietly dismissed by his university.

Cassandra's death had occurred while she was investigating Coach Robert Daniels, a Columbia University athletic director accused of serial sexual assault. Daniels himself had died years later from anaphylactic reaction to contaminated supplements— a death that had been ruled accidental despite occurring shortly after Cassandra's "suicide."

Two sisters. Two tragedies involving sexual assault. And two men connected to those tragedies who'd subsequently died under circumstances that appeared natural but which had occurred at moments when they were vulnerable to exposure or facing potential consequences.

Hale pulled out a fresh notepad and began documenting what he was seeing:

Dr. Marcus Webb - died of heart failure, 10 years ago, shortly after Sierra Sinclair's assault Coach Robert Daniels - died of anaphylactic reaction, 7 years ago, shortly after Cassandra Sinclair's death Richard

Blackwood - died of cardiac arrest, 3 months ago, during confrontation with Alira Sinclair

Three men with predatory histories. Three deaths that appeared natural or justified. And all three deaths connected, however distantly, to the Sinclair family.

The pattern was circumstantial and wouldn't support any kind of official investigation. But the pattern was also compelling enough that Hale couldn't simply dismiss it as coincidence.

He opened a new file on his computer and labeled it "Pattern Analysis—Miscellaneous." Professional caution prevented him from being more explicit—if his theory was correct, if Alira Sinclair really was systematically eliminating predatory men through methods sophisticated enough to appear completely natural, then documenting that suspicion in official police systems would be premature and potentially actionable.

But Hale's detective instincts demanded that he begin tracking the pattern, documenting connections, and watching for additional data points that might either confirm or refute his emerging theory about what Alira Sinclair actually was.

As he closed the Blackwood file and prepared to move on to other cases demanding his attention, Hale's phone buzzed with a news alert: Senator William Hayes, a three-term senator with significant influence over legislation affecting women's rights, had been hospitalized after suffering what appeared to be a minor stroke. The senator was expected to recover fully, and his office had released a statement attributing the health scare to stress and demanding work schedule.

Hale read the alert with mild interest, then returned his attention to active cases. He had no reason to connect Senator Hayes to his theoretical pattern analysis, no indication that Hayes's health issues were anything other than the natural consequence of a high-stress political career.

But somewhere in the city, Alira Sinclair was beginning surveillance on her next target, planning an elimination with the same methodical precision she'd applied to removing three previous predators from positions of power and privilege.

The pattern would continue, evolving and adapting with each new challenge, until either Sinclair was caught or Hale's suspicions developed into something more substantial than theoretical connections between unrelated deaths.

The hunt was ongoing, and Detective Marcus Hale had just taken his first step toward recognizing what he was actually tracking—not a lucky survivor who'd defended herself against one predator, but a systematic hunter who'd been eliminating powerful men for years without anyone recognizing the pattern beneath apparently natural deaths.

The game had begun in earnest, though neither hunter nor detective yet understood how their confrontation would ultimately conclude.

Chapter 1

The Senator's Shadow

Three months had passed since Richard Blackwood's death, and Alira Sinclair had used every day of that time to study her next target with the methodical precision that had made her first kill so successful. The research process had become almost meditative—a daily routine of documentation, analysis, and strategic planning that transformed abstract moral conviction into concrete operational objectives.

Senator William Hayes commanded a different kind of power than Richard Blackwood's mere wealth. Where Blackwood had wielded money and legal connections to silence his victims, Hayes possessed political authority that could reshape laws, destroy careers, and silence inconvenient truths through mechanisms far more sophisticated than simple financial settlements. His predatory nature was an open secret in Capitol Hill corridors—whispered about in private conversations, acknowledged through euphemism and careful phrasing, but never spoken aloud in contexts where it might actually threaten his position or influence.

On a Thursday afternoon in late April, Alira sat in the public gallery of the Senate chamber, watching Hayes deliver what the media would describe as a "passionate and moving" speech about protecting families and traditional values. His silver hair caught the light from the chamber's elaborate chandeliers as he gestured emphatically, his voice carrying the practiced cadence of a man who'd spent three decades convincing people to believe in things that served his interests rather than theirs.

"We must safeguard our most vulnerable citizens," Hayes declared, his hand pressed dramatically over his heart in a gesture that would photograph beautifully for campaign materials. "Our children, our elderly, our women—they depend on us to create a society where they can feel safe and protected from those who would exploit their vulnerability for personal gratification."

The irony was so profound that Alira had to suppress a smile. Through three months of intensive research, she'd uncovered a pattern of predatory behavior spanning Hayes' entire political career—twenty-three years in the House of Representatives followed by ten years in the Senate, each position providing new opportunities to exploit the young women who worked in his offices or sought his political patronage.

The victims followed a consistent profile: women in their early to mid-twenties, politically ambitious, economically vulnerable, and lacking the kind of family wealth or professional connections that might provide protection against retaliation. Hayes targeted staffers, interns, campaign volunteers, constituent services coordinators—women whose careers and financial stability depended entirely on maintaining good relationships with powerful men like himself.

Alira had documented at least sixty-two credible accusations against Hayes spanning his thirty-three years in public office. The actual number was likely much higher—her research had identified numerous young women who'd left Hayes' employ abruptly, their careers derailed or abandoned entirely, but who'd never filed formal complaints or pursued legal action against him.

The pattern of abuse was sickeningly methodical. Hayes would identify vulnerable women whose careers or objectives required his political support, then deploy a sophisticated grooming process designed to create psychological dependence and confusion about appropriate professional boundaries. He presented himself as a mentor and protector, offering career guidance and political access that seemed genuine and valuable. He built trust gradually, mixing professional development with increasingly personal attention in ways that made victims question their own perceptions about when mentorship crossed the line into harassment.

The actual assaults, when they occurred, were never violent in the conventional sense. Hayes didn't use physical force to overpower resistance—instead, he created psychological conditions where resistance seemed impossible or counterproductive. He isolated victims in private settings where their word would be pitted against his if they reported his conduct. He emphasized the professional consequences of making accusations against a powerful senator. He framed his sexual demands as natural extensions of mentorship relationships, using therapeutic language about trust and vulnerability to normalize behavior that was actually predatory.

And when victims did resist or report his conduct, Hayes deployed the full machinery of political power to destroy their credibility and professional futures. His chief of staff would contact their references, planting doubts about their stability and professionalism. His attorneys would threaten defamation lawsuits that victims couldn't afford to defend. His media contacts would publish stories questioning their motivations and mental health. His political allies would ensure they were blacklisted from other positions in Washington's tight-knit political community.

The institutional protections surrounding Hayes were even more sophisticated than what Blackwood had enjoyed. Where Blackwood had relied primarily on private attorneys and confidential settlement agreements, Hayes had the full apparatus of political power at his disposal. Party leadership valued his legislative effectiveness and fundraising capabilities more than his victims' wellbeing. Congressional ethics investigations moved slowly when they moved at all, hobbled by political considerations and Hayes' seniority. Media outlets that depended on political access were reluctant to pursue stories that might alienate a powerful senator.

But institutional power, while extensive, wasn't absolute. Hayes's security measures and political protections were designed to defend against conventional threats—angry constituents, political opponents, activists seeking to embarrass him through public protest. They weren't designed to protect against someone like Alira, who'd learned exactly how to kill powerful men in ways that appeared natural, undetectable, and completely disconnected from any motive for murder.

As Hayes concluded his speech to polite applause from his colleagues, Alira studied his body language with the analytical detachment she'd developed over three months of surveillance. He moved with the fluid grace of a natural politician, transitioning seamlessly from passionate oratory to casual conversation as he worked the chamber floor. He shook hands with junior senators, shared private jokes with committee chairs, made each person feel like the most important individual in the room through carefully calibrated attention and apparent interest.

It was a masterful performance from a man who'd built his career on making people believe he was something he wasn't—a dedicated public servant rather than a predator who used political authority to hunt vulnerable women with complete impunity.

Alira's phone buzzed with a text message from Dr. Patricia Vance, the therapist she'd been seeing as part of her "recovery" from the traumatic experience with Richard Blackwood. The therapy sessions served multiple purposes—they established Alira as a genuine trauma survivor seeking legitimate mental health treatment, they provided professional validation of her victim status, and they created opportunities for strategic conversations that could be leveraged for her evolving mission.

"How are you feeling about our discussion last week regarding channeling your experience into advocacy work? Remember, healing isn't linear, but engaging with causes you're passionate about can be very therapeutic and empowering."

Dr. Vance had been encouraging Alira to consider advocacy work for several weeks, suggesting that transforming personal trauma into public service could be an important part of her recovery process. The therapist had mentioned several times that Senator Hayes was known for his victim advocacy work and might be receptive to hearing from survivors who wanted to share their stories.

Perfect timing. Alira had been waiting for exactly this kind of opening—a legitimate introduction to Hayes that would come with professional credibility and wouldn't raise any suspicions about her actual intentions.

She typed her response carefully, maintaining the persona of a trauma survivor cautiously exploring ways to find meaning in her painful experience: "I've been thinking about what you said. I actually saw Senator Hayes speaking today in the Senate chamber about protecting vulnerable citizens. His passion about these issues made me wonder if I might be ready to share my story with someone who could actually make a difference in how the system treats assault survivors."

The reply came within minutes: "That sounds like a very positive and empowering step forward in your healing journey. Senator Hayes has an excellent reputation for victim advocacy and has been instrumental in strengthening protections for assault survivors. Would you like me to help facilitate an introduction? I know his office accepts referrals from mental health professionals who work with trauma survivors."

Alira allowed herself a small smile. Dr. Vance's recommendation would provide the perfect introduction to Hayes—a genuine referral from a licensed therapist would lend credibility to her approach and ensure that Hayes' staff took her request for a meeting seriously.

"Yes, please. I think I'm finally ready to turn my pain into something meaningful and potentially helpful for other women who've experienced what I went through."

As Alira left the Capitol building and made her way toward the Metro station, she reflected on how perfectly the pieces were falling into place. Hayes had no idea that he was being studied, catalogued, and prepared for elimination by someone who understood exactly how predators like him operated. He believed his political power made him invincible, that his victims were too frightened or professionally dependent to pose any real threat to his continued abuse.

But Alira wasn't trying to challenge Hayes through legal channels or political pressure—methods that had failed countless victims over three decades. She was planning to eliminate him entirely, using methods that would make his death appear so natural that investigators would never suspect murder.

The planning was more complex than what she'd done with Blackwood. Hayes had government security, sophisticated protective protocols, and a public profile that would attract media attention to any suspicious death. The fake identity approach that had worked with Blackwood wouldn't be appropriate for a prominent politician whose associates would notice and investigate any unusual new relationships.

Instead, Alira would need to approach Hayes as herself—or rather, as a carefully crafted version of herself that would appeal to his predatory instincts while providing legitimate reasons for private meetings and personal access. She would present as a trauma survivor seeking his political support for advocacy work, someone vulnerable but intelligent, damaged but determined to transform her pain into purpose.

Hayes would interpret her vulnerability as opportunity. He would see another young woman whose emotional damage and need for validation made her an ideal target for his particular form of manipulation. He would believe he was grooming a victim when he was actually allowing a hunter to get close enough to strike.

That evening, sitting in her apartment surrounded by research files on Hayes' medical history, security protocols, and behavioral patterns, Alira began drafting the letter she would send to his office requesting a meeting. The letter needed to strike exactly the right tone—grateful for his advocacy work, hopeful about the possibility of contributing to important causes, and subtly conveying the kind of vulnerability that Hayes found irresistible in potential victims.

"Dear Senator Hayes," she wrote, "My name is Alira Sinclair, and I am writing at the recommendation of my therapist, Dr. Patricia Vance, who suggested that you might be willing to meet with an assault survivor interested in advocacy work..."

The letter continued for two carefully constructed paragraphs, describing her "experience" with assault (the fictional attack that had supposedly occurred during her encounter with Richard Blackwood), her recovery process through therapy, and her growing conviction that sharing her story might help strengthen protections for other survivors.

It was perfect—sincere without being desperate, intelligent without seeming threatening, vulnerable without appearing completely broken. Hayes would read it and see exactly what Alira intended him to see: another damaged young woman seeking validation and guidance from a powerful man who could provide the political platform and personal attention she craved.

She printed the letter on quality stationery, signed it in her careful script, and placed it in an envelope addressed to Senator Hayes' personal office. Tomorrow, she would mail it along with a brief supporting note from Dr. Vance confirming that Alira was her patient and that the therapist believed political advocacy might be beneficial for her continued healing.

Within a week, Alira expected to receive a response from Hayes' office scheduling an initial meeting. Within a month, she anticipated having sufficient access to Hayes to begin implementing the actual elimination plan. And within three months, if everything proceeded according to her carefully developed strategy, Senator William Hayes would be dead from apparent natural causes, his predatory career finally ended, and his victims finally freed from the fear of continued abuse or professional retaliation.

As Alira sealed the envelope and set it aside for mailing, she thought about Sierra in Riverside Care Facility, working on her paint-by-numbers pictures with the careful concentration of someone whose brilliant mind had been reduced to childlike simplicity. Dr. Marcus Webb had destroyed Sierra and faced no consequences during his lifetime. Richard Blackwood had destroyed forty-three women and would have continued indefinitely if Alira hadn't stopped him.

But Senator William Hayes had destroyed sixty-two documented victims over thirty-three years, and he would continue exploiting vulnerable women until someone ended his career permanently. The legal system had failed comprehensively to hold him accountable—congressional ethics investigations that went nowhere, media exposés that were buried through political pressure, victims who were intimidated into silence through coordinated campaigns of professional destruction.

Hayes believed his political power made him invincible. He was about to learn that some consequences couldn't be avoided through institutional protection or political influence.

The second sin was being carefully prepared, and when it was committed, it would be even more sophisticated and undetectable than the first.

Senator William Hayes was living on borrowed time, though he would never suspect it until the moment when his cardiovascular system began failing and he realized, too late, that his death had been engineered by someone he'd underestimated as just another vulnerable victim.

Alira went to bed that night feeling the familiar mixture of moral certainty and tactical satisfaction that had become the foundation of her new existence. She was no longer just Sierra's sister seeking justice for one woman's destroyed life. She had transformed into something unprecedented—a systematic hunter of predators who would continue eliminating powerful men until either she was stopped or institutions reformed themselves sufficiently that extrajudicial action was no longer necessary.

The hunt continued, and the second target had been identified, studied, and marked for elimination.

Senator Hayes would fall, and the women he'd victimized would finally see consequences delivered to a predator who'd believed himself untouchable.

Chapter 2

The Approach

Alira woke at 6:15 AM on the morning of her scheduled meeting with Senator Hayes, her alarm interrupting a dream in which she'd been standing in the Senate chamber watching Hayes deliver a speech that only she could understand was actually a confession to decades of predatory behavior. The symbolism was obvious enough that she dismissed it immediately—her subconscious processing the research and planning that had consumed her waking hours for the past three months.

She lay in bed for several minutes, mentally rehearsing the performance she would need to deliver in approximately four hours. The meeting was scheduled for 10:30 AM at Hayes' Capitol Hill office, arranged through Dr. Vance's professional referral exactly as Alira had anticipated. Hayes' scheduler had called personally to confirm the appointment, her voice warm and encouraging as she'd explained that the Senator was "very moved" by Alira's letter and "eager to discuss how he might support her advocacy goals."

The phrasing had been calculated to make Alira feel special and valued—exactly the kind of attention that would appeal to a genuine trauma survivor seeking validation and purpose. Hayes was already deploying his grooming tactics through his staff, establishing himself as a compassionate mentor before their first face-to-face meeting.

But Alira wasn't a genuine trauma survivor seeking Hayes' mentorship. She was a hunter preparing to get close to prey that had evaded accountability for three decades.

She rose from bed and began her preparation routine with the same meticulous attention to detail that had characterized her approach to Richard Blackwood. Every element of her appearance and demeanor needed to communicate specific messages that would appeal to Hayes' psychology while maintaining her cover as a legitimate assault survivor interested in advocacy work.

The outfit she'd selected was carefully calculated—a conservative navy blazer over a cream-colored blouse, knee-length gray skirt, modest pearl necklace that had supposedly belonged to her grandmother, minimal makeup that suggested sincerity rather than seduction. The overall impression was professional but not intimidating, attractive but not provocative, put-together but with subtle signs of someone still struggling with trauma and self-confidence.

Alira had learned from her research into Hayes' previous victims that he preferred women who presented as intelligent and capable but fundamentally insecure about their own value. He enjoyed the process of "building up" their confidence while simultaneously creating psychological dependence on his approval and guidance. The contradiction was the point—victims who believed they were being empowered while actually being manipulated into increasing vulnerability.

As she applied her makeup with careful restraint, Alira practiced the facial expressions and vocal patterns she would need to maintain throughout the meeting. Her reflection showed exactly what she'd intended—a young woman who was trying to project confidence while still carrying visible traces of trauma and uncertainty. Someone who needed saving, or at least someone Hayes would believe needed saving.

She left her apartment at 9:15 AM, allowing extra time for the Metro ride to Capitol Hill and the security screening process that preceded any visit to Senate offices. The early departure also provided buffer time if she encountered any delays—arriving flustered and apologetic would be acceptable for a nervous trauma survivor, but arriving late and composed would contradict the persona she needed to maintain.

The metro was moderately crowded with the typical Thursday morning mix of federal workers, tourists, and lobbyists heading toward the political heart of the city. Alira stood near the door, watching her reflection in the train window and making subtle adjustments to her posture and expression. Shoulders slightly hunched to suggest someone still carrying trauma's physical weight. Eyes that looked around nervously as if anticipating threat. Hands that occasionally touched her necklace in a self-soothing gesture that psychological research indicated was common among anxiety sufferers.

She arrived at the Hart Senate Office Building at 10:02 AM, passing through security screening that required surrendering her phone temporarily and walking through metal detectors that confirmed she carried no weapons or recording devices. The security protocols were routine for Senate buildings, but Alira noted them carefully as potential obstacles for future planning. If her ultimate elimination method required bringing any materials into Hayes' office, she would need to account for these screening procedures.

The elevator to Hayes' third-floor office suite was marble-paneled and moved with the smooth silence of expensive engineering. Alira shared the ride with a group of middle-aged constituents wearing visitor badges and discussing their excitement about meeting with their senator's staff. Their innocent enthusiasm was touching in its naivety—they believed political power was exercised transparently through official meetings and documented decisions, with no comprehension of the private abuses and institutional failures that defined so much of Washington's actual operation.

Hayes' office suite was designed to impress visitors with its heavy wooden furniture, thick carpeting that muffled sound, and walls covered with framed photographs documenting his political career. The images told a carefully curated story of public service—Hayes shaking hands with three different presidents, Hayes speaking at important legislative sessions, Hayes receiving awards from various advocacy organizations and civic groups.

What the photographs didn't show were the victims he'd created during those same years—the sixty-two women whose careers and psychological wellbeing he'd destroyed through systematic exploitation of his political authority.

The waiting area contained six leather chairs arranged around a coffee table displaying current political magazines and promotional materials about Hayes' legislative achievements. Two other visitors were already seated—an elderly couple who appeared to be constituents seeking assistance with a federal benefits issue. They looked up briefly as Alira entered, then returned to their quiet conversation about paperwork and deadlines.

Behind a substantial desk positioned to control access to the inner offices sat the receptionist—a pleasant-looking woman in her late forties who'd probably worked for Hayes for years and had learned to navigate his office politics through careful attention to unspoken hierarchies and behavioral expectations.

"Good morning," the receptionist said with practiced warmth. "How can I help you?"

"I'm Alira Sinclair," she replied, her voice carrying just the right note of nervous uncertainty. "I have a 10:30 appointment with Senator Hayes."

The receptionist's expression shifted to something more personal, suggesting she'd been briefed about the nature of Alira's visit. "Of course, Miss Sinclair. Senator Hayes is looking forward to meeting with you. Please have a seat, and someone will come get you in just a few minutes."

Alira settled into one of the leather chairs, positioning herself so she could observe the office dynamics while appearing to be simply waiting nervously for her meeting. Over the next fifteen minutes, she watched staffers move through the space with the purposeful efficiency of people working in a high-pressure political environment.

Most of the staffers were young—mid-twenties to early thirties—and the gender ratio was notably skewed toward women. This wasn't unusual for congressional offices, where young female staffers and interns provided much of the actual labor that kept legislative operations functioning. But given Hayes' documented history, the prevalence of young women in his office took on more sinister implications.

At 10:27 AM, a young woman emerged from the inner office area and approached Alira with a professional smile that didn't quite reach her eyes. She was Asian-American, mid-twenties, dressed in the kind of conservative business attire that was standard for Capitol Hill, and carrying herself with the careful posture of someone who'd learned to navigate a workplace where every interaction carried potential consequences.

"Miss Sinclair? I'm Sarah Chen, one of Senator Hayes' legislative aides. The Senator is ready to see you now."

Alira had researched Sarah Chen as thoroughly as she'd researched every other member of Hayes' staff. Twenty-four years old, master's degree in political science from Georgetown University, hired eight months ago as a legislative aide focusing on women's issues and family policy. Bright, ambitious, and exactly the profile that Hayes typically targeted for exploitation.

As Alira stood and followed Sarah toward the inner offices, she studied the young woman's body language carefully. Sarah moved with practiced efficiency, but there was a tension in her shoulders that suggested someone operating under constant stress. Her smile was professional but contained no genuine warmth. Her eyes held the particular wariness that Alira had observed in other women who'd learned to be constantly alert to potential threats in their environment.

"Senator Hayes has been very moved by your letter," Sarah said as they walked down a corridor lined with more photographs and framed commendations. "He takes victim advocacy very seriously and is always honored when survivors feel comfortable sharing their stories with him."

The phrasing was carefully neutral, but something in Sarah's tone suggested the words were rehearsed rather than spontaneous. She'd delivered this message before, probably to other women who'd sought Hayes' assistance, and the repetition had drained it of any authentic emotion.

They arrived at a heavy wooden door with a brass nameplate reading "Senator William Hayes." Sarah knocked once, waited for a response from inside, then opened the door and gestured for Alira to enter.

"Miss Alira Sinclair, Senator."

Senator William Hayes rose from behind a massive mahogany desk that dominated the office, his smile warm and paternal as he moved around the furniture to greet his visitor. He was taller than Alira had expected from photographs—just over six feet, with the kind of distinguished appearance that came from decades of professional grooming and image management. His silver hair was perfectly styled, his navy suit was impeccably tailored, and his movements carried the practiced grace of someone who'd spent his entire adult life in the public eye.

"Miss Sinclair, thank you so much for coming," Hayes said, his voice carrying the resonant warmth that had helped him win election after election for over three decades. "Dr. Vance spoke very highly of your courage in reaching out, and I was genuinely moved by your letter describing your experience and your desire to transform pain into purpose."

He extended his hand for a handshake that Alira accepted, noting the firm grip that lasted just slightly longer than would be appropriate for a purely professional greeting. His palm was warm and dry, his fingers applying gentle pressure that was meant to convey both strength and reassurance.

"Thank you for agreeing to meet with me, Senator," Alira replied, her voice soft with the carefully practiced tremor of nervousness. "I know how busy you must be, and I'm grateful you'd take time for someone like me."

"Never too busy for something this important," Hayes assured her, releasing her hand and gesturing toward a seating area away from his imposing desk. "Please, let's sit somewhere more comfortable. I find that conversations about difficult topics are easier when we're not separated by formal furniture."

The seating area consisted of two burgundy leather chairs positioned at slight angles to each other across a low mahogany coffee table. The arrangement was more intimate than the desk setup would have been, designed to create an atmosphere of personal connection rather than official business. But it also positioned Hayes so that he could study his visitor closely while maintaining control over the physical space and psychological dynamic.

As Alira settled into her chair, she conducted her own analysis of the office environment. The space was designed to project authority and success—floor-to-ceiling bookshelves filled with leather-bound legislative volumes, framed degrees from prestigious universities, photographs showing Hayes with various political and cultural luminaries. But there were also subtle touches meant to humanize the powerful senator—family photographs on his desk, a small collection of what appeared to be gifts from grateful constituents, fresh flowers in an expensive vase.

Everything in the office told a story of a dedicated public servant who cared deeply about the people he represented while also commanding the respect and influence that came with three decades of political power. It was a masterful construction that concealed the predatory reality beneath the surface.

"First, I want to say how sorry I am about what you experienced," Hayes began, his expression shifting to appropriate sympathy. "Sexual assault is a terrible violation, and the fact that our system failed to provide you with justice adds insult to injury. No survivor should have to endure what you've described in your letter."

"Thank you," Alira said, ducking her head as if overwhelmed by his compassion. "Most days I still struggle with feeling like somehow it was my fault, like I should have known better or done something differently to prevent what happened."

"That's a very common response to trauma," Hayes said, leaning forward slightly with apparent concern. "Survivors often blame themselves because taking responsibility feels less terrifying than accepting that we live in a world where terrible things can happen to good people through no fault of their own. But I want you to understand something very clearly: what happened to you was not your fault. The blame lies entirely with your attacker and with a system that failed to hold him accountable."

The words were exactly what a trauma counselor might say, delivered with practiced sincerity that would have been convincing if Alira hadn't known about the sixty-two women Hayes had victimized using similar therapeutic language to normalize his own predatory behavior. He was already establishing himself as an understanding mentor figure, someone who could help her process her trauma while gradually creating the psychological dependence that would make exploitation possible.

"Dr. Vance has been helping me understand that," Alira said. "But it's different hearing it from someone with your experience and authority. You've worked with so many survivors over the years—you understand the legal and political dimensions of these issues in ways that most people can't."

The compliment was calculated to appeal to Hayes' ego while positioning Alira as someone who valued his expertise and authority. Hayes' expression showed satisfaction at being recognized for his supposed victim advocacy work.

"I've been privileged to work with many survivors over the course of my career," Hayes said, his voice taking on the practiced cadence of someone who'd delivered similar speeches many times before. "And one thing I've learned is that healing isn't just about individual therapy—it's about transforming systemic failures that allow predators to operate with impunity. That's why survivor testimony is so crucial for building political support for stronger protections and accountability measures."

"That's what I want to help with," Alira said, her voice strengthening slightly as if drawing courage from Hayes' encouragement. "I keep thinking about how many other women might go through what I did, and how the system's failures aren't just individual tragedies—they're evidence of structural problems that need political solutions."

"Exactly right," Hayes confirmed, his approval palpable. "You have an unusually sophisticated understanding of these issues for someone so young. Tell me about the specific failures you experienced. What should have been different in how the system responded to your assault?"

For the next twenty minutes, Alira wove a carefully constructed narrative that drew on her research into how the legal system typically failed assault survivors while incorporating elements that would resonate with Hayes' public persona. She described police who'd questioned her account with obvious skepticism, prosecutors who'd been more concerned about protecting her attacker's reputation than seeking justice, defense attorneys who'd used aggressive tactics to discredit her testimony during depositions.

It was a masterful performance, incorporating real details from cases she'd studied while personalizing them in ways that made the story feel authentic and emotionally resonant. She hit every note that would appeal to Hayes' supposed commitment to victim advocacy—institutional indifference, victim-blaming attitudes, legal procedures that retraumatized survivors rather than helping them heal.

Throughout her narrative, Alira watched Hayes carefully for his reactions. Unlike Richard Blackwood's obvious hunger when presented with female vulnerability, the Senator's interest was subtle and professionally masked. His expression conveyed appropriate sympathy and concern. His body language suggested engaged listening and emotional connection. His occasional questions demonstrated understanding of trauma psychology and legal procedure.

But there were tells that revealed the predatory calculation beneath the compassionate mentor façade. His gaze lingered just a moment too long when Alira shifted in her seat, his attention drawn to the movement of her legs crossing. His pupils dilated slightly when she described feeling powerless during the assault, responding to vulnerability with something that wasn't quite sympathy. His posture leaned incrementally forward when she spoke about needing guidance from someone who understood power dynamics, reading her expressed need as opportunity rather than appeal for help.

"That's exactly the kind of systemic failure I've been working to address through legislation," Hayes said when Alira finished her account. "The Violence Against Women Act needs substantial updating to address the kinds of institutional indifference and victim-blaming you've described. And survivor testimony is absolutely crucial for building political support for those reforms.

Would you be willing to share your story in a more formal setting—perhaps testimony before a Senate committee or interviews with key staffers who work on these issues?"

Alira allowed anxiety to show on her face, her hands gripping the arms of her chair with apparent tension. "I don't know if I'm ready for something that public. The thought of facing cameras, having reporters ask questions, dealing with scrutiny from people who might not believe me or might blame me for what happened... it's terrifying."

"Of course, of course," Hayes said quickly, his voice soothing. "I completely understand those concerns. We don't need to rush into anything public. Perhaps we could start with smaller steps—private briefings with key staffers, helping you build confidence gradually before considering any public appearances. I'd be there to support you every step of the way, making sure you never felt pressured or uncomfortable."

The hook was perfectly set. Hayes was offering exactly what Alira had expected—private meetings, personal attention, the gradual building of dependence that was always the first step in his predatory process. He was positioning himself as protector and mentor while actually creating opportunities for exploitation.

"That might be possible," Alira said slowly, as if considering the proposition carefully. "Though I have to warn you—I sometimes have panic attacks when talking about what happened in detail. I might need to stop suddenly, or take breaks to compose myself. I don't want to waste your time or seem unreliable."

"You could never waste my time," Hayes assured her, his tone carrying the warm conviction that had made him such an effective politician. "And needing breaks or time to process difficult emotions isn't unreliability—it's a completely normal response to trauma. We'll go at whatever pace feels comfortable for you. This is about empowering you, not retraumatizing you or pushing you into situations where you don't feel safe."

They spoke for another fifteen minutes about potential next steps, with Hayes outlining various ways Alira could contribute to advocacy work while she expressed cautious interest mixed with appropriate anxiety. The Senator was skilled at making his suggestions seem spontaneous and responsive to her needs rather than following a predetermined script for grooming potential victims.

When their scheduled time was nearly up, Hayes walked Alira to the door personally—a gesture that she knew would be noted by his staff and interpreted as evidence of his special compassion for this particular constituent. His hand rested briefly on her shoulder as they reached the doorway, the touch lasting just long enough to establish physical contact while remaining plausibly appropriate for a supportive mentor.

"Miss Sinclair," he said as they emerged into the corridor where Sarah Chen was working at a desk positioned to monitor access to Hayes' private office, "I hope you'll consider having dinner with me next week. Nothing formal—just a chance to continue our conversation in a more relaxed setting. I find that some people are more comfortable discussing difficult topics outside the formal atmosphere of Capitol Hill offices."

Sarah looked up from her computer at the invitation, her expression carefully neutral, but Alira caught the brief flicker of something in her eyes—concern, perhaps, or recognition of a pattern she'd observed before. The young staffer's reaction confirmed what Alira had suspected: Hayes' invitation to private dinners was part of his standard operating procedure, and Sarah had learned to recognize the signs even if she couldn't or wouldn't openly acknowledge what they meant.

"That's very kind of you, Senator," Alira replied, maintaining her uncertain but grateful demeanor. "Though I should mention—I don't drink alcohol anymore. Since the assault, it makes me feel unsafe, like I'm not fully in control of myself."

It was a calculated disclosure meant to serve multiple purposes. The admission reinforced her trauma survivor persona while also establishing a boundary that Hayes would interpret as both evidence of her vulnerability and a potential challenge to overcome. Men like Hayes were attracted to victims who set boundaries precisely because it gave them opportunities to demonstrate their power by gradually eroding those limits.

"Completely understandable," Hayes said, his voice carrying appropriate sympathy. "Many trauma survivors develop sensitivities around substances that impair judgment or control. I know a quiet restaurant with excellent food and a very discreet atmosphere. You'd feel perfectly safe, and we could have a thoughtful conversation without any pressure or expectations beyond discussing your potential advocacy work."

The phrasing was carefully constructed to be reassuring while also establishing the private, isolated nature of what Hayes was proposing. "Discreet atmosphere" meant few witnesses to whatever might occur. "No pressure or expectations" was meant to lower Alira's defenses while actually laying groundwork for future pressure once she was more deeply invested in the relationship.

"That sounds lovely," Alira said, allowing herself to appear touched by his continued attention. "I'd appreciate the opportunity to learn more about how I might contribute meaningfully to advocacy work."

As Sarah escorted Alira back through the office suite toward the exit, the young woman's professional mask slipped slightly. When they were out of earshot of other staff members, Sarah spoke quietly without looking directly at Alira.

"Be careful with private dinners," she said, her voice barely above a whisper. "The Senator can be very... intense when he's focused on someone. Just remember to maintain professional boundaries, even when he seems very understanding and supportive."

The warning was oblique but unmistakable. Sarah had recognized something in Hayes' attention to Alira that concerned her—whether from personal experience or observation of previous patterns, the young staffer understood that private meetings with Senator Hayes carried risks that went beyond normal professional interactions.

"Thank you," Alira replied softly. "I appreciate the advice."

Sarah's expression suggested she wanted to say more but couldn't, constrained by whatever combination of non-disclosure agreements, professional loyalty, and fear of retaliation kept Hayes' staffers from speaking more directly about his predatory behavior.

As Alira left the Hart Senate Office Building and emerged into the bright April afternoon, she reflected on how perfectly the first meeting had proceeded. Hayes had followed his documented pattern precisely—establishing himself as a compassionate mentor, isolating his target through private meeting invitations, deploying therapeutic language to normalize boundary violations, and creating psychological conditions where resistance would seem ungrateful or neurotic.

Most importantly, she'd gained confirmation that Hayes' current staffers were aware of his predatory behavior even if they couldn't speak about it openly. Sarah Chen's warning suggested she'd either experienced Hayes' exploitation personally or had observed it happening to others, and her inability to be more direct indicated that Hayes had successfully created an office culture where victims remained silent through some combination of incentives and intimidation.

The hunt was proceeding exactly as Alira had planned. Hayes believed he was grooming another vulnerable victim, gradually building trust that he would eventually exploit for sexual gratification and psychological domination. He had no idea that his supposed victim was actually studying him with cold analytical precision, documenting his methods and identifying vulnerabilities that would ultimately be used to engineer his death.

Over the next several weeks, Alira would continue cultivating her relationship with Hayes while conducting deeper surveillance on his private routines, medical history, and security protocols. She would accept his dinner invitation and allow him to escalate his grooming behavior in ways that would create opportunities for her actual objective.

And when the time was right, when she'd gathered sufficient intelligence and developed an elimination method that would appear completely natural, Senator William Hayes would die believing he'd successfully manipulated another victim into submission—never realizing that he'd actually allowed a predator far more dangerous than himself to get close enough to strike.

The second sin was being carefully prepared, and Alira Sinclair was patient enough to ensure that when it was committed, it would be as undetectable and successful as the first.

Senator Hayes had made the fatal mistake of underestimating someone he'd categorized as just another damaged young woman seeking validation from powerful men. That underestimation would cost him his life, though he would never understand why or how until the moment his cardiovascular system began to fail and consciousness faded into permanent darkness.

GULA *Gluttony*

_____

"Some men consume everything they touch and call it appetite."

Chapter 3

The Study Continues

Alira spent the week following her initial meeting with Senator Hayes conducting deeper surveillance on his private routines and personal security measures. Unlike Richard Blackwood's relatively simple lifestyle—a wealthy bachelor whose only real protection had been building security and the isolation of his penthouse—Hayes moved within multiple layers of institutional protocol and government protection that would make any elimination attempt significantly more challenging.

The surveillance operation required more sophisticated methods than what she'd employed with Blackwood. Hayes was a public figure whose movements were documented by staff, security personnel, and occasionally media. His home address was publicly available information, but accessing his Georgetown townhouse for observation required careful planning to avoid drawing attention from neighbors, security patrols, or the Capitol Police protection detail that occasionally monitored residences of senior senators.

Alira had rented a small studio apartment in Georgetown under one of her carefully constructed false identities, positioning herself three blocks from Hayes' townhouse in a building that provided convenient access for surveillance while maintaining sufficient distance to avoid suspicion. The apartment was sparsely furnished with only what was necessary for her operational purposes—high-powered binoculars, a telephoto camera with night vision capabilities, a laptop for logging observations, and encrypted storage for the detailed profiles she was building.

She established a routine that allowed her to observe Hayes' patterns without creating her own suspicious pattern that might be noticed by security personnel or neighbors. Some mornings she would position herself in a coffee shop with clear sightlines to Hayes' residence, watching as he departed for Capitol Hill. Other evenings she would conduct walking surveillance, following his car service from a distance as it transported him between political events and personal appointments. On weekends, she would observe from various positions around Georgetown, documenting who visited his townhouse and how long they stayed.

The surveillance revealed that Hayes maintained a carefully managed double life that would have been impressive if it weren't so morally repugnant. His public persona was that of a devoted family man—married to Margaret Hayes for thirty-two years, father of three adult children, grandfather to five. His wife appeared regularly at his side during official functions, presenting the image of a supportive political spouse who'd stood by her husband throughout his career.

But Margaret Hayes spent most of her time at the couple's estate in McLean, Virginia, a substantial property that she'd apparently claimed as her primary residence years ago. According to property records and social media activity that Alira had carefully analyzed, Margaret maintained an active social life in Virginia's horse country, serving on charity boards and hosting events that had nothing to do with her husband's political career.

The separate residences suggested an arrangement that was common among long-married political couples—staying together for appearances and shared interests while maintaining largely independent personal lives. Whether Margaret knew about her husband's predatory behavior was unclear, but her systematic absence from Washington provided Hayes with exactly the kind of privacy he needed to continue exploiting vulnerable women without spousal oversight.

Hayes' Georgetown townhouse was a three-story brick structure in one of the neighborhood's most exclusive areas, purchased fifteen years ago for what would now be considered a bargain price but was then a significant investment demonstrating his financial success. The property was protected by a security system that appeared to be high-quality but not excessive—cameras covering the entrances, motion sensors for the ground floor, and reinforced locks on doors and windows.

More importantly for Alira's planning purposes, the security detail that occasionally monitored senior senators' residences did not maintain constant surveillance on Hayes' home. The Capitol Police conducted periodic drive-bys and responded to any triggered alarms, but there were no permanent guards stationed outside and no real-time monitoring of who entered or departed the property.

This relative lack of security made sense from an institutional perspective—Hayes wasn't in leadership positions that would warrant dedicated protection, he'd never received credible threats that justified enhanced security measures, and the Capitol Police had limited resources to spread among hundreds of federal officials. But from Alira's perspective, the security gaps represented vulnerabilities that could be exploited when the time came to eliminate him.

On Thursday evening of her surveillance week, Alira positioned herself in a small park across from Hayes' townhouse, sitting on a bench with a book that provided cover for her actual activity of observing his residence. The spring weather was pleasant enough that her presence wouldn't seem suspicious—Georgetown parks were popular with residents and students from the nearby university during evening hours.

At 11:23 PM, well after dark, Alira observed a young woman departing Hayes' townhouse through the front entrance. Even from across the street, the woman's body language told a comprehensive story—quick, furtive movements suggesting someone fleeing rather than simply leaving, head down to avoid eye contact with anyone who might be watching, shoulders hunched in the defensive posture of someone who'd just experienced something traumatic or deeply uncomfortable.

The woman was in her mid-twenties, professionally dressed in what had probably been a smart business outfit when she'd arrived but now looked disheveled in ways that suggested physical struggle or at minimum very aggressive contact. Her blouse was partially untucked, her jacket was draped over her arm rather than worn properly, and she moved with the particular unsteadiness of someone whose equilibrium had been disrupted by stress or fear.

Alira rose from her bench and followed at a discrete distance, maintaining sufficient separation to avoid detection while keeping the woman in sight. The young woman walked quickly through Georgetown's well-lit streets, her pace suggesting someone who wanted to put maximum distance between herself and Hayes' townhouse as rapidly as possible.

Three blocks from Hayes' residence, the woman stopped under a streetlight and made a phone call. Alira positioned herself near enough to hear the conversation while appearing to be simply another pedestrian checking her own phone.

"Mom? I need to come home for a few days." The woman's voice was thick with suppressed tears, carrying the particular quality of someone trying desperately to maintain composure while emotionally devastated. "No, everything's fine with the job, I just... I think I made a mistake taking this position. I need some time away from Washington to think about things."

There was a pause while the woman listened to her mother's response, her free hand pressed against her mouth as if physically holding back sobs.

"Please don't ask questions right now, okay? I just need to come home and be somewhere safe where I can think clearly. Can you pick me up from the train station tomorrow afternoon?"

The woman was crying openly by the time she ended the call, standing alone under the streetlight with the particular stillness of someone whose understanding of the world had just shifted fundamentally. Alira recognized the look—she'd studied it in photographs of assault survivors, had practiced it herself for her victim persona, and now was observing it in real-time on someone who'd just experienced whatever Hayes did to women in the privacy of his townhouse.

After several minutes, the woman composed herself enough to begin walking again, heading toward the Metro station that would take her back to wherever she lived. Alira didn't follow further—she'd seen everything she needed to confirm that Hayes was actively continuing his predatory behavior and that his victims experienced profound trauma from their encounters with him.

Back in her surveillance apartment, Alira researched the woman's identity using facial recognition software and cross-referencing with Hayes' office staff directory. Jennifer Walsh, twenty-four years old, master's degree in public policy from American University, hired as a legislative correspondent eight months ago. Another bright young woman whose career was now being derailed by Senator Hayes' sexual exploitation.

Alira documented Jennifer's information in her growing file on Hayes' recent victims, noting the pattern that was consistent with his documented history—young staffers or recent hires who were invited to private meetings at the townhouse under professional pretenses, then subjected to sexual harassment or assault that left them psychologically devastated and professionally compromised.

The observation had served multiple purposes. It confirmed that Hayes was actively escalating his predatory behavior despite his advancing age and the increased risks of discovery in the current political climate. It demonstrated the security vulnerabilities in his townhouse operations—no witnesses, no documentation, no oversight of who entered or what occurred inside. And most importantly, it reinforced

Alira's conviction that eliminating Hayes was morally necessary and strategically justified.

The next morning brought a phone call from Senator Hayes' office. Sarah Chen's voice was professionally pleasant as she confirmed the dinner reservation that Hayes had proposed during their initial meeting.

"Miss Sinclair, Senator Hayes asked me to confirm that you're still available for dinner this Saturday evening at 7:30 PM. He's reserved a private dining room at Tosca, an Italian restaurant in Penn Quarter. He thought you'd be more comfortable with complete privacy for your conversation about advocacy opportunities."

The phrasing was carefully neutral, but Alira detected subtle stress in Sarah's voice—a slight hesitation before "private dining room," a particular emphasis on "complete privacy" that suggested Sarah understood the implications of what was being arranged.

"That's very thoughtful of the Senator," Alira replied, maintaining her grateful but slightly uncertain persona. "I have to ask, though—is this the kind of meeting Senator Hayes typically has with potential advocates? I don't want to monopolize his time or seem like I'm asking for special treatment."

There was a brief but significant pause before Sarah answered, during which Alira could almost hear the young woman choosing her words carefully to navigate between honesty and professional loyalty.

"Senator Hayes is... very committed to the causes he supports. He believes that personal connection is essential for effective advocacy, and he often meets individually with people whose stories might inform his legislative work. You certainly aren't the first person he's taken a special interest in helping."

The carefully constructed response told Alira everything she needed to know. Sarah was aware of Hayes' pattern of private meetings with young women but had learned to describe it in language that maintained plausible professional justification while avoiding direct acknowledgment of the predatory subtext.

"I understand," Alira said. "Please tell Senator Hayes that I'm grateful for his personal attention and I look forward to learning more about how I might contribute meaningfully to advocacy work."

"I'll let him know," Sarah replied, and Alira detected what might have been relief that the conversation was ending without requiring her to navigate any more ethically complicated territory.

After hanging up, Alira spent several hours researching Tosca restaurant and the implications of Hayes' choice of location. The establishment was upscale Italian cuisine in a neighborhood known for expense-account dining and political power lunches. More significantly, the availability of private dining rooms meant Hayes was continuing his pattern of isolating potential victims from witnesses while maintaining the appearance of professional mentorship.

But Alira's research into Hayes had revealed that the restaurant dinner was typically just another step in his grooming process, not the setting where actual assaults occurred. Hayes used public venues to build trust and create relationship history that would complicate any later accusations—if victims reported inappropriate behavior at his townhouse, he could point to previous professional dinners as evidence that their relationship had been consensual and mutually beneficial.

The actual assaults occurred later, once Hayes had sufficiently cultivated psychological dependence and confusion about appropriate boundaries. The pattern was sophisticated and demonstrated years of practice refining his methods to minimize legal risk while maximizing his opportunities for exploitation.

Over the following days, Alira began researching exotic compounds that could be used to eliminate Hayes in ways that would appear to be natural death or medical emergency. The method she'd used with Blackwood— potassium chloride injection during a violent struggle— wouldn't be appropriate for Hayes. The Senator was more cautious, more paranoid about his safety, and operated in environments where sudden physical confrontation would be more difficult to engineer and explain.

She needed something that could be administered gradually without Hayes' knowledge, that would mimic natural medical conditions common in men of his age and stress levels, and that wouldn't be detected in standard toxicology screens unless investigators had specific reason to suspect poisoning.

After extensive research into forensic toxicology and exotic poisons, Alira settled on tetrodotoxin—a powerful neurotoxin derived from certain species of pufferfish and other marine organisms. The compound was perfect for her purposes: it was colorless, virtually tasteless when properly diluted, extremely potent in small doses, and most importantly, it mimicked the symptoms of stroke or cardiac arrest when administered in carefully calculated amounts.

Tetrodotoxin worked by blocking sodium channels in nerve cells, progressively paralyzing the neuromuscular system until respiratory failure occurred. In controlled medical settings, the symptoms looked identical to stroke—progressive weakness, difficulty speaking, respiratory distress, and eventually cardiac arrest as the brainstem's respiratory control centers failed.

More importantly for Alira's purposes, tetrodotoxin wasn't included in standard toxicology panels. Medical examiners routinely tested for common drugs, alcohol, and standard poisoning agents like arsenic or cyanide. But exotic marine toxins required specialized testing that would only be ordered if investigators had specific reason to suspect that particular type of poisoning.

If Hayes died showing symptoms consistent with stroke—a medical emergency that was common in men of his age, stress level, and lifestyle—there would be no reason for medical examiners to suspect poisoning, let alone test for an exotic compound derived from tropical fish.

The challenge would be obtaining the toxin and developing a delivery method that would allow gradual administration without Hayes' knowledge. Tetrodotoxin was tightly controlled due to its extreme toxicity, available only to licensed researchers through specialized scientific suppliers who carefully documented every purchase.

But Alira had become skilled at creating false identities with sufficient documentation to withstand casual verification. Over the next week, she constructed a comprehensive persona as Dr. Elena Vasquez, a marine biology researcher affiliated with a small university conducting neurological research on sodium channel blockers. The identity included forged academic credentials, a fabricated research proposal studying neurotoxin mechanisms, and even a fake university email address that would respond appropriately if suppliers attempted to verify her credentials.

The persona was sophisticated enough to withstand the kind of routine verification that chemical suppliers conducted—checking that researchers were affiliated with legitimate institutions and had plausible reasons for ordering controlled substances. It wouldn't survive intensive investigation by law enforcement, but there would be no reason for such investigation unless Alira made mistakes that drew attention to her activities.

She placed her order for 50 milligrams of purified tetrodotoxin with a specialized research supplier, presenting her carefully constructed credentials and explaining that the compound was needed for neurological research into sodium channel function. The supplier's verification process consisted of confirming that Dr. Vasquez was listed as faculty at the institution she claimed, that her research proposal seemed legitimate, and that she had appropriate laboratory facilities for handling hazardous materials.

The order was approved within forty-eight hours, with delivery scheduled for the following week to the commercial mailbox that Alira maintained under her false identity. The entire transaction would create a paper trail that led to a nonexistent researcher at a university that had no record of anyone named Elena Vasquez, making the purchase effectively untraceable if anyone ever looked for it—which they wouldn't, because Hayes' death would appear completely natural.

While waiting for the tetrodotoxin delivery, Alira continued her surveillance of Hayes' routines and began developing a more detailed plan for how she would administer the poison without his knowledge. The Saturday dinner at Tosca would be an important opportunity to study Hayes' behavior in private settings, assess his caution level about food and drink, and determine whether he showed any of the paranoid hypervigilance that would make gradual poisoning difficult.

She also needed to develop a relationship with Sarah Chen that would provide access to Hayes' office environment and daily routines. Sarah's warning about maintaining boundaries suggested the young woman had experienced or witnessed Hayes' predatory behavior firsthand, which meant she might be receptive to approaches that positioned Alira as an ally or potential friend rather than just another of Hayes' victims.

On Friday afternoon, two days before the scheduled dinner with Hayes, Alira called Sarah Chen's office number directly rather than going through the Senator's main office line.

"Sarah Chen speaking."

"Sarah, this is Alira Sinclair. I hope I'm not catching you at a bad time—I wanted to thank you again for being so helpful during my visit to Senator Hayes' office last week."

"Of course, Miss Sinclair. I'm glad I could help facilitate your meeting with the Senator." Sarah's tone was professionally pleasant but contained the slight wariness that Alira had observed during their previous interactions.

"I also wanted to thank you for the advice you gave me when you walked me out," Alira said carefully, lowering her voice slightly as if worried about being overheard. "About maintaining professional boundaries even when someone seems understanding and supportive. That was... really thoughtful of you to mention that."

There was a pause during which Alira could almost hear Sarah processing the implications of this acknowledgment—whether Alira was genuinely grateful for the warning or was attempting to probe for information about Hayes' behavior with other women.

"I just think it's important for people to be aware that professional relationships can sometimes become complicated," Sarah said finally, her phrasing careful and deliberately vague. "Especially in political environments where power dynamics aren't always obvious or clearly defined."

"I appreciate your concern," Alira replied. "Actually, I was wondering if you might be willing to meet for coffee sometime? Not in any official capacity—I just thought it might be helpful to talk with someone who understands the political world better than I do. I'm still figuring out whether advocacy work is something I'm emotionally ready for, and it would be nice to have someone I could ask questions without feeling like I'm imposing on Senator Hayes' time."

The request was calculated to appeal to Sarah on multiple levels. It positioned Alira as someone seeking guidance rather than making accusations, it acknowledged Sarah's expertise and experience in ways that would be flattering, and it created an opportunity for private conversation away from Hayes' office where Sarah might feel more comfortable speaking candidly.

"I think I could do that," Sarah said after a moment's consideration. "How about Tuesday afternoon? There's a coffee shop near Georgetown University—Café Luna—that I go to sometimes when I need to work outside the office environment."

They arranged to meet at 3:00 PM on Tuesday, which would give Alira time to conduct her Saturday evening dinner with Hayes and assess how he escalated his grooming behavior in private settings before having a potentially revealing conversation with one of his current staff members.

As Alira ended the call, she reflected on how the multiple threads of her operation were beginning to converge. The tetrodotoxin would arrive next week, providing the weapon she needed to eliminate Hayes. The Saturday dinner would give her crucial intelligence about his private behavior and security consciousness. The Tuesday meeting with Sarah would potentially provide access to Hayes' office routines and might even reveal information about other victims or patterns that could be exploited.

Most importantly, the careful cultivation of relationships with both Hayes and Sarah was creating the foundation for an elimination method that would be far more sophisticated than what she'd employed with Richard Blackwood. Where Blackwood's death had required engineering a single violent encounter with immediate consequences, Hayes' death would result from patient, invisible administration of poison over time, with no sudden confrontation or dramatic moment that might raise suspicions.

That evening, Alira visited Sierra at Riverside Care Facility, finding her sister working on a jigsaw puzzle in the common room. The puzzle featured a pastoral scene with horses grazing in a meadow—simple enough for Sierra's damaged cognitive capacity but engaging enough to hold her attention for extended periods.

"Alira!" Sierra exclaimed with unfiltered joy when she spotted her sister entering the room. "I'm almost done with my puzzle! Just need to find three more pieces!"

"That's wonderful, Sierra," Alira said, sitting beside her sister and studying the nearly completed image. "You're getting so good at these. The horses look beautiful."

Sierra beamed with pride, returning her attention to the scattered pieces as she searched for the ones that would complete her picture. Her concentration was absolute—the puzzle represented the full extent of her current intellectual capacity, a task that the brilliant graduate student she'd been before Dr. Webb's assault would have completed in minutes without conscious thought.

Watching Sierra work, Alira felt the familiar mixture of grief and rage that motivated everything she was doing. Webb had destroyed Sierra's brilliant mind and faced no consequences during his lifetime. Blackwood had destroyed forty-three women over twenty-eight years before Alira had finally stopped him. And Hayes had destroyed sixty-two documented victims over thirty-three years, continuing his predatory behavior even now despite the increased risks and changing social attitudes about powerful men's conduct.

The legal system had failed comprehensively to protect any of these victims or hold their attackers accountable. Institutional mechanisms designed to deliver justice had instead protected predators while punishing anyone who dared challenge powerful men.

But Alira had learned that some forms of justice required working outside institutional frameworks that were fundamentally corrupted. Senator William Hayes would die believing he'd successfully groomed another victim, never understanding that he'd actually invited a far more dangerous predator to study him closely enough to engineer his elimination.

"Are you working on something important?" Sierra asked, looking up from her puzzle with the innocent curiosity of a child.

"Yes," Alira replied honestly. "I'm working on making sure that bad people who hurt vulnerable women face consequences for what they've done."

Sierra nodded solemnly, her damaged mind processing this explanation through the simplified moral framework that was all her brain injury had left her. "That's good. Bad people should face consequences. They shouldn't be allowed to hurt people and just get away with it."

"No, they shouldn't," Alira agreed. "And I'm going to make sure they don't."

As she left Riverside Care Facility that evening, Alira felt renewed certainty about what she was planning. Hayes had spent thirty-three years exploiting vulnerable women while protected by institutional power and political influence. His victims had suffered in silence, their careers destroyed, their psychological wellbeing shattered, their trust in justice permanently undermined.

But that pattern was about to end. Senator William Hayes would fall, and the women he'd victimized would finally see consequences delivered to a predator who'd believed himself untouchable.

The study was complete, the weapon was being prepared, and the hunter was ready to strike.

Chapter 4

Reading Sarah Chen

Three days after her initial meeting with Senator Hayes, Alira found herself in Café Luna, a small coffee shop near Georgetown University that was popular with graduate students and young professionals seeking a quieter atmosphere than the more crowded establishments in the main commercial district. The café occupied the ground floor of a converted townhouse, with exposed brick walls, mismatched vintage furniture, and enough ambient noise to allow private conversations without the risk of being overheard by nearby patrons.

Alira arrived fifteen minutes early, selecting a corner booth that would provide privacy while allowing her to observe the entrance and identify Sarah Chen when she arrived. She ordered a black coffee and settled in with a notebook and pen, creating the appearance of someone working on academic research while actually reviewing her mental notes about Sarah Chen's background and likely psychological state.

Sarah was twenty-four years old, had graduated summa cum laude from Georgetown's School of Foreign Service, and had been hired by Senator Hayes eight months ago as a legislative aide focusing on women's issues and family policy. Her academic record was exceptional, her recommendations from professors had been glowing, and her career trajectory suggested someone who'd been destined for significant success in political circles.

But something had changed during her eight months working for Hayes. Alira had studied Sarah's social media presence carefully, noting the subtle shifts in tone and content that suggested psychological deterioration. Early posts from when she'd first been hired had been enthusiastic and optimistic— photographs of the Capitol building with captions about fulfilling lifelong dreams, excited updates about policy work, expressions of gratitude for the opportunity to serve.

But over the past several months, the posts had become less frequent and more subdued. The enthusiastic captions had been replaced by generic quotes about resilience and perseverance. The photographs of Capitol Hill had given way to images of empty coffee cups and rainy windows. The overall impression was of someone whose initial excitement about her career had been systematically undermined by experiences she couldn't or wouldn't discuss publicly.

Sarah arrived at 3:07 PM, looking frazzled and carrying herself with the particular tension that Alira had observed during their brief interactions at Hayes' office. She was dressed in the conservative business attire that was standard for Capitol Hill staffers—navy blazer, white blouse, gray slacks—but there was something disheveled about her appearance that suggested she'd come directly from work without taking time to compose herself.

Dark circles under her eyes indicated chronic sleep deprivation or stress. A slight tremor in her hands as she ordered her coffee suggested anxiety or possibly the physiological effects of sustained psychological trauma. Her movements were careful and controlled in ways that suggested someone who'd learned to regulate their external presentation even when internally struggling.

"Sarah, thank you so much for taking time to meet with me," Alira said as the young woman slid into the booth across from her. "I know how busy you must be with the Senator's schedule being so demanding."

"Actually, it's nice to get out of the office for a while," Sarah replied, her smile wan but genuine. "Sometimes that environment can be... intense."

The word choice was careful and deliberate. Not "challenging" or "demanding"—which would be normal descriptors for any high-pressure political job—but "intense" in a way that suggested something beyond standard workplace stress.

"I imagine working for someone as powerful and prominent as Senator Hayes must create a lot of pressure," Alira said gently, watching Sarah's reactions carefully. "Especially as a young woman. I'm sure you have to be very careful about how you present yourself, how you navigate relationships with senior staff and the Senator himself."

Something flickered across Sarah's face—recognition, perhaps, or relief at being understood by someone who seemed to grasp the particular challenges of being a young woman in a male-dominated political environment. Her posture relaxed slightly, her hands loosening their grip on her coffee cup.

"You have no idea," Sarah said, then immediately caught herself. "I mean, Senator Hayes is an excellent boss in many ways. Very dedicated to his legislative work, very committed to the issues he cares about. It's just that the political world can be... demanding in ways that aren't always obvious from the outside."

The self-correction was revealing—Sarah had started to speak candidly, then retreated into the careful diplomatic language that Capitol Hill staffers learned to deploy when discussing their employers. But the brief moment of unguarded honesty suggested she wanted to speak more freely if she could find a way to do so safely.

"I've been worried about exactly that," Alira said, allowing vulnerability to show in her voice. "About putting myself in a position where I'm dependent on

Senator Hayes' approval and support. After what happened to me—the assault and the way the system failed me—the thought of being in another situation where someone has power over me is terrifying."

Sarah's coffee cup rattled slightly as she set it down, her eyes meeting Alira's with sudden intensity. "What do you mean? Has Senator Hayes done something that made you uncomfortable?"

"I don't know exactly," Alira replied carefully. "It's probably just my trauma making me paranoid, but sometimes when Senator Hayes talks to me, I feel like there's something underneath the professional concern. Something that reminds me of... before. Of the man who assaulted me and how he made me feel like he was helping me when he was actually positioning me for exploitation."

Sarah's face had gone pale, her hands clenching tightly in her lap. The reaction was immediate and visceral, suggesting that Alira's description had resonated with Sarah's own experiences in ways that couldn't be faked or misinterpreted.

"Has the Senator ever..." Sarah began, then stopped herself, looking around the café nervously as if worried about being overheard. "I'm sorry, I shouldn't ask such personal questions. It's not my place to pry into your interactions with him."

"Has he ever what?" Alira pressed gently, sensing that Sarah was on the edge of revealing something significant.

Sarah looked down at her hands, her voice dropping to barely above a whisper. "Has he ever made you feel like his help comes with... expectations? Like the professional support and advocacy opportunities he's offering aren't really free, that there's an unspoken price you're expected to pay?"

The question was so quietly spoken and so carefully phrased that it took Alira a moment to process the full implications. Sarah wasn't asking whether Hayes had been inappropriate—she was asking whether Alira had experienced the same pattern of manipulation and coercion that Sarah herself had apparently endured.

"I'm not sure," Alira said, reaching across the table to cover Sarah's hand with her own in a gesture of support and solidarity. "But your question makes me think you might have experienced something like that yourself. Am I right?"

For a long moment, Sarah said nothing. Her eyes had filled with tears that she was struggling to control, her breathing had become slightly labored, and her entire body had tensed as if preparing for fight or flight. When she finally spoke, the words came out in a rush that sounded like confession or testimony—something that had been held back for months and was finally being released.

"He has expectations of all of us. The young women on his staff, I mean. He calls it mentorship, professional development, building relationships that will serve our careers in the long term. But it's not that. It's something else entirely. It's about control and power and making us feel like we owe him things that go way beyond normal professional obligations."

"What happened to you, Sarah?" Alira asked softly.

"I can't," Sarah whispered, her voice breaking. "I signed a non-disclosure agreement when I accepted the position. My career, my student loans, my future—everything depends on this job and on not saying anything that could be interpreted as disparaging Senator Hayes or his office. If I violate the NDA, I could be sued for everything I have and everything I'll ever earn."

The mention of a non-disclosure agreement was significant and disturbing. NDAs were common in political offices to protect confidential legislative information and strategic discussions, but requiring staffers to sign agreements that prevented them from discussing their employer's personal conduct was a massive red flag indicating systematic abuse.

"You don't have to give me specific details," Alira said carefully. "But I need to know—am I walking into something dangerous? Is Senator Hayes someone who uses his position to hurt the people who work for him?"

Sarah's tears were flowing freely now, her composure finally breaking after what had apparently been months of maintaining a professional facade while enduring ongoing exploitation. She pulled her hand away from Alira's to wipe her eyes with a napkin, her movements jerky and uncoordinated with emotion.

"He's never violent," Sarah said finally. "That's what makes it so confusing and difficult to name or resist. It's not like he attacks people or uses physical force. It's more... gradual. Persistent. He makes you feel special, chosen, like you're different from all the other staffers. He offers opportunities and access that seem valuable for your career. He talks about trust and vulnerability and how important it is for effective working relationships."

"And then the boundaries shift," Alira said, understanding the pattern that Sarah was describing.

"Yes. Gradually, so you're never quite sure when things crossed from appropriate to inappropriate. A hand on your shoulder that lingers too long. Compliments about your appearance that seem professional until you realize he never makes them about male staffers. Invitations to private meetings in his townhouse that are framed as work sessions but feel... different. Questions about your personal life and relationships that seem like friendly interest until you understand he's actually mapping your vulnerabilities."

Sarah's description was chillingly familiar—it matched the accounts Alira had read from Hayes' previous victims, the pattern she'd identified through months of research, and the grooming techniques that predators like Hayes used to create confusion and psychological dependence that made resistance difficult.

"How many others?" Alira asked. "How many women on the staff have experienced this?"

"I don't know for certain," Sarah replied, her voice steadier now that she'd begun speaking openly. "We don't talk about it directly. But there are signs. Jennifer Walsh left suddenly last month—officially it was for 'family reasons,' but I saw how she looked in the days before she quit. Maria Santos before her transferred to another senator's office after only four months, claiming she wanted different policy experience. And there have been others over the years. The pattern is always the same—young women arrive enthusiastic and capable, then either leave abruptly or become... diminished. Quieter. More withdrawn. Like something inside them has been damaged."

"Why don't people report this?" Alira asked, though she already knew the answer from her research into how Hayes had protected himself over three decades.

"Because he'd destroy us," Sarah said immediately, her voice carrying the certainty of someone who'd thought carefully about this question and understood the stakes. "He has resources, connections, attorneys who specialize in discrediting people who make accusations against powerful men. If any of us went public, we'd face defamation lawsuits we couldn't afford to defend, our professional reputations would be systematically demolished, and we'd be blacklisted from political work throughout Washington. We'd lose everything—careers we've spent years building, student loans we can't pay without professional salaries, references we need for any future employment."

"So you stay silent and endure it," Alira said.

"We stay silent and try to survive it," Sarah corrected. "Try to maintain enough professional competence to do our jobs while managing the psychological damage of being constantly manipulated and violated in ways that are too subtle for most people to recognize or take seriously. We tell ourselves it's temporary, just until we can build enough experience and connections to move on to better positions. But some days I feel like I'm disappearing piece by piece, like the person I was when I took this job is being systematically erased by someone who sees me as an object for his gratification rather than as a human being with dignity and autonomy."

The pain in Sarah's voice was genuine and profound. This wasn't someone being dramatic about workplace stress—this was someone describing ongoing psychological trauma that was fundamentally changing her sense of self and her understanding of her place in the world.

"What if there was a way to stop him?" Alira asked quietly, keeping her voice carefully neutral. "Without destroying your career or violating your NDA? What if someone else came forward—someone without an employment contract or legal agreements that could be used against them?"

Sarah looked up sharply, her expression shifting from grief to something approaching hope mixed with fear. "What do you mean?"

"I mean, what if I reported what happened to me?" Alira said, referring to the fictional assault scenario she'd created for her approach to Hayes. "Not what he's done to his staff, but what he's doing to me as someone seeking his political support. I don't work for him, I haven't signed any agreements, and I have a documented history as a trauma survivor that would make my account credible."

"He'd destroy you too," Sarah said, though her tone suggested she wanted to believe otherwise. "He has lawyers who've been doing this for decades. They know exactly how to make women like you—like us—look unstable, mercenary, motivated by attention-seeking rather than genuine harm. They'd investigate every aspect of your life, find anything that could be used to undermine your credibility, and use it to paint you as someone who's either lying for money or mentally ill and unable to accurately perceive reality."

"Maybe," Alira acknowledged. "But what if he couldn't? What if something happened that made it impossible for him to retaliate or deploy his usual tactics?"

Sarah stared at her for a long moment, her expression showing confusion mixed with growing alarm. "What are you suggesting?"

Alira realized she'd pushed too far, too fast. Sarah was receptive to the idea of Hayes facing consequences, but she was also fundamentally law-abiding and would become suspicious if Alira seemed to be proposing anything that sounded like vigilante action or violence.

"I'm not suggesting anything specific," Alira said quickly, softening her tone. "I'm just saying that predators like Hayes only have power as long as their victims remain isolated and silent. If enough people spoke out, if patterns became undeniable, if the institutional protections broke down... maybe then he'd face real accountability."

Sarah's expression remained troubled, but the immediate alarm faded. "I want to believe that's possible. But I've been in Washington long enough to understand how these things actually work. Powerful men don't fall because victims speak out—they fall when other powerful people decide they're more of a liability than an asset. Hayes has enough political capital and fundraising capability that his party leadership will protect him indefinitely unless he becomes a major public scandal that threatens their broader objectives."

"What would it take to make him that kind of scandal?" Alira asked.

"Probably death or criminal charges," Sarah said with bitter humor. "Those are about the only things that can't be managed through political pressure and legal maneuvering. Short of that, he'll continue doing what he's been doing for thirty-plus years, and the rest of us will continue trying to survive working for him until we can find ways to escape."

The conversation shifted to less dangerous territory after that, with Sarah describing her work on women's policy issues and Alira expressing continued interest in advocacy opportunities while maintaining appropriate uncertainty about her emotional readiness. They spoke for another thirty minutes before Sarah checked her watch and realized she needed to return to the office for a late afternoon meeting.

"Alira," Sarah said as they prepared to leave the café, "I want you to know that talking with you has been...

important. I haven't been able to speak honestly about any of this with anyone, and it means a lot to have someone who understands what it's like to deal with Hayes' particular kind of manipulation."

"Thank you for trusting me with your experience," Alira replied sincerely. "And please know that you're not alone in this. Whatever happens with my advocacy work or my interactions with Senator Hayes, I want you to feel like you have someone you can talk to who won't judge you or use what you share against you."

Sarah's eyes filled with tears again, but this time they seemed to be tears of gratitude rather than grief. "That means more than you know. Working in that office can be so isolating—you're surrounded by people but you can't really talk to any of them about what's actually happening. Having someone who gets it, who understands the complexity and the fear... it helps."

As they parted company outside the café, Alira reflected on how the meeting had exceeded her expectations. She'd confirmed that Hayes was actively exploiting his current staff, that his behavior followed the same patterns she'd documented in historical cases, and that his victims were systematically silenced through a combination of NDAs, economic dependence, and fear of professional retaliation.

More importantly, she'd established a relationship with Sarah Chen that could be leveraged for future intelligence gathering about Hayes' routines, vulnerabilities, and upcoming activities. Sarah viewed Alira as a potential ally and confidant, someone who understood what she was experiencing and might help her find ways to resist or escape Hayes' exploitation.

What Sarah didn't understand—couldn't understand—was that Alira had no intention of challenging Hayes through legal channels or political pressure. She was planning to eliminate him entirely, using methods that would make his death appear so natural that investigators would never suspect murder.

And Sarah, despite her good intentions and genuine suffering, would unwittingly help facilitate that elimination by providing access and information that would allow Alira to get close enough to administer the tetrodotoxin that was currently being prepared for delivery.

That evening, back in her Georgetown surveillance apartment, Alira reviewed her notes from the conversation with Sarah and began developing a more detailed plan for how she would recruit the young staffer's assistance without revealing her actual intentions.

Sarah had mentioned that Hayes often invited staffers to his townhouse for what he called "work sessions" but which actually functioned as opportunities for private exploitation. If Alira could position herself as someone

Sarah trusted, she might be able to get information about when these sessions were scheduled, what Hayes' security routines were during private meetings, and what kinds of materials or substances he regularly consumed that could be used as delivery mechanisms for the toxin.

The key would be making Sarah believe she was helping with legitimate advocacy work or victim support rather than facilitating an assassination. Sarah's moral framework was fundamentally conventional—she believed in working within systems even when those systems failed, and she would be horrified if she understood that Alira was planning murder rather than political accountability.

But Sarah also wanted Hayes to face consequences, wanted her own suffering to mean something, wanted to believe that predators couldn't continue operating with complete impunity forever. That desire for justice could be channeled and exploited, even if Sarah never understood how her assistance was actually being used.

Alira opened a new document on her encrypted laptop and began outlining the psychological approach she would use with Sarah over the coming weeks:

Phase 1 (Current): Establish trust and solidarity through shared understanding of Hayes' predatory behavior.

Phase 2: Gradually introduce the idea of gathering information about Hayes' activities that might be useful for future accountability efforts.

Phase 3: Request specific assistance with seemingly innocent tasks—obtaining Hayes' schedule, learning about his dietary habits or health concerns, identifying patterns in his private meetings.

Phase 4: Use information provided by Sarah to develop and execute the poisoning plan without her knowledge or understanding of what she'd helped facilitate.

Phase 5: Maintain relationship with Sarah after Hayes' death, providing emotional support while ensuring she never suspects her own unwitting complicity in his elimination.

The plan was sophisticated and morally complex in ways that would have troubled Alira before she'd committed her first kill. Sarah was a victim herself, someone who deserved protection and support rather than manipulation. Using her suffering as a tool for facilitating Hayes' murder represented exactly the kind of exploitation that Alira claimed to be fighting against.

But Alira had learned that achieving justice for the many sometimes required accepting moral compromises that protected individual victims while eliminating predators. Sarah would never know she'd helped kill Senator Hayes, would never bear the psychological burden of complicity in his death, and would ultimately benefit from his elimination even if she couldn't be told how it had been accomplished.

The greater good sometimes required using people who couldn't be trusted with complete truth, and Alira had accepted that moral calculus when she'd decided to become a systematic hunter of predators rather than simply seeking justice for her sister through conventional means.

As she prepared for bed that night, Alira thought about the Saturday evening dinner with Hayes that was now just three days away. The meeting with Sarah had provided crucial intelligence about Hayes' methods and psychology, confirming that he was continuing to escalate his predatory behavior even as social attitudes shifted and the risks of discovery increased.

But it had also revealed the extent of Hayes' institutional protections and the sophistication of his legal defenses. He'd been operating with impunity for thirty-three years not through luck or oversight, but through systematic exploitation of power structures that protected wealthy, prominent men while destroying anyone who challenged them.

The legal system wouldn't stop Hayes. Political pressure wouldn't stop him. Public exposure might embarrass him temporarily, but his party leadership valued his legislative effectiveness and fundraising capabilities enough to protect him through any scandal short of criminal conviction.

Only death would stop Senator William Hayes from continuing to victimize vulnerable women, and Alira was prepared to deliver that consequence through methods that would ensure he never saw it coming.

The second sin was being carefully prepared, and every conversation, every surveillance session, every strategic relationship was bringing Alira closer to the moment when she would eliminate another predator who believed himself untouchable.

Sarah Chen wanted justice but lacked the moral courage or practical means to deliver it. Alira would provide that justice while protecting Sarah from ever understanding her own role in facilitating it.

The hunt continued, and the prey remained completely unaware that he was being studied by someone far more dangerous than any of the victims he'd spent decades exploiting.

FIAT JUSTITIA *Let Justice Be Done*

_____

"Well-behaved women seldom make history." — Laurel Thatcher Ulrich

Chapter 5

The Innocent Favor

Two weeks passed after Alira's conversation with Sarah Chen in the Georgetown café, during which she carefully cultivated her relationships with both the young staffer and Senator Hayes while waiting for the tetrodotoxin delivery and developing the specific methodology she would use to administer the poison without detection.

The Saturday dinner with Hayes at Tosca had proceeded exactly as Alira had anticipated—the Senator had been charming and attentive in the private dining room, his conversation mixing genuine interest in her supposed advocacy goals with increasingly personal questions designed to map her psychological vulnerabilities and assess her potential as a victim. He'd touched her hand repeatedly during dinner, his fingers lingering in ways that were meant to seem supportive but actually functioned to establish physical familiarity and test her boundaries.

Most significantly, Hayes had consumed wine freely throughout the meal—two glasses of an expensive Barolo without any apparent concern about how the alcohol might impair his judgment or make him vulnerable. His casual consumption of substances provided by restaurants suggested he wasn't paranoid about being poisoned, which was crucial for Alira's developing plan. Hayes also complained extensively during their dinner about his chronic fatigue, the demands of his legislative schedule, and his wife's "nagging" about seeing a cardiologist for a full workup.

"Margaret thinks I'm going to drop dead of a heart attack if I don't get every possible test," Hayes had said with obvious irritation. "She doesn't understand that I can't just take time off whenever I feel a little tired. The work we're doing on victim advocacy legislation is too important to interrupt for medical appointments that will probably just tell me what I already know—that I need to lose weight and reduce stress."

The admission had been revealing on multiple levels. It confirmed that Hayes had documented cardiovascular concerns that would make stroke or heart attack seem like plausible natural causes of death. It demonstrated that his wife was actively worried about his health and trying to get him to take preventive measures. And it showed that Hayes himself was resistant to medical advice and unlikely to be suspicious of health interventions as long as they didn't require significant time commitment or acknowledgment that his lifestyle might actually be dangerous.

The dinner had concluded with Hayes inviting her to a "private policy briefing" at his Georgetown townhouse the following week, framed as an opportunity to learn more about his legislative work on victim advocacy issues. Alira had accepted with appropriate gratitude mixed with nervous uncertainty, playing her role perfectly while internally cataloguing every detail that would inform her eventual elimination strategy.

Her relationship with Sarah had deepened through regular text message exchanges and two additional coffee meetings, during which Sarah had shared increasingly personal details about the toxic work environment in Hayes' office and her growing desperation to find another position. Sarah had mentioned her mother several times during these conversations—a retired schoolteacher living in Virginia who worried constantly about her daughter working in such a high-pressure political environment.

"My mother keeps asking if Senator Hayes treats his staff well," Sarah had said during one of their meetings. "I don't know what to tell her. He's not openly abusive or anything that would be easy to explain, but the atmosphere is just... unhealthy. She can hear it in my voice when we talk, even when I try to hide how stressed I am."

The mention of Sarah's mother had registered with Alira as potentially useful information—family members who were concerned about a loved one's wellbeing often became invested in solutions that might improve difficult situations. If Alira could position Sarah's mother as someone worried about both Sarah's stress levels and Hayes' health, it might create additional opportunities for manipulation.

On the twelfth day after her dinner with Hayes, Alira received notification that her tetrodotoxin order had been delivered to the commercial mailbox she maintained under her Dr. Elena Vasquez identity. She retrieved the package that evening, carefully transporting it back to her Georgetown apartment where she could work with the compound in complete privacy.

The tetrodotoxin arrived in a small amber vial containing fifty milligrams of purified compound suspended in a stable pharmaceutical-grade solution. The supplier had included detailed documentation about the compound's properties, safety protocols for handling, and proper storage requirements—all written for legitimate researchers conducting neurological studies rather than for someone planning to weaponize the substance for murder.

Alira spent the next three days conducting intensive research into tetrodotoxin pharmacology, dosing calculations, and delivery mechanisms that would ensure lethal accumulation while mimicking the progressive symptoms of stroke or cardiac arrest. The compound worked by blocking sodium channels in nerve cells, progressively paralyzing the neuromuscular system until respiratory failure occurred. In controlled medical settings, the symptoms were virtually indistinguishable from stroke—progressive weakness, difficulty speaking, respiratory distress, and eventually cardiac arrest as the brainstem's respiratory control centers failed.

The critical challenge was calculating doses that would accumulate to lethal levels over several days while avoiding immediate acute symptoms that might trigger emergency medical intervention or poison screening. Tetrodotoxin was extraordinarily potent—the lethal dose for an average adult male was approximately 1-2 milligrams total. But administering that amount in a single dose would cause immediate, dramatic symptoms that would obviously indicate poisoning.

Instead, Alira needed to spread the lethal dose across multiple days, allowing the compound to accumulate in Hayes' tissues while producing symptoms that would be attributed to stress, overwork, or progressive cardiovascular disease. Based on her research into Hayes' body weight, general health status, and documented medical conditions, she calculated that daily doses of 0.15 milligrams would achieve lethal accumulation within nine to eleven days while producing symptoms that would seem consistent with stroke.

The first three or four days would produce subtle neurological effects—mild tingling in extremities, slight coordination difficulties, fatigue beyond what Hayes' normal stress levels would explain. He would likely attribute these symptoms to his demanding schedule and pre-existing health issues rather than suspecting poisoning.

Days five through seven would bring more pronounced symptoms—progressive weakness, difficulty speaking clearly, respiratory challenges that he would interpret as stress-related breathing problems. Still nothing that would necessarily trigger emergency medical care or comprehensive toxicology screening, just the gradual deterioration of someone whose cardiovascular system was failing under political pressure.

By days nine through eleven, the accumulated tetrodotoxin would trigger catastrophic neuromuscular failure. Hayes' respiratory system would progressively shut down, his heart rhythm would become increasingly erratic, and he would experience what would appear to be a massive stroke complicated by cardiac arrest. Emergency responders would find a senior politician with documented cardiovascular risk factors dying of apparent natural causes exacerbated by stress and overwork.

The medical examination would reveal nothing suspicious unless investigators specifically ordered testing for exotic marine toxins—something that would only occur if they had particular reason to suspect that specific type of poisoning. Standard toxicology panels tested for common drugs, alcohol, and conventional poisoning agents like arsenic or cyanide, but not for tetrodotoxin unless there was obvious reason to suspect exposure to marine organisms or deliberate poisoning with exotic compounds.

After completing her dosing calculations, Alira purchased a bottle of legitimate CardioVital supplements from an upscale health food store in a neighborhood where she'd never conducted any other activities related to her operations. She paid with cash, avoiding any transaction records that might later be traced. The supplements came in large gel capsules that would be perfect for her purposes—easy to open and reseal, opaque enough to conceal tampering, and similar in appearance to countless other vitamin supplements that wouldn't draw special attention.

Working in her apartment wearing latex gloves and using equipment purchased specifically for this purpose, Alira set up a makeshift laboratory on her kitchen table. She'd covered the surface with disposable plastic sheeting, arranged her tools in careful order, and prepared the binding agents that would allow her to convert the liquid tetrodotoxin into powder form that could be sealed inside capsules.

The process required extreme precision and caution. Tetrodotoxin was lethal in minute quantities, and even accidental skin contact with concentrated solution could cause serious harm or death. Alira worked slowly and methodically, using micro-pipettes to measure exact amounts of the toxin solution, mixing it with pharmaceutical-grade binding agents that would hold the compound in stable powder form, then allowing the mixture to dry completely before handling.

Each weaponized capsule required approximately thirty minutes to prepare. Alira would carefully open a CardioVital capsule by gently twisting the two halves apart, pour out the original supplement powder into a waste container, then fill the empty capsule with precisely measured amounts of her tetrodotoxin mixture. The powder looked and felt nearly identical to the original supplement contents—slightly grainy, off-white in color, with no distinctive odor that would alert Hayes to tampering.

After filling each capsule, Alira would carefully reseal it by pressing the two halves back together, then inspect it under bright light to ensure there were no visible signs of tampering. The process was tedious and required absolute focus—a single miscalculation in dosing could either fail to achieve lethal accumulation or produce such dramatic acute symptoms that poisoning would be immediately obvious.

She prepared thirty capsules over the course of two evenings—more than enough to ensure lethal accumulation even if Hayes missed occasional doses or if the kill required longer than her initial calculations suggested. The remaining capsules in the CardioVital bottle were left untampered, creating a mixture where roughly one-third of the bottle's contents were weaponized while two-thirds remained legitimate supplements.

This mixing strategy served multiple purposes. If the supplements were tested after Hayes' death, random sampling might not detect the poisoned capsules among the legitimate ones. The presence of actual CardioVital contents in most capsules would support the narrative that these were genuine health supplements rather than weaponized delivery mechanisms. And the gradual consumption of mixed legitimate and poisoned capsules would create irregular symptom progression that would further obscure the pattern of deliberate poisoning.

With the weaponized supplements prepared and carefully stored in her apartment, Alira turned her attention to the more complex challenge of getting Hayes to actually consume them without creating any direct connection between herself and the delivery of potentially lethal substances. She couldn't simply give the supplements to Hayes herself—that would make her an obvious suspect if anything went wrong. She needed an intermediary who would provide them to Hayes, encourage consistent consumption, and never suspect that they'd been weaponized for murder.

Sarah Chen was the obvious choice, but the approach would require sophisticated psychological manipulation to ensure Sarah took ownership of the idea rather than simply following Alira's suggestion. The difference was crucial—if Alira directly proposed that Sarah give supplements to Hayes, Sarah might later remember that suggestion as suspicious if Hayes died shortly after starting to take them. But if Sarah independently decided to provide health supplements as part of her own concern for Hayes' wellbeing, she would have no reason to question her actions or suspect she'd been manipulated into facilitating murder.

On a Tuesday afternoon, exactly sixteen days after her initial meeting with Hayes, Alira arranged to meet Sarah for coffee at Café Luna. She'd spent the previous evening rehearsing exactly how she would plant the information and concerns that would lead Sarah to independently propose the supplement solution.

"Thanks for meeting me," Alira said as Sarah settled into their usual corner booth, looking even more exhausted than during their previous meetings. "I've been worried about something and I wanted to get your perspective on it."

"Of course. What's going on?" Sarah's tone was warm but carried the chronic fatigue that had become her baseline state after eight months working for Hayes.

"It's about Senator Hayes," Alira said, allowing genuine concern to color her voice. "I had dinner with him last weekend, and I have to tell you, he looked terrible. Not just tired—actually unwell. Gray complexion, moving slowly, that kind of general deterioration that suggests serious health problems rather than just stress and overwork."

Sarah's expression shifted to something more complicated—concern mixed with what might have been bitter satisfaction. "He has been looking progressively worse over the past few months. Working incredible hours, eating nothing but takeout and coffee, refusing to acknowledge that his body can't maintain the pace he's setting."

"Does he have any documented health problems?" Alira asked, as if the question was motivated purely by concern rather than by reconnaissance for her elimination plan.

"High blood pressure, elevated cholesterol, family history of heart disease," Sarah replied. "His wife has been trying to get him to see a cardiologist for a full workup, but he keeps putting it off because he says he's too busy. He actually complained about her 'nagging' during our staff meeting last week, as if being concerned about your spouse's health is somehow unreasonable."

Alira shook her head with what appeared to be sympathetic frustration. "That sounds exactly like my father. Same symptoms, same resistance to medical advice, same attitude that his work was too important to interrupt for preventive care."

"You've mentioned your father before," Sarah said gently. "I'm sorry you lost him. Was it sudden, or...?"

"Heart attack," Alira replied, her voice taking on the grief-stricken quality she'd practiced for this conversation. "Massive cardiac arrest at fifty-six, completely preventable if he'd just listened to his doctor and taken basic precautions. The worst part is that his cardiologist had given him specific recommendations months before—dietary changes, stress management techniques, cardiovascular supplements that could have supported his heart health while he worked on the bigger lifestyle modifications."

"What kind of supplements?" Sarah asked, her interest clearly piqued.

"There was this brand called CardioVital that his doctor specifically prescribed," Alira said, as if recalling a painful but important memory. "It contained CoQ10, magnesium, omega-3 fatty acids—all the nutrients that research shows support cardiovascular function and help prevent the kind of acute events that killed my father. He took them consistently for about three months, and he said they made a real difference in his energy levels and overall health. But then he convinced himself he was fine and didn't need them anymore, and he stopped taking them."

Alira paused, allowing emotion to show in her voice. "Two months later, he was dead. The autopsy showed that his heart disease had progressed significantly during those two months, and his cardiologist said that if he'd just stayed on the supplement regimen, it might have bought him enough time to implement the larger lifestyle changes that could have actually saved his life."

Sarah was quiet for a long moment, clearly processing the story and its implications for Hayes' situation. "I'm so sorry. That must be incredibly painful—knowing that something so simple could have prevented his death."

"It is," Alira confirmed. "And that's why seeing Senator Hayes displaying the same symptoms my father had— the exhaustion, the deteriorating appearance, the refusal to take preventive measures seriously—brings back all those feelings of helplessness. It's like watching someone walk toward a cliff while refusing to acknowledge that the edge exists."

"I know exactly what you mean," Sarah said, her voice carrying genuine frustration. "Working with Senator Hayes can be maddening because he's clearly intelligent enough to understand that his lifestyle is unsustainable, but he refuses to admit it or do anything about it. His wife calls the office at least twice a week trying to schedule cardiology appointments, and he tells us to make excuses about scheduling conflicts."

Alira leaned forward slightly, lowering her voice as if sharing a difficult truth. "Can I be honest about something? Part of me wonders if people like my father and Senator Hayes actually want to ignore their health problems because addressing them would mean acknowledging vulnerability or mortality. It's easier to pretend everything is fine and just push through the symptoms than to admit they're not invincible."

"That's probably exactly right," Sarah agreed. "Senator Hayes has built his entire identity around being strong, capable, in control of everything. Admitting he has health problems that require medical intervention would contradict that self-image."

They sat in silence for a moment, both contemplating the psychology of men who'd rather die than admit weakness. Then Alira carefully planted the next seed.

"The thing that frustrates me most is that taking basic supplements isn't even really admitting weakness—it's just supporting your body's ability to handle stress and maintain function. My father's cardiologist explained it as being similar to getting oil changes for your car. It's not because the car is broken; it's preventive maintenance that keeps everything running smoothly so bigger problems don't develop."

"That's a good analogy," Sarah said thoughtfully.

"But try explaining that to someone who's convinced that any form of health intervention means they're sick or weak," Alira continued with apparent frustration. "My father wouldn't listen, and from what you're telling me, Senator Hayes is the same way. It's tragic because they're not just hurting themselves—they're hurting everyone who depends on them. When my father died, it devastated my mother and our entire family. If Senator Hayes has a heart attack or stroke, it won't just affect him—it'll affect everyone who works in his office, everyone who depends on his legislative work, everyone whose lives would be disrupted by losing someone in his position."

Sarah's expression had shifted to something more troubled as she processed this broader implication. "I hadn't thought about it that way, but you're right. If something happens to Senator Hayes, it doesn't just affect his family—it affects dozens of staffers whose careers are tied to working in his office, constituents who depend on his advocacy, legislation that might not move forward without his involvement."

"Exactly," Alira said. "Which makes his refusal to take basic preventive measures even more irresponsible. He's not just risking his own health—he's risking all the work and all the people who depend on him being functional and alive."

They talked for another twenty minutes, with Alira carefully reinforcing the themes she'd introduced—her father's preventable death, the effectiveness of CardioVital supplements, Hayes' concerning health symptoms, the broader impact his potential death would have on people beyond just himself. She was planting information and concerns that Sarah would continue processing after their conversation ended, germinating ideas that would eventually lead Sarah to independently propose a solution.

As they prepared to leave the café, Sarah seemed lost in thought, her expression troubled in ways that suggested she was still contemplating everything they'd discussed.

"Alira," she said as they stood to go, "do you think supplements like the ones your father took would actually help someone like Senator Hayes? I mean, would they make enough difference to matter?"

"I can't say for certain," Alira replied carefully, not wanting to seem too eager to push a specific solution. "Every person's health situation is different. But my father's cardiologist believed they were valuable for anyone with cardiovascular risk factors, especially people dealing with high stress and poor lifestyle habits. They're not a substitute for proper medical care or lifestyle changes, but they can provide important nutritional support that helps the body handle stress and maintain function."

Sarah nodded slowly, clearly filing this information away for future consideration. "Thanks for sharing all this. I know it must be painful to talk about your father, but hearing about his experience actually helps me understand better what might be going on with Senator Hayes."

Over the next three days, Alira waited patiently for Sarah to process their conversation and develop her own response to the concerns they'd discussed. She resisted the temptation to follow up or push harder on the supplement idea—that would risk making Sarah feel manipulated rather than allowing her to reach her own conclusions about what should be done.

On the fourth day after their coffee meeting, Sarah sent Alira a text message: "Can we talk? I've been thinking about our conversation about Senator Hayes' health and I want to run something by you."

They arranged to meet that evening at a wine bar near Georgetown, where Sarah arrived looking more animated than Alira had seen her in weeks.

"I've been researching CardioVital since we talked," Sarah said after they'd ordered drinks. "The ingredients you mentioned—CoQ10, magnesium, omega-3s— they're all supplements that legitimate cardiologists recommend for cardiovascular health. There's actual peer-reviewed research showing they can improve heart function and reduce the risk of cardiac events."

"I'm glad the research supports what my father's doctor told him," Alira said neutrally.

"But here's what I'm struggling with," Sarah continued. "I want to suggest that Senator Hayes start taking something like this, but I know he'll dismiss it if it comes from me. He already thinks I'm overstepping when I try to schedule medical appointments for him—if I suggest supplements, he'll probably accuse me of playing doctor and tell me to focus on legislative work."

Alira nodded sympathetically. "That does sound like a difficult position. You can see he needs help, but you don't have the credibility or relationship to make suggestions he'll actually take seriously."

"Exactly," Sarah said, her frustration evident. "Which is why I've been thinking about whether there might be another approach. What if the suggestion came from someone he actually listens to—like his wife?"

This was even better than Alira had hoped. Sarah wasn't just proposing to give supplements to Hayes herself; she was thinking strategically about how to get him to actually take them through the involvement of his wife, which would add yet another layer of separation between Alira and the delivery of the poisoned substances.

"That could work," Alira said carefully. "Does his wife call the office often enough that you could mention your concerns to her?"

"She calls at least twice a week," Sarah replied. "Usually trying to schedule cardiology appointments or asking me to convince the Senator to come home earlier for dinner. We've actually developed kind of a rapport—she knows I'm trying to help manage his schedule in ways that might be better for his health."

"Then maybe you could mention to her that you've been reading about cardiovascular supplements and wondering if they might help with his fatigue and stress symptoms," Alira suggested, making it seem like she was just helping Sarah develop her own idea rather than directing her toward a specific course of action.

Sarah's expression brightened. "That's good—frame it as something I'm learning about rather than something I'm specifically recommending for him. Mrs. Hayes might be more receptive to that kind of information-sharing than she would be to me directly telling her what her husband should do."

"And if she decides on her own to purchase supplements and encourage him to take them, he might be more willing to listen to her than he would be to anyone on his staff," Alira added.

"Exactly!" Sarah said, clearly excited by the developing plan. "Mrs. Hayes has been trying to get him to take his health seriously for years. If I can provide her with specific, research-backed information about something that might actually help, she could be the one to implement it."

They spent another thirty minutes discussing exactly how Sarah would approach Mrs. Hayes with the information, with Alira providing subtle guidance while making sure Sarah felt ownership of the strategy. By the time they parted that evening, Sarah was committed to raising the supplement issue with Mrs. Hayes during their next phone conversation.

Two days later, Sarah called Alira with an excited update.

"I talked to Mrs. Hayes this morning," Sarah said, her voice carrying genuine satisfaction. "I mentioned that I'd been reading about cardiovascular health because I was concerned about how exhausted the Senator has been looking, and I asked if she knew anything about supplements like CoQ10 and omega-3s."

"How did she respond?" Alira asked.

"She was actually really interested," Sarah replied. "She said she'd been trying to get the Senator to see a cardiologist for months, but that he keeps refusing. She asked me if I thought supplements might help, and I told her about CardioVital specifically—that a friend's father had taken it and found it really beneficial for his energy levels and heart health."

Alira felt a surge of satisfaction that she carefully controlled. Sarah had adapted the story about "Alira's father" into "a friend's father," creating an additional layer of separation that would make the information seem less personally motivated and more like general knowledge Sarah had acquired.

"That was smart to frame it that way," Alira said. "Did she seem receptive to the idea?"

"Very receptive," Sarah confirmed. "She said she was going to research the supplements herself and talk to her own doctor about whether they might be appropriate for the Senator. She seemed grateful that someone on his staff was paying attention to his health and willing to share information that might actually help."

Over the next week, the plan continued to unfold exactly as Alira had hoped. Mrs. Hayes researched CardioVital, consulted with her personal physician about its appropriateness for someone with her husband's health profile, and ultimately purchased a bottle from a high-end health food store in McLean, Virginia.

Sarah provided regular updates through text messages: "Mrs. Hayes bought the supplements and is bringing them to the Senator's office tomorrow." Then, the following day: "The Senator was resistant at first, said he didn't need vitamins from a health food store. But Mrs. Hayes told him it was non-negotiable—either he starts taking basic preventive measures or she's going to start attending all his medical appointments with him to make sure he actually listens to doctors."

The detail about Hayes' initial resistance was important—it demonstrated that he hadn't been eager to take the supplements, which would make his eventual compliance seem reluctant rather than suspicious. When he died after taking them for a week or more, investigators would see a pattern of a stubborn man who'd been pressured by his wife into finally accepting basic health interventions, not someone who'd eagerly consumed substances provided by a potential enemy.

The final piece of information came in Sarah's next message: "Mrs. Hayes is calling me every morning to confirm the Senator actually took his supplement with breakfast. She's treating this like a serious health intervention, not just a casual suggestion. I think we might have actually gotten through to him!"

Alira's response was warmly supportive: "That's such wonderful news! Your suggestion to Mrs. Hayes might have literally saved his life by getting him to finally take his health seriously. You should feel really good about having made that connection."

What Sarah didn't know—what she could never be allowed to know—was that the CardioVital bottle sitting on Senator Hayes' desk would need to be replaced with Alira's carefully prepared weaponized version. The legitimate supplements that Mrs. Hayes had purchased would need to be swapped for the poisoned capsules that would kill her husband within nine to eleven days of consistent consumption.

The substitution would require access to Hayes' office when neither he nor his staff were present, but Alira had been carefully developing exactly such an opportunity through her growing relationship with Sarah. The young staffer had mentioned several times that the office was sometimes empty on weekend mornings when Hayes was in Virginia and the staff were either taking personal time or attending training sessions and retreats.

The opportunity presented itself sooner than Alira had expected. On Friday afternoon, Sarah sent a text message: "Staff retreat tomorrow morning 9 AM - 1 PM at the Capitol Visitor Center. The Senator isn't attending because he's in Virginia with his wife. Office will be completely empty if you need a quiet place to work on your advocacy materials."

The invitation was perfectly innocent—Sarah knew that Alira had been developing written materials about her assault experience for potential use in advocacy work, and she was offering access to a quiet, professional workspace where Alira could focus without distractions. Sarah had no idea she was providing the opportunity Alira needed to commit murder.

Alira's response was carefully casual: "That's really thoughtful of you! I actually might take you up on that— my apartment has been too noisy for focused writing lately. Would I need a key, or will someone be there to let me in?"

"I can give you my spare office key," Sarah replied. "Just drop it back in my desk drawer when you're done. The building security will let you in if you show ID and say you're working in Senator Hayes' office."

That evening, Alira prepared for the substitution with the same meticulous attention to detail that had characterized all her planning. She dressed in professional attire that would make her appear to be a legitimate staffer or consultant working on official business. She packed her laptop and notebooks to support the cover story that she was working on advocacy materials. And most importantly, she carefully packed the weaponized CardioVital bottle in her bag, cushioned with bubble wrap to prevent any accidental damage to the poisoned capsules.

Saturday morning arrived with clear skies and moderate temperatures. Alira took the Metro to Capitol Hill, arriving at the Hart Senate Office Building at 9:47 AM— late enough that the staff retreat would have started but early enough that she'd have ample time to complete the substitution before anyone returned.

Building security checked her ID and confirmed that she was expected in Senator Hayes' office, then allowed her to proceed to the elevators. The third-floor corridor was silent and empty, all the other offices closed for the weekend. Alira used Sarah's key to enter the office suite, her heart rate elevated slightly despite her confidence in her planning.

The office was exactly as she'd observed during her previous visits—the receptionist's desk with its organized files and appointment calendar, the hallway leading to the individual staff offices and Hayes' private office at the end. Alira moved quickly but carefully, heading directly toward Hayes' office while noting the locations of security cameras and ensuring her movements would appear consistent with someone working on legitimate business.

Hayes' private office was unlocked—apparently he didn't bother securing it when the entire office suite was locked and empty. Alira entered and immediately spotted the CardioVital bottle sitting on his desk next to a small crystal water glass and a leather-bound legislative calendar.

She extracted her own bottle from her bag and set it beside the legitimate one, comparing them carefully to ensure they were identical in appearance. The labels matched perfectly—same brand, same formulation, same lot number that she'd carefully replicated using her graphic design software. The bottles themselves were the same size, shape, and color.

Working quickly, Alira opened both bottles and examined the capsule counts. Mrs. Hayes had purchased a full bottle containing ninety capsules, and Hayes had apparently taken four so far—one for each of the four mornings since his wife had delivered them. That left eighty-six capsules in the legitimate bottle.

Alira's weaponized bottle contained exactly eighty-six capsules—a mixture of thirty poisoned capsules and fifty-six legitimate ones that she'd carefully counted out to match whatever quantity she expected to find in Hayes' current bottle. The mixture ensured that random testing wouldn't necessarily detect the poisoned capsules while guaranteeing that Hayes would consume sufficient toxin to achieve lethal accumulation.

She performed the swap in less than thirty seconds, placing her weaponized bottle exactly where the legitimate one had been sitting and putting the legitimate bottle in her bag for later disposal. Then she stepped back and examined the desk carefully, ensuring everything appeared exactly as it had when she'd entered.

The entire substitution had taken less than three minutes from entering the office to completing the swap. Alira spent another hour in the office suite, actually working on her advocacy materials at a desk in the main area, establishing legitimate reasons for her presence in case anyone asked Sarah about it later. She made sure to leave some papers on the desk, create some document files on her laptop that were timestamped to Saturday morning, and generally ensure that her cover story would hold up under even moderate scrutiny.

At 11:23 AM, Alira left the office suite, carefully locking the door behind her and returning Sarah's key to the desk drawer as instructed. She departed the building through normal security procedures, nodding pleasantly at the weekend guards who barely glanced at her.

By noon, she was back in her Georgetown apartment, the legitimate CardioVital bottle already disassembled and its contents disposed of in multiple locations—capsules flushed down different toilets throughout the city, the bottle itself crushed and deposited in a public trash bin miles from her apartment or Hayes' office.

The substitution was complete. When Hayes returned to his office on Monday morning and took his daily supplement with breakfast, he would be consuming the first poisoned capsule that would begin the gradual accumulation of tetrodotoxin in his system. Mrs. Hayes would continue calling Sarah each morning to confirm he'd taken his supplement, never suspecting that her well-intentioned health intervention was actually administering a lethal dose of exotic poison.

Sarah would continue feeling good about having helped connect Mrs. Hayes with information that might improve the Senator's health, never understanding that her innocent suggestion had facilitated murder. And Hayes himself would take his daily CardioVital capsules believing they were helping support his cardiovascular health, not realizing that each dose was bringing him closer to the catastrophic neuromuscular failure that would end his predatory career permanently.

That evening, Alira sent Sarah a thank-you text message: "Thanks so much for letting me use the office this morning! I got so much done on my advocacy materials in that quiet, professional environment. You're a really good friend for thinking of me."

Sarah's response was warm: "Of course! I'm glad it helped. And I'm really happy that we were able to work together to help Senator Hayes take better care of his health. Sometimes I feel like the small things we do— like suggesting supplements or creating quiet workspaces for friends—don't matter much, but they can actually make a real difference in people's lives."

The irony of Sarah's message was profound and tragic. She believed she'd helped save Hayes' life by facilitating his wife's health intervention, when in reality she'd helped end it by providing the access Alira needed to substitute poisoned supplements for legitimate ones. Her innocent intentions had been weaponized by someone who understood exactly how to manipulate good people into facilitating evil outcomes without ever understanding their complicity.

But Sarah would never know. She would grieve sincerely when Hayes died, would never suspect that her helpful suggestion to Mrs. Hayes had been part of an elaborate murder plot, and would be protected from the moral burden of knowing she'd helped kill someone even if that someone had been a predator who'd victimized her and dozens of other women.

The innocent favor had been orchestrated through layers of psychological manipulation and misdirection that would protect everyone involved except the man who deserved death for thirty-three years of systematic exploitation. And when Senator William Hayes died showing symptoms consistent with stroke, no one would have any reason to suspect that his death had been engineered by a trauma survivor he'd underestimated as just another potential victim.

The second sin was being committed with surgical precision, and the countdown to Hayes' death had officially begun.

VERITAS *Truth*

_____

"The truth does not change because it is silenced."

Chapter 6

The Perfect Delivery

Monday morning arrived with unseasonably warm weather for late April, the kind of spring day that made Washington feel almost optimistic despite the political tensions and institutional failures that defined the city's actual operations. Alira woke at her usual time, went through her morning routine with deliberate calm, and then settled at her kitchen table with coffee to wait for the confirmation that Senator William Hayes had begun consuming the poisoned supplements.

The text message arrived at 8:34 AM, exactly when Alira had anticipated based on Sarah's established pattern of morning check-ins with Mrs. Hayes.

"Mrs. Hayes just called to confirm the Senator took his supplement with breakfast this morning. She sounded really pleased that he's being consistent about it. Day 5 of his new health routine!"

Alira smiled at the message's innocent enthusiasm. Sarah believed she was tracking Hayes' progress toward better health management, celebrating each day of compliance as evidence that her helpful suggestion was making a positive difference. She had no idea she was actually documenting a murder in progress, providing a detailed timeline that would show exactly when Hayes began consuming the poison that would kill him.

From Sarah's perspective, this was Day 5 of Hayes taking CardioVital supplements. But in reality, it was Day 1 of Hayes consuming weaponized capsules containing carefully measured doses of tetrodotoxin. The four days he'd taken legitimate supplements before Alira's Saturday morning substitution were irrelevant to the poisoning timeline—those capsules had contained nothing but the standard cardiovascular nutrients that Mrs. Hayes had purchased from a Virginia health food store.

Alira replied with appropriate warmth: "That's wonderful! Consistency is so important with supplements. I'm really glad he's taking this seriously."

Over the following days, Sarah continued providing regular updates that allowed Alira to track Hayes' consumption of the poisoned supplements with precision. Each morning brought a new message confirming that Mrs. Hayes had called, that Hayes had taken his daily capsule, and that the Senator's "health routine" was proceeding exactly as planned.

Day 2 (Tuesday): "Mrs. Hayes called again. Senator took his supplement. She's so happy he's finally taking preventive health seriously."

Day 3 (Wednesday): "Daily check-in complete. Mrs. Hayes says the Senator seems to have a bit more energy lately. She thinks the supplements might already be helping!"

The comment about increased energy was interesting and slightly concerning. Alira knew from her research that tetrodotoxin shouldn't produce any positive effects—the compound was purely toxic, progressively disrupting neuromuscular function without providing any beneficial impacts. But the placebo effect was powerful, and Hayes might genuinely feel better simply because he believed he was doing something good for his health. Alternatively, Mrs. Hayes might be engaging in wishful thinking, interpreting normal day-to-day variation in her husband's energy levels as evidence that her health intervention was succeeding.

Day 4 (Thursday): "Mrs. Hayes reported Senator took his supplement. She mentioned he's been sleeping better. I think we really did help him!"

Again, the reported improvement was likely placebo effect or confirmation bias rather than any actual benefit from the supplements. But Alira noted it carefully in her encrypted research log, tracking every detail of Hayes' condition as the poison accumulated in his system.

Day 5 (Friday): "Morning check-in done. Mrs. Hayes noticed Senator seemed a bit distracted during their phone call last night, but she thinks he's just stressed about upcoming committee hearings. He took his supplement as usual."

This was more significant. "Distracted" could be an early neurological symptom of tetrodotoxin accumulation—mild cognitive disruption as the compound began affecting neural function. But it was subtle enough to be easily attributed to stress or work pressure, exactly as Mrs. Hayes had apparently done.

Day 6 (Saturday): "Mrs. Hayes called even though it's the weekend. Senator took his supplement. She mentioned he seemed tired again, but she thinks it's because he worked late Friday night."

The return of fatigue symptoms after the brief period of reported increased energy suggested the placebo effect was wearing off and the actual toxic effects were beginning to manifest. Tetrodotoxin's progressive disruption of neuromuscular function would naturally present as fatigue and weakness as the body struggled to maintain normal activity levels despite compromised neural signaling.

Day 7 (Sunday): "Weekly check-in complete. Mrs. Hayes sounds a bit concerned—said the Senator seemed to have some trouble with coordination this morning, nearly dropped his coffee cup. But he insisted he's fine, just didn't sleep well."

Alira's pulse quickened slightly as she read this message. Coordination difficulties were a classic early symptom of tetrodotoxin poisoning, indicating that the compound was beginning to disrupt the precise neural control required for fine motor skills. The fact that Hayes had nearly dropped something was significant— it suggested his neuromuscular function was deteriorating enough to produce observable effects, though still subtle enough to be dismissed as simple clumsiness or fatigue.

She replied to Sarah with carefully calibrated concern: "I hope the Senator is okay. Sometimes when people first start supplements, their body needs time to adjust. But if his symptoms get worse, maybe he should check in with his doctor just to be safe."

The response served multiple purposes. It demonstrated appropriate concern for Hayes' wellbeing, which Sarah would remember as evidence of Alira's innocent intentions. It planted the idea that some initial adverse effects might be normal when starting supplements, which could delay recognition that something was seriously wrong. And it suggested medical consultation if symptoms worsened, which would make Alira seem like someone genuinely worried about Hayes' health rather than someone engineering his death.

Sarah's response came quickly: "That's good advice. I'll mention to Mrs. Hayes that some adjustment period might be normal, but that she should watch for worsening symptoms. She's pretty vigilant about his health anyway, so I'm sure she'll notice if anything concerning develops."

Day 8 (Monday): "Mrs. Hayes called this morning sounding more worried. Senator took his supplement, but she said he complained about tingling in his hands and feet. He told her it's probably just stress or sitting in uncomfortable chairs during long meetings. She's not sure whether to push him to see a doctor or trust his judgment."

The tingling in extremities was a textbook symptom of tetrodotoxin poisoning—the compound's blockade of sodium channels in peripheral nerves created abnormal sensations that patients typically described as tingling, numbness, or "pins and needles" feelings. The fact that Hayes was experiencing this on Day 8 of consuming the poisoned supplements was exactly consistent with Alira's dosing calculations.

More importantly, Hayes' dismissal of the symptoms as stress-related meant he wasn't yet considering the possibility that something was seriously wrong with his health. His attribution of neurological symptoms to benign causes would delay medical intervention and allow the poisoning to progress further before anyone recognized the severity of his condition.

Alira responded to Sarah: "Tingling in extremities can sometimes be related to vitamin deficiencies, actually. The supplements might be helping his body recognize deficiencies that were already there. But if it persists or gets worse, he should definitely see a doctor. Better to be overly cautious with neurological symptoms."

The explanation was deliberately misleading— suggesting that the tingling might actually be related to the supplements in a way that indicated their helpfulness rather than their toxicity. If Sarah shared this interpretation with Mrs. Hayes, it might delay their recognition that the supplements themselves could be causing problems rather than solving them.

Day 9 (Tuesday): "This morning's call was concerning. Mrs. Hayes said the Senator seemed to have difficulty speaking clearly during breakfast—slightly slurred words, like he couldn't quite coordinate his mouth properly. He insisted it was nothing, that he just bit his tongue slightly. But she's really worried now and is insisting he see a doctor this week."

Alira felt a mixture of satisfaction and carefully controlled excitement as she read this update. Slurred speech indicated that the tetrodotoxin was now affecting the complex neuromuscular coordination required for clear articulation—a sign that the poisoning had progressed from peripheral nerves to more central neural functions. Hayes was entering the critical phase where his symptoms would become increasingly difficult to dismiss as benign stress effects.

The fact that Mrs. Hayes was now insisting on medical consultation was both predictable and potentially problematic. If Hayes saw a doctor while still alive and coherent enough to provide medical history, there was a slight risk that an astute physician might recognize the constellation of symptoms—fatigue, coordination difficulties, tingling extremities, speech problems—as indicating something more serious than simple stress or cardiovascular disease.

However, Alira's research had shown that even if doctors suspected neurological disease, their first assumptions would be stroke, multiple sclerosis, or other relatively common conditions rather than exotic poisoning with a rare marine toxin. Standard neurological workups would include brain imaging and blood tests for conventional markers, but not specialized toxicology screening for tetrodotoxin unless there was obvious reason to suspect that specific compound.

She replied to Sarah: "It's good that Mrs. Hayes is pushing for medical evaluation. Even if it's nothing serious, it's better to rule out anything concerning. Please keep me posted on what the doctors say—I'm worried about him."

Day 10 (Wednesday): "Mrs. Hayes called in tears this morning. The Senator collapsed in his office last night around 9 PM. He's at Georgetown University Hospital. They're saying it looks like a stroke—he's having trouble breathing and his heart rhythm is irregular. They have him on life support while they run tests."

The message arrived at 8:52 AM, and Alira read it three times to ensure she'd understood correctly. Hayes had collapsed on Day 10 of consuming the poisoned supplements—exactly within the timeframe her dosing calculations had predicted for catastrophic neuromuscular failure. The symptoms Sarah described—respiratory distress and cardiac arrhythmia—were classic manifestations of advanced tetrodotoxin poisoning as the compound progressively shut down the brainstem's control of vital autonomic functions.

The fact that doctors were interpreting his condition as stroke was perfect. Stroke and tetrodotoxin poisoning presented with remarkably similar symptoms—sudden neurological deterioration, respiratory compromise, cardiac instability. Unless physicians had specific reason to suspect poisoning, they would pursue the much more common diagnosis of cerebrovascular accident rather than ordering the exotic toxicology testing that would reveal the true cause.

Alira's response to Sarah was carefully crafted to convey shock and appropriate concern: "Oh my God, that's terrible! Is he going to be okay? What are the doctors saying about his prognosis?"

Sarah's reply came twenty minutes later: "They don't know yet. Mrs. Hayes is devastated. The doctors are saying the next 24-48 hours are critical. If he survives, there could be permanent neurological damage. I can't believe this happened—he was just taking supplements to help his health, and now he's dying."

The guilt and confusion in Sarah's message was palpable. She was trying to reconcile the fact that Hayes had collapsed shortly after beginning a health intervention that was supposed to prevent exactly this kind of medical crisis. The cognitive dissonance was understandable—from Sarah's perspective, Hayes should have been getting healthier from the supplements, not suffering a catastrophic stroke.

"This is not your fault," Alira wrote back firmly. "Strokes happen to people with cardiovascular risk factors regardless of what preventive measures they're taking. The supplements you helped Mrs. Hayes provide were legitimate health products—there's no way they could have caused this. If anything, he might have had the stroke sooner if he hadn't been taking them."

The reassurance was calculated to prevent Sarah from developing the kind of guilty suspicions that might lead her to question the supplement timeline or mention it to investigators. If Sarah believed the stroke was completely unrelated to the CardioVital regimen, she would have no reason to bring up the supplements during any conversations with hospital staff or medical examiners.

Sarah's response suggested the reassurance was working: "Thank you for saying that. I keep running through the timeline in my head, wondering if there was something different I should have done. But you're right—he had high blood pressure, family history of heart disease, terrible stress levels. This was probably inevitable regardless of what anyone did to help him."

Over the next thirty-six hours, Sarah provided regular updates on Hayes' condition as his situation progressively deteriorated. The medical team at Georgetown University Hospital was treating him for massive stroke, administering standard interventions for cerebrovascular accidents while monitoring his failing respiratory and cardiac systems.

"Doctors say the stroke was massive—affecting multiple areas of his brain," Sarah reported on Wednesday afternoon. "They're not optimistic about recovery even if he survives. Mrs. Hayes is making decisions about end-of-life care."

"Brain imaging shows extensive damage," came the update on Wednesday evening. "His breathing is completely dependent on the ventilator. Cardiac function is becoming increasingly unstable despite medication."

"They're talking about withdrawing life support," Sarah wrote on Thursday morning. "Mrs. Hayes doesn't want him to suffer, and the doctors say there's essentially no chance of meaningful recovery. His brain function is too compromised."

At 3:17 PM on Thursday afternoon—Day 11 of consuming poisoned supplements and approximately forty-two hours after his initial collapse—Senator William Hayes was pronounced dead. The immediate cause of death was listed as cardiac arrest secondary to massive ischemic stroke. His body was transferred to the medical examiner's office for the autopsy that was standard procedure for any sudden death of a prominent public figure.

Sarah's message announcing his death was brief and devastated: "He's gone. Senator Hayes died this afternoon. Mrs. Hayes was with him when they withdrew life support. I don't know what to feel. He was terrible in so many ways, but I never wanted this."

Alira's response was carefully sympathetic: "I'm so sorry, Sarah. This must be incredibly complicated for you emotionally. Take whatever time you need to process. And remember—none of this is your fault. You tried to help, which is more than most people would have done."

The medical examiner's autopsy was conducted on Friday morning, and the preliminary findings were exactly what Alira had anticipated. The examination revealed extensive cerebrovascular damage consistent with massive stroke, cardiac tissue showing signs of acute stress and arrhythmia, and brain imaging demonstrating the kind of catastrophic neural damage that explained Hayes' rapid deterioration and death.

The toxicology screening was routine—testing for common drugs, alcohol, and standard poisoning agents. The results showed therapeutic levels of Hayes' prescribed blood pressure and cholesterol medications, no alcohol or recreational drugs, and no indication of conventional poisons like arsenic, cyanide, or common pharmaceutical overdoses.

Tetrodotoxin wasn't included in the standard toxicology panel. Testing for exotic marine toxins required specialized procedures that would only be ordered if investigators had specific reason to suspect that particular type of poisoning. And there was no such reason—Hayes had died of apparent stroke, a medical event that was entirely consistent with his documented cardiovascular risk factors, his high-stress lifestyle, and his family history of heart disease.

The medical examiner's final report, released the following Tuesday, listed the cause of death as "massive ischemic stroke with resulting cardiac arrest" and noted contributing factors of hypertension, hyperlipidemia, and chronic occupational stress. The manner of death was classified as natural.

No one questioned the CardioVital supplements sitting on Hayes' desk. No one thought to test them for contamination or tampering. No one suspected that a seemingly innocuous health intervention had actually been a sophisticated murder weapon disguised as preventive care.

Sarah received a copy of the medical examiner's report and shared the relevant details with Alira: "The official cause was stroke, just like the doctors thought. The ME said his cardiovascular disease was more advanced than anyone realized, and the stress of his work probably triggered the catastrophic event. Nothing could have prevented it—it was just a matter of time before his heart or brain gave out under the strain."

The conclusion was exactly what Alira had engineered through her careful selection of poison, dosing strategy, and delivery mechanism. Hayes' death appeared to be a tragic but unremarkable consequence of the lifestyle and health factors that killed thousands of men his age every year. The medical establishment had no reason to suspect murder because every aspect of his death was consistent with natural causes.

Sarah's final message on the topic came three days after the medical examiner's report was released: "Mrs. Hayes called to thank me personally for trying to help the Senator take better care of his health. She said knowing that people cared enough to make suggestions about supplements and preventive care made her feel less alone in trying to get him to take his health seriously. She doesn't blame anyone—she knows he was stubborn about medical care and that the stroke was going to happen eventually regardless of what anyone did."

The irony was profound and tragic. Mrs. Hayes was thanking Sarah for facilitating the very intervention that had killed her husband, believing that the supplements represented a good-faith effort to prevent exactly the kind of catastrophic health event that they had actually caused. Sarah felt validated in her helpful suggestion, believing she'd done everything possible to support Hayes' health even though the outcome had been tragic.

And Alira, the architect of the entire operation, remained completely invisible to everyone involved. She was just a trauma survivor who'd shared concerns about Hayes' health based on her own father's experience, someone who'd provided information that Sarah had independently decided to act on, someone whose involvement in Hayes' supplement regimen was so indirect and innocent that no one would ever think to question it.

The perfect delivery had been achieved through layers of psychological manipulation and institutional assumptions that protected Alira while condemning Hayes. Sarah had delivered the poison believing she was delivering help. Mrs. Hayes had ensured consistent consumption believing she was saving her husband's life. And Hayes himself had taken his daily supplements believing they supported his cardiovascular health while they actually destroyed his neuromuscular system.

On the evening after the medical examiner's final report was released, Alira sat in her Georgetown apartment reviewing the complete timeline of Hayes' poisoning and death. From the initial conversation with Sarah about her father's supplements to Hayes' final collapse in his office, the operation had proceeded with remarkable precision.

Day 1-4: Hayes consumed legitimate supplements purchased by Mrs. Hayes, establishing the routine and pattern.

Day 5 (actually Day 1 of poisoning): Alira substituted weaponized supplements; Hayes began consuming tetrodotoxin.

Days 6-8: Progressive accumulation of toxin producing subtle symptoms—fatigue, coordination difficulties, tingling extremities.

Days 9-10: Advanced symptoms—slurred speech, significant motor coordination problems, progressive neurological deterioration.

Day 11: Catastrophic failure—collapse, respiratory distress, cardiac arrhythmia, death.

The timeline was clinically precise, demonstrating that her dosing calculations had been accurate and that tetrodotoxin behaved exactly as the research literature had predicted. More importantly, the progression of symptoms had been gradual enough to avoid triggering immediate suspicion of acute poisoning while being rapid enough to prevent Hayes from surviving long enough to receive the kind of comprehensive medical investigation that might have revealed the true cause.

Alira opened her encrypted files and added Senator William Hayes to her list of completed eliminations:

Target #1: Richard Blackwood

- Date of death: January 11, 2024
- Method: Potassium chloride injection during assault
- Official cause: Cardiac arrest during physical struggle
- Status: Case closed, natural causes

Target #2: Senator William Hayes

- Date of death: May 2, 2024
- Method: Tetrodotoxin poisoning via weaponized supplements
- Official cause: Massive ischemic stroke with cardiac arrest
- Status: Case closed, natural causes

Two predators eliminated, two investigations concluded without any suspicion of murder, two sets of victims finally freed from the men who'd destroyed their lives. The success rate was perfect, the methods were increasingly sophisticated, and Alira's skills were evolving rapidly with each operation.

But there was no time for self-congratulation or complacency. The mission was far larger than just two eliminated predators—there were hundreds of powerful men operating with similar impunity throughout the country, destroying vulnerable women while protected by institutional failures and social structures that valued male authority over female safety.

Alira closed her files on Hayes and opened a new folder labeled "Target #3: Preliminary Research." The next elimination would need to be different again—a new method, a new approach, a new set of circumstances that would make the death appear completely natural and unconnected to the previous two kills.

She was becoming a master of invisible justice, learning to engineer deaths that looked like accidents or natural causes while actually representing carefully calculated consequences for men who'd believed themselves untouchable. The legal system had failed comprehensively to hold these predators accountable, but Alira had learned that some forms of justice required working outside institutional frameworks.

Senator William Hayes was dead, his predatory career ended, his victims liberated from fear of continued exploitation or retaliation. Sarah Chen would grieve the complicated loss of an employer who'd been both professionally important and personally harmful, never understanding that his death represented justice delivered through her own innocent assistance.

And Alira Sinclair would continue her work, refining her methods and expanding her operations until either she was stopped or the institutional protections for powerful predators were reformed sufficiently that extrajudicial action was no longer necessary.

The perfect delivery had been completed with surgical precision, leaving no evidence, no suspicions, and no trail that could ever lead investigators back to the woman who'd engineered a senator's death through weaponized supplements disguised as preventive healthcare.

The second sin was complete, and the hunter was already identifying her next prey.

VINDICTA *Vengeance*

———————

"She did not become a monster. She became the thing that monsters fear."

Chapter 7

The Reckoning

The news of Senator William Hayes' death broke across major media outlets within hours of his passing, transforming from brief hospital updates to comprehensive obituaries that would define his legacy for posterity. Alira watched the coverage unfold from her Georgetown apartment, monitoring multiple news sources simultaneously to track how the narrative was being constructed and whether any suspicious elements were emerging that might threaten her operational security.

CNN's breaking news alert appeared at 3:47 PM on Thursday, exactly thirty minutes after Hayes had been pronounced dead: "BREAKING: Senator William Hayes (D-VA) has died at Georgetown University Hospital following massive stroke. He was 58."

The initial coverage was respectful and focused on Hayes' legislative accomplishments—his three decades of public service, his work on various Senate committees, his reputation as an effective dealmaker who could build bipartisan coalitions on difficult issues. The early reports made no mention of his history of sexual misconduct or the predatory behavior that had destroyed dozens of women's careers over his political lifetime.

But as the evening progressed and journalists had time to develop more comprehensive stories, the coverage began incorporating the more complicated aspects of Hayes' legacy. By 7 PM, the Washington Post had published an extensive obituary that included carefully worded references to "controversies" and "allegations of inappropriate workplace behavior" that had periodically emerged throughout his career.

The New York Times went further, publishing a piece at 8:34 PM titled "Senator William Hayes Dies at 58; Career Marked by Legislative Success and Harassment Allegations." The article provided a detailed accounting of the settlement payments, the former staffers who'd left his employment under questionable circumstances, and the pattern of accusations that had been consistently dismissed or buried through legal and political mechanisms.

Most significantly, several women who'd previously been silenced by non-disclosure agreements began speaking to reporters on background, providing anonymous accounts of Hayes' predatory behavior now that his death had eliminated the threat of retaliation. The stories were remarkably consistent—Hayes had used his position to manipulate vulnerable young women into sexual relationships, deployed psychological tactics to create dependence and confusion about appropriate boundaries, and systematically destroyed the careers of anyone who resisted or reported his conduct.

"He made you feel special at first," one former staffer told the Post. "Like you were the most talented person he'd ever worked with, like your career was going to be extraordinary if you just trusted his guidance and mentorship. And then slowly, incrementally, the relationship would become inappropriate. But it happened so gradually that you'd question your own perceptions—was this normal political mentorship, or was it something darker? By the time you realized it was exploitation, you were already so invested in the relationship and so dependent on his support that leaving seemed impossible."

Another anonymous source described the retaliation process: "When I tried to report his behavior, his chief of staff made it very clear what would happen if I pursued official complaints. My references would be contacted and told I was unstable. My professional reputation would be destroyed through whisper campaigns. I would be blacklisted from political work throughout Washington. The message was unmistakable—accept what happened and move on quietly, or have your entire career demolished."

The accumulation of these accounts, published within hours of Hayes' death by women who no longer feared his power, created a media narrative that was far more damning than anything that had emerged during his lifetime. Hayes' obituary was being written not as a celebration of public service, but as a cautionary tale about how political institutions protected predatory men while silencing their victims.

Alira read through the coverage with a mixture of satisfaction and careful attention to whether any journalists were raising questions about the timing or circumstances of Hayes' death. But the media focus remained entirely on his predatory behavior and the institutional failures that had enabled it—no one was suggesting that his stroke had been anything other than a tragic but unremarkable medical event.

By Friday morning, the coverage had evolved to include reactions from victim advocacy organizations, statements from political leaders about the need for stronger workplace protections, and speculation about how Hayes' death might affect pending legislation he'd been working on. The Washington political establishment was engaged in the complicated dance of acknowledging a colleague's death while also grappling with revelations about behavior that could no longer be ignored or minimized.

Senator Rebecca Martinez, who would temporarily assume Hayes' committee positions, issued a statement that walked the careful line between respect for the deceased and acknowledgment of his victims: "Senator Hayes' death is a loss for his family and constituents. However, the accounts emerging from former staffers remind us that we have a responsibility to create workplace environments where young people can pursue public service without fear of exploitation. We must honor those who've come forward by implementing stronger protections and accountability measures."

The political response was particularly interesting to Alira because it suggested that Hayes' death might actually accelerate reforms that his victims had been unable to achieve while he was alive. Dead, Hayes could no longer deploy his political capital to block workplace protection legislation or threaten retaliation against accusers. His death had created space for honest conversations about predatory behavior in political environments—conversations that his institutional power had previously suppressed.

Sarah Chen called Alira on Friday afternoon, her voice carrying the emotional exhaustion of someone who'd spent two days processing complicated grief while also managing the practical chaos of a senator's sudden death.

"I don't know if you've been following the news coverage," Sarah said, "but it's been... a lot. All these women coming forward with stories about the Senator's behavior, and suddenly everyone's acting like they always knew he was a predator. But where were all these people when we were actually working for him and dealing with his harassment? Why does it take someone's death before people are willing to acknowledge the truth?"

"Because powerful men are protected while they're alive," Alira replied quietly. "The same institutional mechanisms that enabled Hayes' behavior for three decades also ensured that speaking truth about him was professionally dangerous. His death removed the threat of retaliation, which freed people to finally be honest about what he'd done."

"I know you're right," Sarah said. "But it's still infuriating. All these politicians releasing statements about workplace safety and protecting young staffers—they could have done something while he was alive, while those of us working in his office were actually dealing with his abuse. Instead, they waited until he was dead and it was politically safe to condemn his behavior."

The anger in Sarah's voice was entirely justified, and Alira let her continue venting about the hypocrisy of political leaders who'd ignored Hayes' predatory behavior for years but were now positioning themselves as advocates for reform.

"How are you holding up personally?" Alira asked when Sarah's initial outpouring of frustration had subsided.

"I honestly don't know," Sarah admitted. "Part of me feels guilty for being relieved that he's dead. Like, I know I'm supposed to feel sad about losing my boss, but mostly I just feel... free. I don't have to go to work on

Monday and worry about being called into his office for a 'private meeting.' I don't have to manage his schedule and make excuses when his wife calls trying to get him to come home for dinner. I don't have to participate in the collective fiction that he was a dedicated public servant rather than a predator who used his position to hurt people."

"You're allowed to feel relieved," Alira said firmly. "You're allowed to acknowledge that his death ended your ongoing victimization, even if that's not a socially acceptable thing to say at funerals and memorial services. Hayes spent eight months making your work environment toxic and exploiting your vulnerability. His death means that toxicity is finally over."

"Thank you for saying that," Sarah replied, her voice breaking slightly. "Everyone else keeps telling me I should focus on his legislative accomplishments and try to find meaning in the work we did together. But that feels like just another form of erasure—pretending that the abuse didn't matter as long as he passed some bills."

They talked for another twenty minutes, with Alira providing the kind of validation and emotional support that Sarah clearly wasn't receiving from her political colleagues or the institutional structures managing Hayes' death. By the time they ended the call, Sarah sounded marginally more stable, though still processing the complicated grief of losing someone who'd been both professionally important and personally harmful.

That evening, Alira visited Sierra at Riverside Care Facility, finding her sister working on a large puzzle featuring various breeds of dogs. Sierra's face lit up with her characteristic unfiltered joy when she spotted Alira entering the common room.

"Alira! Look at all the puppies I'm putting together! There's a golden retriever and a beagle and a dalmatian!" Sierra's enthusiasm was pure and uncomplicated, untouched by any awareness of the complex moral calculations that occupied her sister's thoughts.

"They're beautiful, Sierra," Alira said, settling into a chair beside her sister and studying the partially completed puzzle. "You're getting so good at these complicated ones."

They worked on the puzzle together for a while, with Alira helping Sierra locate pieces while her mind processed everything that had happened over the past two weeks. Senator William Hayes was dead, killed by poison Alira had carefully administered through an elaborate scheme that had made his death appear completely natural. His victims were beginning to speak publicly about their experiences, freed from fear of retaliation by his death. And the political establishment was engaging in performative discussions about reform while continuing to protect other predatory men whose power remained intact.

"Did something good happen?" Sierra asked suddenly, looking up from the puzzle with her intuitive sensitivity to Alira's emotional state.

"Why do you ask that?" Alira replied, curious about what her sister had detected.

"You seem... lighter. Like something heavy that was bothering you isn't bothering you anymore." Sierra's damaged cognitive capacity couldn't understand complex causation, but her emotional intelligence remained remarkably intact.

"Something did happen," Alira confirmed carefully. "Someone who was hurting a lot of people can't hurt them anymore. The people he damaged are starting to feel safe enough to talk about what happened to them."

Sierra nodded solemnly, her expression showing the simplified moral clarity that her brain injury had left intact. "That's good. People who hurt others should face consequences. And the people they hurt should be able to tell their stories without being scared."

The innocence of Sierra's moral framework was both heartbreaking and validating. She understood fundamental principles of justice and accountability with perfect clarity, uncomplicated by the institutional compromises and legal nuances that allowed predators to operate with impunity in the world beyond Riverside Care Facility.

"Yes," Alira agreed. "That's exactly right."

As she left the care facility that evening, Alira reflected on the profound gap between the simple moral truths that Sierra articulated and the complex realities of actually achieving justice in systems designed to protect powerful men. Sierra believed people who hurt others should face consequences—a principle that was theoretically foundational to legal systems but practically abandoned whenever accountability threatened institutional power or political interests.

Alira had learned that bridging the gap between theoretical justice and practical accountability sometimes required working outside the very systems that claimed to deliver fair outcomes. Hayes had faced no legal consequences during his lifetime despite three decades of documented predatory behavior. But he had faced ultimate consequences through Alira's careful administration of exotic poison disguised as preventive healthcare.

The weekend brought additional media coverage as journalists continued investigating Hayes' history and developing more comprehensive accounts of his predatory pattern. The Saturday Washington Post published a major investigative piece titled "A Career of Harassment: How Senator William Hayes Exploited

Power for Three Decades," featuring on-the-record interviews with five former staffers who'd previously been bound by non-disclosure agreements but were now willing to speak publicly.

The article detailed specific incidents that painted a devastating picture of systematic abuse:

Jennifer Walsh described being invited to Hayes' Georgetown townhouse for what was supposed to be a policy briefing, only to find herself subjected to aggressive sexual advances that she'd been too frightened and professionally vulnerable to resist. "He made it very clear that my career depended on my compliance," Walsh told the Post. "He said he could make me a rising star in Democratic politics or ensure I never worked in Washington again. Those were my options—submit to his demands or have my professional future destroyed."

Maria Santos recounted a pattern of escalating harassment that had begun with seemingly innocent compliments about her appearance and gradually progressed to explicit sexual propositions and unwanted physical contact. "He framed it as mentorship and professional development," Santos explained. "He'd tell me that building intimate relationships with powerful men was how women succeeded in politics, that I needed to be 'flexible' and 'understanding' about the realities of Washington culture. It took me months to recognize that I was being groomed and exploited."

The accumulation of these firsthand accounts, published with the credibility of the Washington Post behind them, ensured that Hayes' legacy would be defined primarily by his predatory behavior rather than his legislative accomplishments. The political obituary was being rewritten in real time, transforming from respectful remembrance to cautionary tale about institutional failure and the protection of powerful abusers.

On Monday morning, exactly four days after Hayes' death, Alira received a phone call from Detective Marcus Hale—the same detective who'd investigated Richard Blackwood's death four months earlier. The call came at 9:23 AM, early enough to suggest it was among Hale's first tasks of the workday.

"Miss Sinclair, this is Detective Marcus Hale from the Metropolitan Police. We spoke several months ago regarding the death of Richard Blackwood. Do you have a few minutes to talk?"

Alira's pulse quickened slightly, though she kept her voice calm and slightly confused. "Of course, Detective. Is there something new about Mr. Blackwood's case? I thought that was closed."

"The Blackwood case is closed," Hale confirmed. "I'm actually calling about an unrelated matter. I understand you'd been working with Senator William Hayes on advocacy issues prior to his death last week. I'm conducting some routine follow-up interviews with people who'd had recent contact with the Senator, just to help complete our understanding of his final weeks."

The explanation sounded reasonable and bureaucratic, exactly the kind of administrative task that police departments conducted after the death of prominent public figures. But Alira noted carefully that Hale had specifically mentioned her connection to both Blackwood and Hayes, which suggested he'd identified that link and found it at least minimally interesting.

"I'd be happy to help however I can," Alira replied. "Though I have to say, I didn't know Senator Hayes very well. We'd only met a couple of times to discuss potential advocacy work."

"That's my understanding," Hale said. "I just have a few basic questions about your interactions with him. Would you be available to meet briefly sometime today or tomorrow? I can come to you, wherever is convenient."

They arranged to meet at 2 PM that afternoon at a coffee shop in Dupont Circle—neutral territory that would seem appropriately casual for what Hale was framing as routine follow-up rather than formal interrogation. After ending the call, Alira spent several hours reviewing her cover story and ensuring that every detail of her interactions with Hayes would withstand scrutiny.

The meeting with Detective Hale was scheduled to be brief and unremarkable, but Alira understood that even routine questions could become problematic if she provided answers that created inconsistencies or raised additional questions. She needed to maintain her persona as a trauma survivor who'd sought Hayes' political support for advocacy work, someone whose connection to the Senator had been professional, recent, and completely innocent.

At 1:45 PM, Alira arrived at the designated coffee shop and selected a table near the window where she could observe Detective Hale's approach. He arrived precisely at 2 PM, looking much as she remembered from their previous encounter—mid-forties, weathered appearance suggesting years of difficult police work, expression that conveyed professional competence without revealing personal reactions.

"Miss Sinclair, thank you for meeting with me," Hale said as he settled into the chair across from her. "I appreciate your willingness to help with this follow-up."

"Of course," Alira replied. "Though I'm not sure how much help I can actually be. My connection to Senator Hayes was pretty limited."

Hale pulled out a small notebook and pen, the analog tools suggesting he wasn't recording their conversation or treating this as formal interrogation. "I understand you were referred to Senator Hayes by your therapist, Dr. Patricia Vance, approximately six weeks ago. Is that correct?"

"Yes, that's right," Alira confirmed. "Dr. Vance thought I might benefit from channeling my trauma recovery into advocacy work, and she knew Senator Hayes had a reputation for supporting assault survivors who wanted to contribute to policy discussions."

"And how many times did you actually meet with Senator Hayes?"

"Twice," Alira said, having anticipated this question and prepared her answer carefully. "Once in his Capitol Hill office for an initial conversation about my experience and potential advocacy opportunities. Then once for dinner at a restaurant in Penn Quarter where we discussed more specifically what kind of testimony or policy input might be helpful."

"And those meetings were...?" Hale consulted his notes. "October 28th for the office meeting and November 4th for the dinner?"

The dates were wrong—Hale was apparently testing whether she'd correct them or accept his timeline. "I think the office meeting was earlier than that—sometime in mid-April, maybe around the 15th or 16th? And the dinner was the following weekend, so probably

April 22nd. But I'd have to check my calendar to be certain about exact dates."

Hale made a note, his expression neutral. "And after those two meetings, did you have any further contact with Senator Hayes?"

"Just a few text messages and one phone call," Alira replied. "He'd invited me to attend a committee hearing where assault survivors were going to testify, and we'd discussed whether I might be comfortable participating. But I was still feeling uncertain about going public with my story, so I'd been putting off making a final decision."

"When was the last time you communicated with him?"

Alira pretended to think back carefully. "I think the last text message was maybe two weeks ago? He'd sent me information about the hearing schedule, and I'd replied saying I was still considering whether I was ready. Then I saw the news about his stroke, and obviously that ended any plans about testimony."

Hale nodded, making additional notes. "During your interactions with Senator Hayes, did he ever seem unwell or mention any health problems?"

This was a more significant question—Hale was probing for whether Hayes had displayed symptoms that might have presaged his stroke. Alira considered her answer carefully, balancing the need to seem observant and honest with avoiding any statements that might draw attention to the poisoning timeline.

"He seemed tired during both meetings," she said finally. "Kind of run down, like he wasn't sleeping well or was under a lot of stress. During the dinner, he mentioned that his wife was worried about his health and wanted him to see a cardiologist, but he seemed dismissive about it—said he was too busy for medical appointments. I remember thinking he looked older than his photographs, more worn down."

"Did he mention taking any medications or supplements?"

Alira's pulse quickened slightly, though she maintained her expression of neutral recollection. "Not that I recall. We mostly talked about my potential advocacy work and his legislative priorities. His personal health wasn't really a topic of conversation beyond his brief mention that his wife was worried."

Hale made another note, then looked up with an expression that seemed designed to appear casual. "I understand you've had some difficult experiences over the past year. The assault you reported involving Richard Blackwood, now losing a potential advocate in Senator Hayes. That must be challenging to process."

The statement was phrased sympathetically, but Alira recognized it as a probe—Hale was noting the connection between Blackwood and Hayes, observing that both men had died shortly after interacting with her, and assessing her reaction to having this pattern pointed out.

"It has been difficult," Alira agreed, allowing vulnerability to show in her voice. "Mr. Blackwood's death was traumatic in complicated ways—I defended myself against his assault, but I never wanted him to die. And Senator Hayes was someone I'd hoped would help me find meaning in my trauma by contributing to policy work. Losing that opportunity feels like another door closing on my recovery process."

"Have you continued working with Dr. Vance on these issues?"

"Yes, we meet weekly. She's been helping me process the complicated emotions around both deaths—guilt about Blackwood even though I was defending myself, and disappointment about Hayes because I'd invested hope in the idea that advocacy work might help my healing."

Hale nodded sympathetically. "That sounds like healthy processing. I'm glad you have professional support." He closed his notebook with a gesture that suggested the interview was concluding. "I think that's all I needed to ask. Thank you for your time, Miss Sinclair."

"Can I ask what this is about?" Alira said, maintaining appropriate curiosity. "Is there some question about Senator Hayes' death? I thought he died of a stroke."

"He did," Hale confirmed. "This is just routine follow-up—getting a complete picture of his final weeks for our records. When prominent public figures die, we conduct these kinds of interviews to document their activities and state of mind, particularly when there might be questions about whether work stress contributed to medical events."

The explanation was plausible and bureaucratic, exactly the kind of administrative procedure that police departments might conduct. But Alira noted that Hale had chosen to interview her personally rather than delegating to a junior detective or conducting the follow-up by phone, which suggested at least mild interest in her connection to both Blackwood and Hayes.

As they parted company outside the coffee shop, Hale offered a final observation that seemed carefully casual: "You know, Miss Sinclair, you've had remarkable bad luck with men in positions of power over the past few months. First Blackwood assaults you and then dies during the attack. Then Hayes offers to help with advocacy work and dies before you can participate. That's a lot of loss and trauma concentrated in a short time period."

"I've thought about that a lot," Alira replied quietly. "My therapist says it's important not to take on responsibility for things beyond my control—that Mr. Blackwood's heart attack and Senator Hayes' stroke were medical events that would have happened regardless of my involvement with them. But it's hard not to feel like I'm somehow cursed, like people around me keep dying and I'm left to process the aftermath."

Hale's expression was sympathetic but also assessing, his detective's instincts clearly evaluating whether her response seemed genuine or performed. "Your therapist is right that you can't control other people's health issues. Take care of yourself, Miss Sinclair. And feel free to call if you remember anything else that might be relevant to our understanding of Senator Hayes' final weeks."

After Hale departed, Alira remained at the coffee shop for another thirty minutes, reviewing the conversation and assessing whether she'd made any mistakes or created any inconsistencies that might warrant additional scrutiny. The interview had been brief and seemingly routine, but Hale's final comment about her "remarkable bad luck" suggested he'd at least noticed the pattern of powerful men dying shortly after interacting with her.

The connection wasn't necessarily problematic—both deaths had been thoroughly investigated and conclusively attributed to natural causes, and Alira's involvement in each case had been documented and deemed innocent. But the fact that a detective was noticing patterns meant she would need to be even more careful about her future operations, ensuring that the methods and circumstances varied enough to avoid creating obvious links between seemingly unrelated deaths.

That evening, Alira conducted a thorough review of her operational security, examining every element of the Hayes elimination for potential vulnerabilities or traces that might eventually lead investigators back to her involvement. The analysis was methodical and comprehensive:

The Tetrodotoxin Purchase: Ordered under false identity (Dr. Elena Vasquez) using forged credentials that couldn't be traced to Alira's real identity. The supplier had documentation showing a legitimate researcher ordering materials for legitimate purposes. Even if investigators somehow became suspicious about the tetrodotoxin and traced the purchase, the trail would lead to a nonexistent person affiliated with a university that had no record of that researcher.

The Supplement Substitution: Conducted alone in Hayes' office using Sarah Chen's key, but framed as working on advocacy materials in a quiet workspace. Sarah would remember lending her key for innocent purposes and would have no reason to connect that favor with Hayes' death. The building security footage would show Alira entering and leaving at times consistent with her cover story.

The Weaponized Supplements: Prepared in Alira's apartment using equipment and materials purchased with cash in locations far from her residence or any of her known activities. The supplements themselves had been disposed of after Hayes' death—the bottle on his desk contained only the legitimate CardioVital capsules that Mrs. Hayes had purchased, mixed with the poisoned capsules that were chemically identical in appearance.

The Delivery Mechanism: Orchestrated through Sarah Chen and Mrs. Hayes, both of whom believed they were helping improve Hayes' health. Neither woman had any knowledge of the substitution or any reason to suspect that the supplements they'd encouraged Hayes to take were actually poisoned. Their involvement created multiple layers of separation between Alira and the actual administration of the lethal substances.

The Medical Investigation: Concluded that Hayes died of natural causes—massive stroke consistent with his cardiovascular risk factors and lifestyle. The toxicology screening hadn't included testing for tetrodotoxin because there was no reason to suspect exotic poisoning. Even if investigators later became suspicious and ordered comprehensive testing, they would find that most of the capsules in the bottle were legitimate supplements, making it appear that any contamination was either accidental or the result of manufacturing defects rather than deliberate poisoning.

The operational security was comprehensive, with multiple redundancies and misdirections that would protect Alira even if investigators became suspicious and began looking more closely at the circumstances of Hayes' death. But Detective Hale's observation about her "remarkable bad luck" suggested that future operations would need to be even more carefully planned to avoid creating patterns that might eventually trigger deeper investigation.

As Alira prepared for bed that night, she opened her encrypted files and began developing preliminary research on potential future targets. The elimination of Hayes had been more sophisticated than Blackwood's death, incorporating gradual poisoning, multiple unwitting accomplices, and exploitation of institutional assumptions about natural causes. The next operation would need to be different again—a new method, new circumstances, new ways of achieving elimination that couldn't be connected to previous kills.

But that planning could wait. For now, Alira allowed herself to feel satisfaction about what she'd accomplished. Senator William Hayes was dead, his predatory career ended, and his victims were finally beginning to speak publicly about their experiences without fear of retaliation. Sarah Chen was freed from ongoing exploitation, even if she didn't fully understand how her liberation had been achieved. And the political establishment was engaging in uncomfortable but necessary conversations about workplace protections and accountability that Hayes' living presence had previously suppressed.

The second sin was complete, and the consequences of Hayes' three decades of predatory behavior had finally caught up with him in ways that no amount of political power or institutional protection could prevent.

Two targets eliminated, two investigations closed as natural causes, and a growing understanding of how to engineer deaths that appeared completely unremarkable while actually representing carefully calculated justice for predators who'd operated with impunity.

The mission would continue, evolving and adapting with each new challenge, until either Alira was stopped or the institutional failures that necessitated extrajudicial action were reformed sufficiently that her work was no longer necessary.

Detective Marcus Hale might be noticing patterns, but patterns alone didn't constitute evidence of murder when every death had been thoroughly investigated and conclusively attributed to natural causes. Alira would need to be more careful going forward, but she would not be deterred.

The hunt continued, and the next predator was already being identified and studied for elimination.

Chapter 8

New Beginnings

Three weeks after Senator William Hayes' funeral, Sarah Chen received notification that she'd been offered a position as senior legislative aide in Senator Rebecca Martinez's office. The appointment was effective immediately, and the salary represented a fifteen percent increase over what she'd been earning under Hayes—a gesture that Martinez's chief of staff explained was intended to recognize Sarah's experience and to help compensate for the difficult working conditions she'd endured in her previous position.

Sarah called Alira with the news on a Tuesday afternoon, her voice carrying genuine excitement for the first time since Hayes' death.

"I got the job with Senator Martinez," she said, barely containing her enthusiasm. "I start next Monday. Her chief of staff was really direct about why they wanted me—she said they specifically sought out former Hayes staffers because they understood we'd been working in a toxic environment and deserved better opportunities."

"That's wonderful, Sarah," Alira replied warmly. "Senator Martinez has an excellent reputation. I think you're going to find the work environment dramatically different from what you experienced with Hayes."

"I already can tell it's going to be different," Sarah said. "During my interview, Senator Martinez asked me directly about my experience in Hayes' office—not in a gossipy way, but like she genuinely wanted to understand what I'd dealt with so she could ensure her office culture was completely different. She said she's implementing new policies around staff boundaries, mandatory harassment training, and anonymous reporting mechanisms that don't require people to risk their careers to report misconduct."

The contrast Sarah was describing represented exactly the kind of institutional reform that Hayes' death had created space for. While he was alive, his political power and seniority had made it difficult for other senators to publicly criticize his office practices or implement policies that might implicitly condemn his behavior. But his death had removed that political constraint, allowing leaders like Martinez to openly acknowledge the toxicity of his workplace culture and position themselves as reformers committed to preventing similar abuse.

"How are you feeling about starting fresh with a new senator?" Alira asked.

"Honestly? Relieved. Excited. A little bit guilty that I'm benefiting professionally from Senator Hayes' death, but mostly just grateful to have an opportunity to work in an environment where I won't spend every day managing anxiety about being called into private meetings or dealing with inappropriate comments disguised as mentorship."

They talked for another twenty minutes about Sarah's new position, the policy areas she'd be working on, and her hope that Martinez's office would become a model for how Senate offices should operate. By the time they ended the call, Sarah sounded more optimistic about her career than Alira had ever heard her during the eight months she'd worked for Hayes.

The political aftermath of Hayes' death continued to unfold in ways that suggested his elimination had achieved consequences beyond simply ending his individual predatory behavior. Over the three weeks since his funeral, additional victims had come forward with accounts of his misconduct, media investigations had revealed the extent of his settlement payments and legal intimidation tactics, and the Senate Ethics Committee had announced a comprehensive review of workplace harassment policies.

Senator Martinez had emerged as a leading voice in these reform discussions, using her new committee positions to advance legislation that would strengthen protections for congressional staffers and create more robust accountability mechanisms for senators accused of misconduct. In interviews, she was careful not to speak ill of Hayes directly—maintaining the political convention that recently deceased colleagues should be remembered charitably—but she was explicit that his death had revealed systemic problems that required urgent attention.

"We've learned that non-disclosure agreements were being used not to protect legitimate confidential information, but to silence victims and enable ongoing abuse," Martinez said in a CNN interview. "We've learned that settlement payments were coming from office budgets in ways that created financial incentives to cover up misconduct rather than address it. And we've learned that young staffers, particularly women, have been bearing the costs of a workplace culture that prioritized protecting powerful men over ensuring safe working environments."

The reform momentum was significant, though Alira understood that institutional change was always fragile and subject to political calculations that might shift as media attention moved to other issues. Hayes' death had created a brief window of opportunity for honest discussions about predatory behavior in political environments, but whether that window would result in lasting change remained uncertain.

What was certain was that Hayes' victims were experiencing liberation that wouldn't have been possible while he remained alive and politically powerful. Jennifer Walsh had returned to Washington after several weeks with her family, accepting a position with a victim advocacy organization where she could channel her own traumatic experience into helping others. Maria Santos had given an on-the-record interview to the Washington Post about her experience in Hayes' office, describing the grooming process and psychological manipulation in ways that were helping other victims recognize similar patterns in their own experiences.

The cumulative effect of these public accounts was a comprehensive rewriting of Hayes' legacy. Where his obituary might have emphasized legislative accomplishments and political effectiveness, the narrative that would define him for posterity focused almost entirely on his predatory behavior and the institutional failures that had enabled it. He would be remembered not as a distinguished public servant, but as a cautionary tale about how power corrupts and how political institutions protect abusers at the expense of their victims.

On the fourth week after Hayes' death, Alira received another call from Detective Marcus Hale requesting a follow-up meeting. The call came at 10:17 AM on a Thursday, and Hale's tone was professional but carried a subtle intensity that suggested this wasn't purely routine administrative follow-up.

"Miss Sinclair, I hope I'm not catching you at a bad time. I was wondering if you might be available for a brief conversation sometime in the next few days. Just tying up some loose ends on the Hayes matter."

They arranged to meet that afternoon at the same coffee shop in Dupont Circle where they'd met previously. Alira spent the intervening hours reviewing her previous statements and ensuring that anything she said during this follow-up would remain consistent with what she'd already told Hale.

The detective arrived at 2 PM precisely, settling into the same seat he'd occupied during their previous meeting. But this time he was carrying a leather folder that suggested more formal documentation than the simple notebook he'd used before.

"Thank you for meeting with me again," Hale said. "I appreciate your continued cooperation with our inquiry."

"Of course," Alira replied. "Though I have to admit I'm curious about what inquiry you're conducting. I thought Senator Hayes' death was conclusively determined to be from natural causes—a stroke related to his cardiovascular disease and stress levels."

"It was," Hale confirmed. "The medical examiner's findings were definitive on that point. This is more about understanding the full context of his final weeks—who he was meeting with, what his state of mind was, whether there were any concerns about his health that might have presaged the stroke."

Hale opened his folder and consulted some notes. "I've been conducting interviews with various people who had contact with Senator Hayes in the month before his death. His wife, his staff members, colleagues, constituents. Just building a comprehensive picture."

"That sounds very thorough," Alira said neutrally.

"One thing that's emerged from these interviews is that Senator Hayes started taking cardiovascular supplements about two weeks before his death. His wife mentioned that one of his staffers—Sarah Chen— had suggested the supplements after learning about them from a friend whose father had found them beneficial for heart health."

Alira's pulse quickened slightly, though she maintained an expression of polite interest. "I think Sarah might have mentioned something about that. She was worried about Senator Hayes' health and wanted to help."

"Did you discuss the supplements with Sarah?" Hale asked, his tone remaining casual but his eyes watching Alira carefully.

"We might have talked about general cardiovascular health at some point," Alira replied, keeping her answer vague. "My father died of a heart attack several years ago, and I remember his doctor had recommended various supplements and lifestyle changes. When Sarah mentioned being concerned about Senator Hayes looking run down, I might have shared what I remembered about my father's experience."

"Do you remember the specific brand of supplements your father took?"

"Not with certainty," Alira said, which was technically true since her father was fictional. "It was several years ago, and I wasn't closely involved in his medical care. Something with 'cardio' in the name, I think? But I'd have to check with my mother to be sure about the exact brand."

Hale made a note, then shifted his questioning. "I spoke with Sarah Chen yesterday. She mentioned that you'd been very helpful to her during a difficult time working in Senator Hayes' office, that you'd provided emotional support and helped her process the complicated feelings she had about his workplace behavior."

"Sarah's a good person who was dealing with a toxic work environment," Alira replied. "I tried to be a friend when she needed someone to talk to who wasn't involved in the political world and wouldn't judge her for acknowledging how difficult her situation was."

"She also mentioned that you'd used Senator Hayes' office on a Saturday morning to work on some advocacy materials. Said she'd lent you her office key so you could have a quiet workspace."

This was more concerning—Hale had identified the exact opportunity when Alira had substituted the poisoned supplements for the legitimate ones. But there was no reason for him to connect that innocent favor with Hayes' death unless he had evidence of the substitution, which should be impossible since Alira had taken extensive precautions to avoid leaving any traces.

"That's right," Alira confirmed. "I was working on written materials about my assault experience—the kind of testimony that Senator Hayes had suggested might be useful for policy discussions. My apartment was too noisy that weekend, and Sarah very kindly offered to let me use the office since it would be empty during a staff retreat."

"And while you were there, did you interact with any of Senator Hayes' personal items or materials on his desk?"

The question was pointed enough to reveal that Hale was specifically interested in the supplements, though Alira couldn't determine whether he had actual evidence of tampering or was simply following a hunch based on the timeline of her office access and Hayes' subsequent death.

"I worked at one of the desks in the main staff area," Alira said carefully. "I didn't go into Senator Hayes' private office. I was there to work on my own materials, not to snoop through his workspace."

Hale nodded, making another note. "I also spoke with Mrs. Hayes about her husband's final weeks. She mentioned that she'd purchased cardiovascular supplements after speaking with Sarah Chen, and that she'd personally delivered them to Senator Hayes' office to ensure he would actually take them consistently."

"That sounds like something a concerned wife would do," Alira said. "Senator Hayes apparently had a history of ignoring medical advice and resisting preventive health measures."

"Mrs. Hayes said she called Sarah every morning to confirm that her husband had taken his daily supplement. She was treating it very seriously, almost like a medical intervention rather than just a casual suggestion."

"I think she was probably right to take it seriously given his cardiovascular risk factors," Alira replied. "Though obviously the supplements didn't prevent the stroke that ultimately killed him."

"No, they didn't," Hale agreed. His expression shifted to something more contemplative. "You know, Miss Sinclair, I've been a detective for fifteen years, and one thing I've learned is that coincidences do happen. People with health problems sometimes die unexpectedly despite taking preventive measures. Stressed politicians sometimes have strokes regardless of what supplements they're taking."

He paused, studying Alira's reaction. "But I've also learned that when you see multiple coincidences clustering around the same person, it's worth paying attention to the pattern even if each individual element seems innocuous."

"What pattern are you seeing, Detective?" Alira asked, maintaining her tone of polite curiosity despite the tension rising in her chest.

"You've had contact with two powerful men in the past six months—Richard Blackwood and Senator William Hayes. Both men died shortly after their interactions with you. Both deaths were thoroughly investigated and conclusively attributed to natural causes—Blackwood's heart attack during an assault, Hayes' stroke related to cardiovascular disease. But both men also had something in common beyond you—they both had documented histories of predatory behavior toward women."

Alira felt the full weight of Hale's scrutiny as he articulated the connection she'd hoped would remain invisible beneath the surface of two apparently unrelated deaths.

"I can see how that might seem like a significant pattern," she said carefully. "But I don't understand what you're suggesting. Are you saying there's some question about whether these deaths were actually natural causes?"

"The medical evidence is clear that both deaths resulted from natural medical events," Hale replied.

"Blackwood's heart attack was consistent with his cardiac condition and the stress of physical struggle. Hayes' stroke was consistent with his cardiovascular disease and lifestyle factors. There's no forensic evidence suggesting anything other than natural causes in either case."

"Then what exactly are we discussing?"

Hale leaned back in his chair, his expression thoughtful. "We're discussing the fact that I'm a detective who notices patterns, and the pattern I'm noticing is that powerful men with histories of sexually predatory behavior seem to experience fatal medical events shortly after coming into contact with you. That could be pure coincidence—you could genuinely be someone with remarkably bad luck in terms of the men you encounter. Or it could be something else."

"Something else like what?" Alira asked, though she knew exactly what Hale was implying.

"I don't know," Hale admitted. "That's what's frustrating about this situation. I have two thoroughly investigated deaths that were conclusively attributed to natural causes. I have no evidence of foul play in either case. But I also have a pattern that my instincts tell me is worth paying attention to, even if I can't articulate exactly what that pattern means."

They sat in silence for a moment, both understanding that Hale had effectively accused Alira of murder while simultaneously acknowledging he had no evidence to support that accusation.

"Detective Hale," Alira said finally, "I understand that your job requires you to be suspicious and to look for patterns in seemingly unrelated events. But from my perspective, what you're describing is the traumatic reality of my life over the past six months. I was assaulted by Richard Blackwood and defended myself, which unfortunately resulted in his death from a heart attack during the struggle. That experience was devastating and terrifying, and it led me to seek therapy and try to find meaning in my trauma through advocacy work. Senator Hayes offered to help with that advocacy, and then he died of a stroke before I could participate in any meaningful way. Those aren't coincidences I've orchestrated—they're losses and traumas that I've had to process while trying to rebuild my life."

The response was perfect—acknowledging Hale's concerns while reframing them through the lens of a victim's experience rather than a perpetrator's strategy. Alira could see in his expression that he recognized the plausibility of her narrative even as his instincts continued suggesting there was more to the story.

"I appreciate your perspective," Hale said after a moment. "And I want to be clear that you're not under investigation for anything. Both deaths have been closed as natural causes, and there's no active criminal inquiry. I'm simply doing my due diligence in understanding these cases as completely as possible."

"I understand," Alira replied. "And I want to cooperate however I can, even though I don't have any information that would change the medical examiners' conclusions about how these men died."

Hale closed his folder and prepared to leave, but then seemed to reconsider. "Miss Sinclair, there is one more thing. As part of my follow-up with Mrs. Hayes, I asked if she still had the bottle of supplements that Senator Hayes had been taking. She said she'd kept it—she was planning to continue taking them herself since her doctor had said they were appropriate for cardiovascular health."

Alira's chest tightened, though she maintained her expression of polite interest.

"I'd like to have those supplements tested," Hale continued. "Just to rule out any possibility of contamination or manufacturing defects that might have contributed to the Senator's medical crisis. It's purely routine—we sometimes test substances that people were consuming shortly before unexpected medical events, especially when the person was taking new supplements or medications."

"That sounds like reasonable due diligence," Alira said, though her mind was racing through the implications. The bottle would contain a mixture of legitimate

CardioVital capsules and the poisoned ones she'd prepared. Random testing might or might not detect the tetrodotoxin, depending on which capsules were selected for analysis.

"Mrs. Hayes was cooperative about providing the bottle," Hale said. "But when I followed up with Sarah Chen to ask if she knew exactly when the Senator had started taking the supplements and whether there had been any concerns about side effects, she mentioned something interesting."

He paused, watching Alira's reaction. "Sarah said that Mrs. Hayes had purchased the supplements from a health food store in Virginia, but that the bottle on Senator Hayes' desk might not have been the original one. Apparently Senator Hayes had mentioned to Sarah about a week before his death that the capsules looked slightly different than what he remembered from when he first started taking them—said they seemed a bit more powdery or something. Sarah thought maybe he'd just started a new bottle from a different manufacturing batch."

The detail about Hayes noticing a difference in the capsules was concerning—Alira had worked hard to ensure the poisoned capsules were visually identical to the legitimate ones, but apparently some subtle variation had been detectable to Hayes even if he'd dismissed it as normal manufacturing variance.

"I wouldn't know anything about that," Alira said carefully. "I never saw the supplements and wasn't involved in Senator Hayes' decision to take them beyond possibly mentioning to Sarah that my father had found cardiovascular supplements helpful years ago."

"Of course," Hale said. "I'm just being thorough in documenting the timeline and details. Sarah mentioned that she'd planned to ask Mrs. Hayes if she wanted her to dispose of the supplements after the Senator's death—apparently there were still quite a few capsules left in the bottle. But Mrs. Hayes wanted to keep them."

Hale stood, preparing to leave. "I'll let you know if the testing reveals anything significant. Though I expect they'll come back as completely normal supplements— CardioVital is a reputable brand sold in health food stores across the country. There's no reason to think there would be any contamination."

As Hale departed, Alira remained seated at the coffee shop, her mind working through the new variables he'd introduced. The supplements were going to be tested, which meant there was a possibility—however small— that the tetrodotoxin contamination would be detected. The bottle contained a mixture of legitimate and poisoned capsules, so random sampling might not hit the contaminated ones. But if testing was comprehensive enough, or if Hale specifically requested screening for exotic toxins, the poisoning could be discovered.

More concerning was Hale's observation about patterns and his clear suspicion that the two deaths were somehow connected to Alira despite the lack of evidence supporting that theory. He was paying attention in ways that could become problematic if she continued her operations without adjusting her methods to avoid creating additional links between seemingly unrelated eliminations.

That evening, Alira conducted a comprehensive risk assessment of her operational security in light of Hale's investigation. The analysis was methodical and unflinching:

Immediate Risk - Supplement Testing:

- Bottle contains mixture of legitimate and poisoned capsules

- Random sampling might not detect contamination

- Even if tetrodotoxin is detected, trail leads to nonexistent Dr. Elena Vasquez

- No direct connection to Alira unless investigators specifically focus on her office access

Medium-Term Risk - Pattern Recognition:

- Hale has identified connection between Alira and two dead predators

- No evidence of foul play in either case, but pattern creates suspicion

- Future eliminations must avoid any connection to Alira personally

- Methods must vary significantly to prevent pattern recognition

Long-Term Risk - Institutional Attention:

- If supplement testing reveals poisoning, full investigation will follow

- Investigators will review Alira's access to Hayes' office

- Sarah will be questioned about lending office key

- Timeline of supplement substitution might be reconstructed

The risk assessment suggested that Alira had been fortunate so far—both eliminations had been investigated and closed as natural causes, and her involvement in each case had been documented as innocent. But Hale's suspicions represented a new variable that required immediate adaptation of her operational strategy.

Most critically, if the supplement testing revealed tetrodotoxin contamination, the entire investigation would be reopened with focus on how poison had been introduced into a bottle purchased by Mrs. Hayes from a legitimate Virginia health food store. The timeline of Sarah lending Alira her office key would become highly relevant, and the substitution strategy that had seemed so clever might actually create an obvious trail pointing directly to Alira's involvement.

She opened her encrypted files and began developing contingency plans for various scenarios:

Scenario 1 - Testing Reveals Nothing:

- Most likely outcome given random sampling methodology

- Continue operations but with more careful attention to avoiding patterns

- Future targets must have no personal connection to Alira

- Methods must vary significantly from previous eliminations

Scenario 2 - Testing Reveals Tetrodotoxin:

- Full investigation will focus on how poison entered supplement bottle

- Alira must have alibi for any questioning

- Sarah will be cooperative witness describing office key loan for innocent purposes

- Dr. Vasquez identity will withstand initial investigation but not intensive scrutiny

Scenario 3 - Hale Becomes Convinced Despite Lack of Evidence:

- Increased surveillance on Alira's activities
- Future operations become significantly more risky
- May need to cease eliminations temporarily or permanently
- Alternative approaches to achieving justice become necessary

As Alira prepared for bed that night, she understood that she'd reached a critical juncture in her mission. Two successful eliminations had freed dozens of women from ongoing predatory abuse and created political momentum for institutional reforms. But those successes had also created patterns that at least one detective was beginning to notice, even if he lacked evidence to support his suspicions.

The question was whether to continue operations despite increased scrutiny, or whether to pause and reassess her approach in light of Hale's attention. The moral imperative remained unchanged—powerful predators continued operating with impunity throughout the country, destroying vulnerable women while protected by institutional failures. But the tactical calculation had shifted now that law enforcement was potentially watching for additional deaths connected to her.

Five days later, the answer arrived in the form of another call from Detective Hale.

"Miss Sinclair, I wanted to update you on the supplement testing. The lab results came back, and I thought you'd want to know what they showed."

Alira's heart rate accelerated, though she kept her voice calm. "Of course. What did they find?"

"The supplements were completely normal," Hale said, his tone carrying a mixture of relief and frustration. "Standard CardioVital formulation, no contamination, no manufacturing defects, nothing that would have contributed to Senator Hayes' stroke. Just vitamins, exactly as labeled."

The relief Alira felt was profound but carefully controlled. The random sampling methodology had apparently missed the poisoned capsules, or the testing hadn't included screening for exotic toxins like tetrodotoxin. Either way, the investigation had concluded that the supplements were innocent, which meant Hayes' death remained classified as natural causes with no suspicious elements requiring further inquiry.

"That's good to hear," Alira said. "I know Sarah was worried that she might have inadvertently contributed to his death by suggesting the supplements. This should help ease her mind."

"I've already informed her and Mrs. Hayes," Hale confirmed. "They were both relieved to know the supplements weren't a factor."

There was a pause, and then Hale added something that suggested his suspicions hadn't been entirely resolved despite the negative test results: "Though I have to say, Miss Sinclair, I find it interesting that Senator Hayes apparently noticed something different about the capsules shortly before his death—mentioned they seemed more powdery than usual. But the lab testing showed nothing abnormal."

"Maybe he was just more aware of them because his wife was making such a point about taking them consistently," Alira suggested. "When you're paying close attention to something, you notice variations that are actually just normal manufacturing differences."

"Possibly," Hale agreed, though his tone suggested he wasn't entirely convinced. "Well, thank you again for your cooperation with this inquiry. The Hayes matter is now officially closed."

After ending the call, Alira sat motionless for several minutes, processing the narrow escape she'd just experienced. If the lab testing had been more comprehensive, if Hale had specifically requested screening for exotic toxins, if the random sampling had happened to select poisoned capsules rather than legitimate ones—any of those scenarios could have revealed the murder and triggered a full investigation that might have eventually traced back to her involvement.

But fortune had favored her operational security, and Hayes' death remained classified as natural causes even after Hale's suspicions had prompted additional testing. The second sin was complete and officially closed, leaving no evidence trail that could threaten Alira's freedom or her ability to continue her mission.

That evening, she received a final text message from Sarah Chen: "Detective Hale told me the supplements were fine—nothing wrong with them at all. I feel so relieved that my suggestion to Mrs. Hayes didn't somehow contribute to Senator Hayes' death. Thank you for being such a good friend through all of this. I don't know what I would have done without your support."

Alira's response was warm and supportive: "I'm so glad the testing confirmed what we knew—that you were trying to help, and that Senator Hayes' stroke was a medical event that would have happened regardless of the supplements. You're starting fresh with Senator Martinez now. Focus on that new beginning and let go of any guilt about things that were beyond your control."

The irony of providing emotional support to someone whose innocent actions had facilitated murder was not lost on Alira, but Sarah's continued trust was both touching and strategically valuable. Sarah viewed Alira as a friend who'd helped her through a difficult time, which meant she would remain a resource who could potentially provide access or information for future operations if needed.

Three weeks later, on a Saturday afternoon in early June, Detective Marcus Hale sat at his desk reviewing the closed case files for both Richard Blackwood and Senator William Hayes. The files were officially concluded—both deaths thoroughly investigated and definitively attributed to natural causes. There was no active inquiry, no outstanding questions, no justification for continuing to devote investigative resources to cases that had been resolved to the medical examiner's satisfaction.

But Hale couldn't shake the feeling that he was missing something important, that the pattern he'd identified represented something more significant than coincidental bad luck for a trauma survivor who happened to encounter powerful predators shortly before they died of natural causes.

He opened a new folder on his computer and labeled it "Pattern Analysis - Sinclair." The folder wasn't an official case file—just his personal documentation of observations and questions that might eventually coalesce into something worth pursuing or might ultimately prove to be nothing more than a detective's overactive pattern recognition creating connections where none actually existed.

He began typing notes about what he knew and what troubled him:

Alira Sinclair - Background:

- Age: 33
- Graduate student (art history)
- Assault survivor (Blackwood incident)
- Seeking therapy with Dr. Patricia Vance
- Interested in victim advocacy work

Deaths Connected to Sinclair:

Richard Blackwood (January 11, 2024):

- Died of cardiac arrest during assault on Sinclair
- Sinclair's account: defended herself, Blackwood collapsed
- ME conclusion: natural causes (heart attack triggered by physical stress)
- Investigation closed: justifiable self-defense, no criminal charges

Senator William Hayes (May 2, 2024):

- Died of massive stroke with cardiac complications

- Sinclair connection: advocacy meetings, possible discussion of supplements with staff

- ME conclusion: natural causes (stroke consistent with cardiovascular disease)

- Supplement testing: negative for contamination

- Investigation closed: natural death, no suspicious circumstances

Pattern Observations:

- Both men had documented histories of sexual predation

- Both died shortly after contact with Sinclair

- Both deaths conclusively attributed to natural medical events

- Both cases thoroughly investigated with no evidence of foul play

- Sinclair's involvement in both cases documented and deemed innocent

Questions:

- Coincidence or something more?

- Why do powerful predators keep dying around Sinclair?

- If not coincidence, what method could leave no forensic evidence?

- How would someone engineer deaths that appear completely natural?

Next Steps:

- Monitor for any additional deaths connected to Sinclair
- Review medical examiner protocols for exotic poisoning detection
- Research methods of killing that mimic natural causes
- Informal inquiry only - no basis for official investigation

Hale saved the file and closed his computer, understanding that his suspicions might never amount to anything more than theoretical pattern recognition. Alira Sinclair appeared to be exactly what she claimed—a trauma survivor who'd defended herself against one predator and sought advocacy support from another who'd died before she could participate meaningfully in his legislative work.

But fifteen years of detective work had taught Hale to trust his instincts even when evidence didn't support them, and his instincts were telling him that Alira Sinclair was more than she appeared to be.

He would be watching, waiting for the pattern to either prove itself coincidental or reveal itself as something far more dangerous and sophisticated than any case he'd encountered in his career.

Meanwhile, three hundred miles away in her Georgetown apartment, Alira Sinclair was conducting her own analysis—not of past cases that were safely closed, but of future targets who deserved consequences for predatory behavior that legal systems had failed to address.

Target #3 was already identified, researched, and being prepared for elimination through methods that would be completely different from her first two kills. No personal connection to Alira, no pattern that could link back to Hayes or Blackwood, no opportunity for Detective Hale or anyone else to recognize that a systematic hunter of predators was operating in plain sight.

The mission would continue, evolving and adapting with each new challenge, until justice was finally delivered to the powerful men who believed themselves untouchable.

The second sin was complete.

The third was about to begin.

Shadows Converging

Detective Marcus Hale locked his office and headed toward the parking garage, his mind still occupied by the Sinclair files he'd been reviewing. It was past 8 PM on a Saturday—far later than he usually worked on closed cases—but something about the pattern kept drawing him back to examine details that seemed innocent individually but potentially significant when viewed collectively.

Two powerful men, both predators, both dead within four months. Both deaths natural causes, both investigations thorough and conclusive. Both connected to the same young woman who appeared to be nothing more than an unfortunate victim of circumstance.

Coincidence? Almost certainly.

But Hale had learned over fifteen years of detective work that "almost certainly" wasn't the same as "definitely," and the cases that haunted him were always the ones where his instincts whispered that obvious answers might be concealing deeper truths.

He reached his car and was about to unlock it when his phone buzzed with an alert from the department's morning briefing system. The notification shouldn't have arrived until tomorrow morning, but someone had flagged it as potentially urgent for detectives working violent crimes and suspicious deaths.

Hale opened the alert and felt his stomach tighten as he read:

PRELIMINARY INCIDENT REPORT Date: June 8, 2024 Location: Elite Fitness Studio, Georgetown Victim: Marcus Sterling, 42, celebrity fitness trainer Incident: Apparent drowning in hydrotherapy pool Status: Under investigation, ME preliminary assessment pending Note: Victim had documented history of harassment complaints from female clients. Circumstances of death being reviewed for suspicious elements.

Marcus Sterling. Hale recognized the name—the celebrity trainer had been featured in several gossip media stories about inappropriate behavior with clients, though no criminal charges had ever been filed. Another powerful man with predatory history, dead under circumstances that would likely be ruled accidental or natural causes.

Hale stood in the parking garage, his mind racing through possibilities. This death had no obvious connection to Alira Sinclair—different city neighborhood, different type of predator, different circumstances entirely. It was probably pure coincidence that another abuser had died shortly after Hayes.

But Hale pulled out his phone and opened the notes he'd been keeping on the Sinclair pattern. He added a new entry:

Potential Target #3: Marcus Sterling Date of death: June 8, 2024 Preliminary cause: Drowning (hydrotherapy pool) Connection to Sinclair: Unknown - requires investigation Pattern significance: TBD

He would follow up on Monday, run some basic checks to see if Sinclair had any connection to Sterling or his fitness studio. Almost certainly the answer would be no—this would prove to be just another coincidence, another powerful predator whose dangerous lifestyle had finally caught up with him.

Almost certainly.

But Hale had stopped believing in too many coincidences a long time ago.

He got in his car and drove home through the quiet Saturday evening streets, his mind already composing the questions he would ask when he inevitably requested another meeting with Alira Sinclair.

The pattern was either becoming clearer or he was succumbing to confirmation bias.

By Monday, he would know which.